# MYSTERY STORIES FOR GIRLS

## 7 SISTER MYSTERIES: TROUBLE IN PARADISE
by Ellen Miles

## MYSTIC LIGHTHOUSE MYSTERIES: THE MYSTERY OF THE MISSING TIGER
by Laura E. Williams

## UNDERCOVER GIRL: SECRETS
by Christine Harris

SCHOLASTIC INC.
New York Toronto London Auckland Sydney
Mexico City New Delhi Hong Kong Buenos Aires

ISBN 0-439-85858-5



12 11 10 9 8 7 6 5 4 3 2 1 6 7 8 9 10 11/0

Printed in the U.S.A. 40

First printing, April 2006

# CONTENTS

# Trouble in Paradise

**Ellen Miles**

*For Julian and Polly, with love*



ISBN 0-439-36006-4



12 11 10 9 8 7 6 5 4 3 2 1 2 3 4 5 6 7/0

Printed in the U.S.A. 40

First Scholastic printing, April 2002

**Welcome to Paradise!**

**Cap'n Teddy and "Duchess" Drysdale welcome**
**you and your family**
**to the most relaxing vacation spot in Vermont:**
**Paradise Cottages!**
**Paddle Paradise Lake in a canoe!**
**Swim from our secluded sandy beach!**
**Hike the nature trails!**
**Or just lie back in your own personal hammock**
**and dream, dream, dream your day away.**
**10 fully furnished cottages on peaceful**
**Paradise Lake**
**Reserve early for the Fourth of July!**

Sounds restful, doesn't it? Serene? Halcyon[1], even? You would think so. *I* would think so. And, the truth is, every *other* Fourth of July week my family has spent at Paradise Cottages has been pretty quiet.

But things are not always what they seem. To be

[1]halcyon: calm, tranquil. Isn't it a great word? A halcyon was originally a mythical bird that had the ability to calm the wind and waves while it nested on the sea. I collect interesting words, and I'll be sharing some of my favorites with you as we go along. Hope you like them!

accurate, the brochure for this year's visit would look something like this:

**Welcome to Paradise!**

**Cap'n Teddy and "Duchess" Drysdale welcome you and your family to the most nerve-racking vacation spot in Vermont: Paradise Cottages!**

**Get your expensive boat stolen!**

**See buildings burn to the ground!**

**Worry that your cottage might be next!**

**Or run around trying your hardest to solve the mystery, putting yourself and your family in danger!**

**10 flammable cottages on crime-ridden Paradise Lake**

**Reserve early for the Fourth of July!**

# Chapter One

"Did I tell you what Daniel thinks about my new bike?" Amanda asked.

I nodded. She had. Daniel thought her new bike was "rad." Amanda and I had been together for a total of two hours. We'd picked her up at the bus station on our way out of town, and now we were driving north to Paradise. I already knew what Daniel thought about lots of things. Such as: her bike, her haircut, the color purple, "posers" who can't really "ride" (skateboards, that is), canned ravioli, and sharks.

(In case you're interested in Daniel's opinions, they are as follows, in order: rad, awesome, funky, totally uncool, it *rules*, and awesome.)

Who's Daniel? Amanda's new boyfriend.

Who's Amanda? One of my best friends ever. We grew up together in Cloverdale, Vermont. That's where I still live, along with my parents and four of my six sisters: Helena and Viola, the nine-year-old twins; Juliet, age eleven; and Katherine, who's fourteen. My oldest sisters, Miranda and Olivia, live on their own nearby.

I'm Ophelia Parker, and I'm thirteen. Amanda

Thompson and I hung out so much together when we were little that people said our names as if they were one: OpheliaandAmanda. The Thompsons lived right next door, and Amanda and I spent most of our waking hours together. Also many of our sleeping ones, if you count sleepovers.

Anyway, about a year ago Amanda's parents got a divorce. Amanda and her mom moved to Connecticut, and her dad moved to Boston. The whole thing was incredibly traumatic for Amanda, and I think it still is, judging by the e-mails she sends me. Her parents don't argue quite as much as they used to, but that's only because they don't live together anymore. According to Amanda, they still bicker and squabble every chance they get. And since most of those chances involve Amanda's visits back and forth, she hears the worst of it.

But during the entire two-hour drive up to Paradise Cottages, Amanda hadn't said a word about her parents. All she could talk about was Daniel.

I'd been so psyched about spending a week with Amanda ever since Mom and Poppy agreed that she could come with us to Paradise. We go there every Fourth of July week; it's a Parker family tradition. But this year, Miranda and Olivia both had to work (Miranda's a cop on the Cloverdale force, and Olivia waitresses in Burlington, where she lives and goes to college), so they'd only be visiting for the actual Fourth. Katherine had decided to go to Martha's Vineyard with her friend Amy's family. So I got to invite Amanda!

I *love* going to Paradise, and I couldn't wait to share it all with Amanda: the sparkling, clear blue lake, the fireworks, the cool little winding paths through the woods . . . We were going to have a blast. At least, that's what I'd thought beforehand. Now, I wasn't so sure.

Amanda had changed.

I saw it right away, as soon as we picked her up at the bus. Her lips were pink and shiny, and blond streaks had appeared (as if by magic!) in her reddish-brown hair. The pink tube top she was wearing made it obvious that she'd "matured" a *lot* since I'd last seen her, and her flared jeans were tight and low-slung. She had on pink platform flip-flops that made her look about a foot taller. Suddenly I felt kind of dowdy in my shorts and T-shirt and Tevas.

But it wasn't just the way she dressed, or how she was doing her hair. It was what she talked about, and most of all, the *way* she talked. "He's a total hottie," she gushed, telling me about Daniel. "I mean, the first time I saw him, I was all, 'Wow.' And he was all, 'Wow,' when he saw me. It was, like, love at first sight. Seriously. I am not even joking." She shoved a picture at me. "Is he not a *com-*

*plete* hottie?" she asked. I caught a glimpse of a shaggy-looking guy in baggy pants before she pulled the picture back and kissed it. Uck. Her lip gloss was probably making it all slimy.

Amanda and I were sitting in the back of our totally overloaded van, which was packed to the roof with all the stuff we'd need for a week. Actually, it was packed *over* the roof, if you count the canoe and the kayak strapped on top. A Beatles CD was blaring (*Revolver*, my favorite), Mom was driving, Poppy was navigating, Helena and Viola were playing Hangman in the first row of seats, and Juliet was sprawled across the second row, reading. She's always been able to read in a moving car, lucky dog. (Speaking of dogs, ours was back home, being taken care of by our pet/housesitter, Kerry. Bob, our dog, *adores* Kerry, and I think Charles and Jenny, our cats, like her pretty well, too. It's always harder to tell with cats.)

I was hoping that Juliet was really absorbed in her book, because I knew how she would react to the things Amanda was saying. Juliet always speaks her mind, and I was sure to get an earful about my Valley Girl friend. Juliet can't stand girls who talk about "hotties." For that matter, neither can I. But this was different. This was Amanda. My friend Amanda.

I would have liked to tell her about my new

friend TJ, but I knew she'd just make a big deal about him being my boyfriend, and he isn't. Not yet, anyway. But there must be *something* we could talk about, other than boys. We'd always had so much in common. Like — reading! "Hey!" I said, interrupting her latest report on The World According to Daniel. "Did you read the new Rachel Vail book? It's *so* good."

"Like, I am so sure," she said. "Me, have time for reading? As *if*." She stroked her hair back from her face. "Daniel says reading is overrated, anyway. Like, real life is more important, and all."

I sighed and turned to look out the window. It was going to be a long week.

We were deep in the country now. Not that Cloverdale is the big city, but when we drive up north, everything looks different. There are more trees and fewer houses, for one thing. And, as you get closer to Paradise, there are little lakes everywhere. Most of them have lots of "camps" (that's what most Vermonters call their little summerhouses) along the shoreline, and they're full of kids splashing in the water, and people fishing off rowboats. Paradise is a little different. For one thing, it's a big lake, not just a pond. It even has an island right in the middle! And it's very quiet there. You can have a motorboat on Paradise Lake, but there's a speed limit so you can only putt along slowly. You can't go fast enough to pull a water-skier, which is too bad in a way since I'd like to try it, but I guess it's worth it for the peace and quiet.

Speaking of peace and quiet, I was wondering if I was going to have any all week. Amanda just kept on chattering nonstop. In the old days, we would have been singing along with the Beatles, or playing cat's cradle or something. Now it looked as if I was in for seven days of "Daniel says . . ."

"Paradise, three miles!" my mom sang out from the front seat.

"Yay!" I yelled. I sat up straighter to look for all the familiar landmarks: the big old falling-down barn, the house with a chain-saw–sculpted statue of a moose in the front yard, the meadow that's always ablaze with orange and purple flowers. "The creemee stand!" I cried, spotting the soft-ice-cream stand on the edge of town. "Can we stop?"

"We'll go next time we come to town," Poppy promised. "Right now I just want to get all our stuff across the lake."

Oh, I forgot to mention the coolest thing about Paradise Cottages. You can't drive there! Instead, you drive to Paradise Village, which we were just entering, and go straight down to the dock. Then you unload all your stuff into a big motorboat that the Drysdales (the owners) send over. Later, if you need any supplies or if you want to go out for pizza or to the Fourth of July parade, you paddle back over to Paradise in a canoe or get another ride in a motorboat.

It makes it really special, I think. We're all kind of marooned over there on the opposite shore. The people who go to Paradise Cottages every year really get to know one another. I was dying to see Sam Drysdale, the owners' granddaughter and my best summer friend. We've spent the Fourth of July together every year since I can remember.

I looked at Amanda, wondering how she and Sam would get along. If you'd asked me a week ago, I would have said, "No problem." Now, I wasn't so sure.

"Look! Patrick's waiting for us!" Juliet said. She'd put her book away and was climbing out of the van, which Mom had just pulled up to the dock. "He brought the big green boat."

Amanda and I were jumping out, too. "Daniel says green is —" she began. Then she saw Patrick.

She never finished her sentence.

# Chapter Two

Patrick *was* kind of cute. Even I had to admit it. He'd changed a lot since last summer. I remembered him as gawky and pale and skinny. This year, he'd lost the gawkiness. He was tan and strong-looking, and his hair was bleached blond from the sun.

Patrick is Sam's sixteen-year-old brother. The two of them have always spent summers with their grandparents at Paradise Cottages. I've never even met their parents. Their dad is a journalist and their mom is a biologist, and both of them travel all the time.

Patrick grinned and waved at us. He jumped off the boat and walked over to the van. "Welcome, Mr. and Mrs. P.," he said. He nodded to the rest of us and I saw his eyes pause on Amanda.

"This is my friend Amanda," I said, realizing I should introduce her. "Amanda, this is Patrick."

She giggled. "Hi," she said, shaking back her hair.

"Hi," said Patrick.

There was a brief silence while they stared at each other.

"So," Poppy said finally, rubbing his hands together. "We've got the usual carload of stuff here. Ready to load 'er up?" He nodded toward the boat.

"Aye, aye," said Patrick, giving Poppy a grin and a little salute.

"'Aye, aye' is right," Amanda whispered to me as she watched Patrick follow Poppy around to the back of the van. I had a feeling I wasn't going to be hearing too much more about Daniel for a while.

It took *forever* to unload all our stuff, hauling it out of the van, down the dock, and into the boat. But finally the van was empty. Patrick helped Poppy take the canoe and kayak off the top. "Nice kayak," he said.

"Thanks!" Poppy beamed. "I made it myself from a kit. Did it this winter."

Patrick was impressed, and we had to stand there in the sun while Poppy told him all about the design and how he'd built it. "Think I'll paddle it over myself," Poppy said finally.

"I'll take the canoe," Mom said. "Who wants to come with me? Ophelia and Amanda?"

Amanda turned to me, pleading with her eyes. I knew what she wanted. "No, we'll ride with Patrick," I said.

Helena and Viola climbed into the canoe with Mom.

"Want to ride on the tube?" Patrick asked Juliet. He had a big old inner tube roped to the back of the boat.

"Definitely!" Juliet took off her sneakers, threw them into the boat, and waded out onto the tube while Amanda and I climbed aboard. Then Patrick started the engine, and our little flotilla[2] moved off.

The lake was as sparkly and clear as always. Little waves danced around us, slapping the sides of the boat as we cruised along. I watched the rocky, tree-lined shore recede as Patrick putted straight across the middle of the lake, leaving Poppy and Mom far behind. Puffy white clouds decorated the blue, blue sky, and there was a gentle breeze lifting my hair. I heard the eldritch[3] sound of a loon calling from the far end of the lake, where they always nest. "Ahh!" I said. "Paradise!"

Patrick smiled down at me from his spot in the stern of the boat, near the motor. "Sam can't wait to see you," he said. "She has all kinds of plans for you." He winked at Amanda as he said that. She giggled.

What was *that* about? Sometimes I don't get this boy-girl stuff.

[2]flotilla: a group of ships
[3]eldritch: weird, ghostly, eerie

I decided to ignore it. I trailed a hand in the water as the boat putted along. I turned to wave at Juliet, who was lying happily in the tube. She waved back, a huge smile on her face. I knew she was looking forward to seeing *her* best summer friend, Sally. They were planning to learn to sail Sally's family's Sunfish.

"Look!" I said. "There's Windswept!" That's always the first sign you see of Paradise Cottages. Windswept is one of the Drysdales' cottages. (They all have totally corny names.) It sits a little off from the others on the far side of a little point that juts out into the lake. Just the sight of it made me happy. It meant summer was really starting.

Before I knew it, Patrick was pulling up to the dock.

"Ahoy!"

"Ahoy!" I called back. I waved at Cap'n Teddy. His yachting cap was pushed back over his thick snowy-white hair, and his wide, sunburned face was as friendly as ever as he grabbed the rope Patrick threw him.

"Welcome!" That was Duchess, his wife. She's such a character! I don't know how she does it, but her silver hair is always beauty-parlor fresh, her makeup is perfect, and her clothes look like a magazine ad for "resort wear." She makes the rest of us look like castaways. Her tiny dog, Brinkley, yapped as we climbed out of the boat. She put him down and he ran up and down the dock, barking like mad.

"Ophelia!" That was Sam, running down the path, her long brown braids flying. "I didn't hear the boat coming. You're here! Yay!" We hugged. Then I introduced Amanda to everyone.

"Welcome, Amanda," said Duchess, standing with an arm around Sam. "I'm sure you'll have a marvelous time. Has Ophelia told you about the swimming races? And Regatta Day? And the parade?"

She nodded. I had told her all about it by e-mail. Fourth of July week at Paradise Cottages is crammed full of activities.

Duchess smiled over at Patrick. "Patrick's going to win the race this year, I'm sure of it," she said. "He's on the swim team at school, and he's been training like mad."

Patrick made an "aw shucks" face. Then he grinned and struck a pose, biceps flexed. I heard Amanda gasp.

Nobody else did, though. Because just then, Rinker drove up on the noisy little tractor that is the only vehicle at the Cottages. Rinker is the Drysdales' handyman. I can never quite get a handle on him. He's tall and thin and there's always this stinky little cloud around him because he smokes a pipe, and he never smiles. He works hard, I know that. He's always hammering away at something, or hauling stones to rebuild a wall.

Rinker (I don't even know if that's his first or last name!) climbed off the tractor and hitched up his overalls. He nodded to me and Amanda and Juliet. Then, without saying a word, he started to unload the boat onto the open wagon that was attached to the tractor. He would be making several trips between the dock and Whispering Pines, hauling all our stuff and stacking it on the porch.

I grabbed a backpack and a duffel jammed with snorkels, masks, and fins. Amanda and Juliet picked out their backpacks, too. Then we all started walking along behind Rinker, in a sort of parade. Rinker putted ahead. Cap'n Teddy and Duchess followed him, Duchess carrying Brinkley. Sam and I strolled along next, with Amanda just behind us. And Juliet, whose friend Sally had just dashed down to the dock, brought up the rear. Patrick stayed with the boat, unpacking the rest of our stuff onto the dock.

"Everything looks just the same!" I said happily as we walked up the white gravel path past the common house, where there's a Ping-Pong table and games and books, toward the little white cottages. Each one has a screened porch, furnished with a hammock and an old couch or some easy chairs, and they all look out at the lake.

"It doesn't change much," Sam agreed.

I sniffed the air. There was a smoky smell. "Bonfire last night?" I asked.

She shook her head.

Duchess overheard my question. "No, dear," she said. "Terrible news. The summerhouse burned down."

"No!" I said. The summerhouse was always one of my favorite things about Paradise Cottages. It was a little open-air gazebo covered in flowering vines. Sam and I played in there for hours at a time when we were little. True, in the last few years we didn't go there as much because it was kind of falling apart, but still. I was sad to hear that it was gone.

Duchess nodded sadly. "Yes, it burned to the ground before we could do a thing," she said. "We're not really sure how the fire started." She lowered her voice. "I think perhaps Rinker was a little careless with a match," she whispered to me.

I looked over at Sam and raised my eyebrows. It sounded as if there might be a mystery in the works! Sam and I both *love* mysteries. In fact, one of the games we used to play in the summerhouse was Nancy Drew. We'd always fight about who got to be Nancy and who had to be her "plump friend" Bess.

Sam didn't seem to catch my meaning, or else she ignored it. "Remember how we used to braid the vines?" she asked. "And sometimes we'd pretend we were in a hut on a tropical island, like the Swiss Family Robinson?"

"I remember cutting out paper dolls," I said. "And putting on little plays with them. We made everybody at the Cottages come to see. They must have been so bored!"

She and I reminisced as we walked along. I glanced over at Amanda once in a while to make sure she didn't feel left out, but she was just walking along with this dreamy expression on her face. I had a feeling she wasn't hearing a word we said.

# Chapter Three

"Ophelia! Is that you?"

I looked up to see where the voice was coming from and saw the familiar porch of Shangri-La. My family stayed in that cottage once. It has a great view of the island.

"Mrs. M!" I cried.

It was Annette Moscowitz, one of my favorite people at Paradise. She and her husband, Carl, have been coming for years. Last summer, she was very, very pregnant. She could barely walk to the common house. But she loved to swim. "I must be part whale," she'd joke as she bobbed around near the main dock.

"Where's your baby?" I asked.

She grinned. "I have a surprise for you," she said. She turned to call in through the screen door. "Carl!"

Her husband appeared, carrying two squirming girls in pigtails. One had purple ribbons in her black hair and the other had pink, but other than that, they looked exactly alike.

"Oh, my God!" I said. "Twins!"

Annette nodded. "Meet Ava and Rose," she

said. "We knew we were having twins, but we kept it a secret. We couldn't wait for you to meet them!"

"Aren't they adorable?" asked Sam. "Annette says we can baby-sit if we want. I already got to watch them for a few hours the other day."

Amanda just yawned. Which was surprising, because she's always been nuts about babies.

I was dying to hold them and ask a million questions about them, but I was also dying to get to our cottage and check everything out. "I'll come back and visit later!" I told Annette. She and Carl smiled and waved. The twins smiled, too, and made "bye-bye" noises.

"So, who else is here?" I asked Sam.

"Lots of people you know," she answered. "The Wallbridges, of course." That was obvious. Juliet's friend Sally, who was walking behind us, is a Wallbridge. She has a kind-of-cute older brother, Derek, who is always drooping around miserably at Paradise because he can't bring his computer.

"And the Greens," Sam went on. "Tessa's going to give Patrick some competition in that swimming race."

"Who?" Amanda chimed in. Hearing Patrick's name seemed to have woken her up.

"Tessa Green," I told her. "She's the most awesome swimmer. She's a little older than Patrick. I think maybe she's eighteen. She usually wins the swim race in her age group."

"Patrick is sixteen," said Amanda, as if she were telling us something important.

"We know," Sam said, rolling her eyes. "Anyway, Tessa's been swimming a lot every day. You should see how fast she is. Even though she's been a little distracted this summer. She has this boyfriend her parents don't like. She's forbidden to see him. It's a whole big drama, I guess."

"Interesting. Anybody else?" I asked.

Sam thought for a moment. "That's most of the regular people," she said.

"I know Poppy said some regulars couldn't afford to come anymore, since the rates were raised." In fact, Poppy had said this might be the last year *we* could come, but I didn't want to tell Sam that. I thought it was kind of unfair of the Drysdales to raise their rates, but Poppy said they had a right to.

Sam sighed. "It's not *that* much more," she protested. "And anyway, they wouldn't have done it if —"

"Sam, darling," Duchess interrupted. She was walking ahead of us, carrying Brinkley. I didn't realize she'd been listening. "Let's not talk business, shall we? It's too lovely a day for such a dull topic. Anyway, don't you think Ophelia would like to hear about some of our wonderful new guests?" She chucked Brinkley under the chin and kissed his tiny nose, murmuring at him.

Sam shrugged. "Sure, Gram," she said.

"Here are some of them now!" said Cap'n Teddy. "Ahoy there!" He waved at a couple who were sitting on the front steps of Seventh Heaven, along with a little redheaded boy in green overalls.

"Sam, introduce your friend," Duchess prompted.

Obediently, Sam introduced us. "This is Ophelia Parker," she said. "And her friend Amanda. Back there are Juliet and Sally. Juliet is Ophelia's sister. You already know Sally."

"We're the Buxtons," said the woman. She was pretty, with short blond hair and a small, cute face. "I'm Susan and this is Mike." She pointed to her husband, a strong-looking guy with a goatee. "And this is our son, Max."

Max grinned and held up four pudgy fingers. "I'm four!" he shouted.

Just then, Mom and Poppy and the twins caught up with us. They must have left their boats tied up at the main dock. "These are my parents," I said, introducing them. "And my sisters Helena and Viola."

"Helena and Viola!" crowed Max, echoing me. He stared at the twins for a moment. Then he jumped up and ran over to Helena. "Pick me up!" he demanded.

Helena looked a little surprised, but she smiled. How could she not? He was totally adorable. "Well, okay," she said. She put her arms around his waist and lifted him. He giggled loudly, then struggled to be let down. "Now you!" he said, turning to Viola.

"I think Max has some new friends," Mike said. He stood up to shake hands with Poppy.

"Is that Buxton, as in 'Build It Better with Buxton'?" Poppy asked. He was talking about the signs that are all over this part of the state. It seemed like Buxton built almost every new house in the area.

Mike laughed and shook his head. "I wish!" he said. "That's my brother. I'm just a carpenter."

"He's a very, very talented carpenter," said Susan, looking at him proudly.

Meanwhile, Max was telling Helena a "secret," buzzing into her ear. She buzzed back at him and he shrieked with laughter.

"Okay, Max," said Susan. "The Parkers probably want to get settled. You'll see them later. Come on over and sit with us again."

Reluctantly, Max obeyed. But he walked backward, staring at Helena and Viola the whole time. Clearly, they'd made a big impression on him.

We said good-bye to the Buxtons and kept walking. By then, Rinker and the tractor were way ahead of us. He was probably already unpacking the first load of our stuff.

I was going over the cottages in my mind. The Drysdales — Cap'n Teddy, Duchess, Sam, and Patrick — must be in the one called Dunrovin'. They always are. The Wallbridges are always in Dew Drop Inn, and the Greens are in Happy Hideaway. The Buxtons were in Seventh Heaven, the Moscowitzes were in Shangri-La, and we were in Whispering Pines. That left Dunworkin', Bide-A-Wee, Sleepy Hollow, and Windswept.

"Who's in Dunworkin'?" I asked Sam. That's the cottage next to Dunrovin'.

"The Carsons," she told me. She bent to pick up a pinecone, then tossed it into the air and caught it as we walked. "Jack and Rita. They've been here before, but never for the Fourth. They're old friends of my grandparents."

"Old?" roared Cap'n Teddy. "Who're you calling old?" He was laughing, and his face glowed red beneath his white hair.

"I mean," Sam said, pretending exasperation, "they've been friends for a long time."

"Practically forever!" Duchess told me. "Why, I knew Rita when she was a chorus girl."

"And I knew Jack when he was a safecracker!" Cap'n Teddy put in.

"A *safe*cracker?" I asked.

"That was before he retired, of course," Cap'n Teddy said.

"Gramps is joking," Sam said, throwing her arms around Cap'n Teddy and giving him an affectionate hug. "Jack just likes to tell stories. I think he actually sold insurance or something."

Cap'n Teddy shrugged. "If that's what you want to believe . . ." he said, giving me a tiny wink as he hugged Sam back.

I took this all in. The Carsons sounded interesting. I couldn't wait to meet them. Then I went back to my list of cottages. "So, that leaves Bide-A-Wee, Sleepy Hollow, and Windswept."

"Rinker is staying in Sleepy Hollow. Windswept is vacant," Duchess said, a little sadly.

"We're going to do some renovations on those two." Cap'n Teddy pushed back his hat and crossed his arms. "They're a little shabby."

I didn't want to say anything, but so far every cottage we'd passed looked a little shabby. Up close, most of them had paint that was peeling, at least one cracked window, and holes in the screen doors. To change the subject, I asked about the cottage he hadn't mentioned.

"Bide-A-Wee? That's the Wilson fellow," said Cap'n Teddy. "Newspaperman. Says he's here to work on a novel."

"His name's Jeremy Wilson," Sam said, filling in the details. "He's really nice. He covers local politics. But he *really* wants to write mysteries. So he brought his laptop up here for some peace and quiet."

"It's plenty quiet," said Cap'n Teddy. "But I haven't seen him doing any writing. Mostly he just paddles around in that fancy boat of his."

"He has a really nice kayak," Sam explained. "It must have cost thousands."

"Poppy built his own," I told her. "It's purple. He let me choose what color to paint it."

"Cool!" Sam smiled at my dad. "Can I try it sometime?"

"How about" — Poppy checked his watch — "in an hour?" I knew he couldn't wait to show off his boat.

"That might be your best chance," Duchess told Sam. "After all, the next few days are going to be very, very busy around here."

"What's the schedule?" Mom asked.

Duchess ticked off the days on her fingers. "Let's see. Tomorrow's July first. You'll spend most of the day settling in, visiting with the other guests. The big swimming race is on the second, the third is Regatta Day, and of course we'll all go to town for the parade and fireworks on the Fourth."

"And we have to spend a night on the island!" I told Sam. "Like always. And pick blueberries. And make fairy castles in the woods, and hunt for heart-shaped rocks, and do dives off the dock, and —"

Sam grinned and nodded. "We'll do all of it," she said. "And more."

"And more," I agreed, thinking about the mystery of the razed[4] summerhouse.

"I'm ready for a nap," said Amanda, who'd been pretty quiet all along. "And, like, is there a place I'll be able to plug in my blow-dryer?"

I looked at Sam.

She looked at me.

I didn't roll my eyes. But believe me, it took a lot of effort. I had a feeling the whole Paradise experience was going to be wasted on Amanda.

[4]razed: funny word. It sounds the same as raised, but it means kind of the opposite: demolished, torn down.

# Chapter Four

"Oh, yay!" I cried. I couldn't help myself. I was so happy to see good old Whispering Pines.

Our little parade had marched right up to it to find Rinker unloading boxes and bags from the tractor. We all pitched in to help, and in a couple of minutes the little trailer was empty, the porch was full, and Rinker had gone off to get another load. Duchess, Cap'n Teddy, and Sam had left, too. "They'll want to settle in, dear," Duchess had said to Sam as they'd gone off arm in arm.

I walked down the porch stairs just to step back and take it all in. Whispering Pines is nestled into a grove of pine trees, so it's all shady and cozy in front. In back there's another porch that gets the early-morning sun. That's the spot to sit in the morning, sipping some tea and looking out at the lake. There's a path that leads straight from the back porch to our own private little dock on the lake, where Poppy's kayak and the canoe would soon be tied up.

There's a hammock on each porch and a bunch of comfy old wooden chairs with overstuffed cushions, perfect for curling up with a good book.

I sighed. "Isn't it the best?" I asked Amanda.

"Don't those cushions get, like, all mildewed?" she asked, wrinkling her nose.

I sighed again, but it was a different kind of sigh. "Actually, I guess they do, a little. They have a certain smell. But I happen to like it." I really do. I guess it's weird, but there's something about that smell that makes me happy. That smell represents summer: long days and warm nights and corn on the cob and ice-cream sandwiches and wet bathing suits and dumb old romance novels to read in the hammock. I love it all.

"Come on in," I told Amanda. "I'll show you around."

She followed me up the porch steps. I pushed open the screen door and took a deep sniff. Ah! That's another smell I love: the scent of the inside of the cottage. It smells of dust and sun-warmed wood and coffee and — I don't know, probably *mice* or something. Okay, so it's not exactly a clean, fresh scent like in the ads for air freshener. But it's one of my favorite smells in the whole world.

I looked around at all the old familiar sights. There were the old couches in the big, open living room, all squashed and soft and cozy and covered in brightly colored but faded Indian-print bedspreads. The fishing nets up on the wall. The tacky sign that says, WELCOME, FRIENDS!

"Where's the TV?" asked Amanda.

"No TV," I told her. "No TV, no phone, no fax, no computer."

"No phone?" She looked a little panicky.

"There's one at the common house," I reassured her. "If you need to check in with your parents or something. And if somebody calls you, they'll come and get you." I knew she wasn't totally happy about that, but what could I do? "Come see the kitchen," I said. I pulled her into a large room to the right. "Isn't that the coolest?" I asked, pointing to the old-fashioned black cookstove.

"You mean, we have to chop wood in order to cook?" Amanda was looking even more panicky now. "Is there running water?"

I laughed. "Yes, there's water," I said. "And *two* bathrooms, one with a shower and everything. Plus a shower outside, for when you're all sandy from the beach. And no, we don't have to chop wood. See? There's a regular stove, too." I glanced around at the kitchen, loving the sight of all the old plates and bowls lined up on the open shelves. The dishes are white enamel with a red rim and a picture of a rooster on them. In the middle of the kitchen is a big old white-painted table, covered with a red-and-white-checked tablecloth. There was a vase of white daisies on the table. Sam had probably picked them and put them there for us.

"Are you hungry?" I asked Amanda, trying to

remember to be a good hostess. I kind of hoped she wasn't, since all the food was still packed in boxes and bags out on the porch.

She shook her head. "Where do we sleep?" she asked. "Do we have, like, a bedroom?"

For a second I felt like saying, "No, we sleep in hammocks out under the trees," just to see her face. But that was mean. "We have the *best* bedroom," I said. "Come see!" I led her out of the kitchen. The living room is two stories high in the middle, but all around it at the second level is a balcony. "The bedrooms are up there," I said, pointing. I headed for the staircase near the back of the cottage, the one that goes up to the right side. There are two bedrooms over there. On the other side, there are two bedrooms and a tiny bathroom.

Amanda and I had the front corner bedroom, the one I usually share with Juliet. Juliet would be in the other one, where Katherine usually sleeps. The twins would sleep in one of the bedrooms on the other side, and Mom and Poppy would be in the other.

I threw open the door to our bedroom. It looked the same as always. There were the two twin beds, covered in the old familiar bedspreads, one blue and one red, both with pictures of horses and lariat-tossing cowboys on them. White curtains billowed at the windows as a pine-scented breeze blew in. There was another little vase of flowers on the big old dresser, which had a lacy white cloth covering at least some of its chipped blue paint.

I drew in a breath. "The shark picture!" I said, pointing to a painting over the dresser. It showed a man clinging to the wreckage of a ship, watching with a frightened face as the fin of a shark drew ever closer. I *love* that picture. I don't know why. I guess it's just part of the whole Paradise thing for me.

"Ew," was Amanda's only comment.

"There aren't any sharks in the lake," I assured her.

She rolled her eyes at me. "Like, I'm not *stupid*," she said.

Just then, my mom called from downstairs, "Ophelia! Amanda! Can you girls come help us unpack?"

I slipped between the sheets later on that night, feeling completely content. We'd unpacked all our stuff, and Poppy had made an excellent dinner. Afterward, Amanda and I had strolled down to the common house for ice-cream sandwiches. Sam had met us there and walked us back, and we'd hung out on the back porch until we were too tired to talk anymore.

I pulled the cowboy blanket up and snuggled down into my bed. Ah, Paradise.

# Chapter Five

It was raining when I woke up. Not hard, just a steady soft rain I could hear on the roof. I didn't mind. It often does that on summer mornings in Paradise. I knew it would clear up soon.

I rolled over to check my watch, which I'd left on the night table. It was only ten after six! No way was Amanda going to want to get up that early. But I couldn't sleep anymore. I slipped out of bed, grabbed some clothes, and padded out onto the balcony to pull them on. Then I tiptoed downstairs, grabbed Juliet's purple rain jacket off one of the hooks near the door, and let myself out.

I walked down the main path, loving the quiet, gentle rain and the way it made everything smell and look so fresh and green. The common house was shut up and quiet, so I went right past it and down to the main dock, where Poppy's kayak and our canoe were tied up, along with a bunch of other boats. I walked to the end of the dock and gazed out at the fog that was just starting to lift off the lake. The water's surface was like a mirror.

Everything was so still. It was preternaturally[5] quiet. I heard a loon call and smiled to myself.

Then I heard a splashing noise. And it kept coming nearer.

For a second, I remembered the scary stories Katherine used to tell me about a lake monster. There was a whole summer when I wouldn't go *near* the water because of those stories. Finally, Poppy found out what I was scared of and set me straight. Katherine got in big trouble: She didn't get any ice cream for a whole week.

The splashing sound was even closer now. Finally, a figure emerged from the fog. It was a swimmer! The person was moving along like a regular motor, with strong, even strokes.

I watched until I could see who it was. "Tessa!" I said as she drew up to the dock.

She looked up, her eyes wide. "Whoa! You scared me! I didn't think anybody would be out this early." Then she pulled herself up onto the dock and shook her head to get the water out of her ears. She was tall and thin and really strong-looking in her blue racing suit. She glanced around. "Training swim," she explained, even though I hadn't asked. "Anybody else up?"

[5]preternatural: beyond the ordinary

"Just me," I said.

She looked relieved, like she didn't want to see anyone else. "How are you, Ophelia?" she asked.

"Great," I said.

She smiled. "Me, too. But I have to go in. I'm freezing!" She didn't have a towel or anything.

"Bye," I said, watching her run off toward Happy Hideaway.

I sat on the dock for a while longer, until the rain let up and the sun started to break through. Then I decided to walk some more. I headed for one of the little winding paths that go through the woods. But before I got there, I smelled that smoky smell. The summerhouse! How could I have forgotten? I had to go check that out.

I walked past the common house again, up a little hill, through a grove of birch trees, past the big, moss-covered boulders Sam and I call Momma and Poppa Bear, and into a little clearing. My stomach lurched when I saw the blackened, charred timbers that were all that was left of the summerhouse.

I tiptoed around, looking for clues. It was probably too late to find much; detectives always say you have to get to a crime scene when it's still fresh. It looked as if a lot of people had trampled through the area; there were way too many different types of footprints for them to be any kind of clue. There were even tire tracks, probably from Rinker's tractor, and marks from someone trying to rake the cinders into a neater pile.

I poked a toe into a pile of logs, moving the top one a little so I could see what was underneath.

Nothing. Just more blackened logs. Poor old summerhouse.

Then a glint of red off to the side caught my eye. I bent down to see what it was and picked up a red metal screw top, about two inches in diameter. Probably just the top off some juice bottle or something. But I put it in my pocket, anyway.

While I was bent over, I saw something else interesting. A small pile of paper matches, bent at weird angles. I felt a little chill run down my spine. This must be the exact spot where somebody started the fire! It hadn't been easy, apparently. There were at least ten matches piled up there.

I looked around some more, but didn't see anything else suspicious. Then I started thinking again about all the things that Sam and I used to do in that summerhouse, and I got so sad I had to leave.

Something about being at Paradise makes me kind of sentimental, I guess.

Anyway, I walked back down toward the common house. Just as I passed it, Sam walked out of

Dunrovin'. "Hey!" I called. "Come for a walk! Better grab your raincoat."

"Don't have one," she said lightly. "Where should we go?"

I was just thinking about the possibilities for our oblectation[6] (the waterfall? the wild apple orchard? the secret cove?) when I heard a commotion down at the dock.

"What's going on down there?" I asked.

Sam shrugged. "Don't know. Somebody banged on our door a little while ago, but I was still half-asleep. Gramps went out, that's all I know."

"Let's go see," I said. We ran down to the dock. A bunch of people were standing around: Cap'n Teddy, Mike Buxton, Derek Wallbridge, and two men I didn't know, one grandfatherly looking and one younger.

"Who're they?" I whispered to Sam. She knew who I meant.

"The old guy is Jack Carson," she whispered back. "The one in the baseball cap is Jeremy Wilson. The reporter?"

I nodded. "He looks mad," I said. Jeremy Wilson seemed to be yelling at Cap'n Teddy.

"He sure does," Sam agreed. She started walking faster, then broke into a run.

[6]oblectation: delight, pleasure

I followed her. Soon we were close enough to hear.

"I'm *not* losing my temper," Jeremy Wilson was saying. "But I might soon. I don't know if you realize how much that boat is worth! If it's been stolen, *your* insurance is going to have to cover it."

"Oh, my God!" Sam said, covering her mouth with her hand as she stared at the dock. "Jeremy's kayak is gone!"

# Chapter Six

First a fire. Now a missing boat. Something was rotten at Paradise Cottages! In all the years I've been coming here, there had never been a crime wave like this one.

Sure, the summer when I was six my stuffed dachshund, Doogie, turned up missing one morning. A toy-napping? Not exactly. In the end I discovered that Mom had taken him over to Paradise Village along with the laundry. A fresh, clean Doogie and I were reunited that very afternoon.

Another time, somebody was helping themselves to ice-cream sandwiches from the freezer in the common house and not leaving money for them (the snack bar is run on the honor system). But that turned out to be Derek Wallbridge, who had spent all his savings on a new computer game and had to wait for his next allowance so he could pay up. He paid; he was forgiven. End of story.

But these were *serious* crimes. And I wanted to be the one to catch the criminal. I *love* mysteries. And what could be better than a real live one, mine for the solving? By the time the rain had stopped and the sun came out, I had assembled my team of detectives.

Sam was totally into it; she was mad at Jeremy for yelling at her gramps and swore that she'd show him by finding his stupid boat. So were Helena and Viola, and their new shadow, Max. Amanda? Not so much. She was more interested in sitting on the dock in her bikini, waiting for Patrick to come by. (He did, by the way. Come by. And, even though he should have been training for his swimming race, he spent most of the afternoon tossing Amanda into the water.)

The rest of us prowled around all afternoon, looking for clues (not that we found any) and kayaks (ditto) and talking about possible suspects (so far, just about everybody at Paradise Cottages). We may not have solved any crimes, but we had a blast.

Little did we know that our criminal had only *begun* his (her???) crime spree.

# Chapter Seven

*"Buenos días, Ophelia! Como estas?"*

I rolled my eyes, but Poppy cheerfully ignored me.

*"Como estas?"* he repeated.

It's another Parker family tradition. Poppy and Mom always come to Paradise with some "project" in mind. They don't believe in estivating[7] during summer vacation. Last year Poppy was into learning to identify ferns, for example, while Mom spent her time rereading all the Greek and Roman myths. They like the family to participate, which is why I can tell a Christmas fern from an ostrich fern, and how I know the story of Narcissus. This year, Poppy is brushing up on his Spanish, which he last studied during the ice age, which is to say when he was in college. He intends to speak nothing but Spanish every morning while we're here. Mom speaks Spanish pretty well already; her goal is to learn how to do watercolors. My parents are extremely chrestomathic[8].

Okay, I can deal with that. Fortunately, I took

[7]estivate: the summer version of hibernate

[8]chrestomathic: devoted to learning useful things

beginning Spanish last year so I remember some stuff, enough to survive. I knew he was asking me how I was. *"Muy bien, gracias, y usted?"* I asked, using the more formal form since I was addressing an elder. (Good, thanks, and you?)

*"Bien, gracias."* Poppy beamed. *"Deseas tu el desayuno?"*

Since he was holding out a box of cereal, it was easy to figure out that he was asking if I wanted breakfast. *"Si, gracias,"* I said. (Yes, thank you.)

Amanda followed my lead and just said all the same things I did. She never took Spanish, but you wouldn't know it. She's smart and picks things up quickly.

We sat down at the table with our cereal. Fortunately, Poppy doesn't remember too much more Spanish, so it was a pretty quiet meal. He studied the Spanish textbook he'd brought, and once in a while he came out with some comment like, *"llueve,"* which means "it's raining."

So it was. Just like the morning before. "I hope it clears up before our race," said Amanda.

"It will," I promised. I glanced at the kitchen clock, which is in the shape of a rooster to match the plates. "Ours doesn't start for a little while. But the first one must be starting soon. It's already nine-thirty."

Just then, we heard a loud *boom*.

Amanda jumped. "What was *that*?" she asked.

"Cap'n Teddy's cannon!" I said. "That means the races are about to begin!" I'd forgotten all about the cannon, but hearing it made me remember all the races of years past. Cap'n Teddy has this little brass cannon — he says it came off a pirate ship — that he just *loves* to shoot off. He uses it instead of a starting pistol. The sound echoes all over the lake, and it never fails to get me all psyched for whatever race is about to start.

"Was that the cannon?" Helena asked, coming into the kitchen, rubbing her eyes. At home, Helena's always the first one up, but she loves to sleep in when we're at the lake. Viola was right behind her.

"Aren't the little kids first?" she asked. "Max will be so bummed if we're not there!"

*"Como estas?"* Poppy asked, a little late. *"Deseas desayuno?"* He shook the cereal box hopefully.

"No time!" said Helena, grabbing a bagel from the counter.

"Let's go!" said Viola, grabbing a yogurt from the fridge.

Juliet ran in just then. "The cannon!" she said. "It went off! Time for the races!" She grabbed a bagel, too.

*"Adios,"* I told Poppy as the five of us headed out the door.

"*Adios*," he said, looking a little forlorn. I knew he'd put his Spanish book away in a moment and follow us down to the dock. Nobody wants to miss the races.

It was still misting a little by the time everyone had assembled near the dock. Patrick, wearing a yellow hooded rain jacket, was helping Rinker get the motorboat ready.

"Can I help?" Amanda asked, going right up to Patrick.

Rinker, his pipe clenched between his teeth, frowned. "Not unless you have a gallon of gas to spare, young lady," he said. He turned away, grumbling.

"He can't find the gas can," Patrick explained. "It's usually locked up in the boathouse, but it's missing."

"It was there yesterday," Rinker said. "Missing its cap, but there all the same. Now it's just plain missing."

Cap? I wondered if that was the cap I'd picked up in the ashes of the summerhouse. If so, somebody had used gas to make sure their fire burned fast and hot. That thought was a little scary.

"I've got some gas," offered Jack Carson. "Hold on, I'll go grab it." He hustled off to his little red motorboat, which was tied up at the small dock in front of Dunworkin'. His boat was named *Jack's*

*Toy.* He leaned into it, pulled out a red gas can, and trotted back to the main dock.

Hmm. A red gas can. Same color as the cap I'd picked up. I filed that fact away.

"Well, then!" said Cap'n Teddy, rubbing his hands together as he watched Rinker fill up the tank. He was standing on the dock, the little cannon at his side. "All set now?" He glanced around. A whole crowd of people had gathered near the dock, practically everyone at the Cottages. Some were there just to watch: Mom and Poppy, who had arrived by then, and the Moscowitzes — or, at least, Annette and the babies, who were napping in a stroller. Others were obviously ready to race, including Max.

"First," bellowed Cap'n Teddy, "is the doggie paddle race. For little ones and nonswimmers."

Max was jumping up and down impatiently. "That's me!" he cried. "That's me!"

"Me, too," said Rita Carson, who was dressed in a frilly red-and-white-polka-dotted suit with a little skirt. She also had on a bathing cap that was covered in huge red rubber roses. She smiled down at Max. "Ready to race?" she asked.

Max grinned. "Ready!"

A couple of other adults had lined up: Mr. Wallbridge, who never learned to swim even though he's a good sailor, and Tessa Green's mom, who's always game for anything.

"Go, Max!" yelled Helena.

He raised his hands like a prizefighter, as if he'd already won the race.

Rinker started the motorboat and putted out to a spot not too far from the dock.

"Out to the boat and back," said Cap'n Teddy. "I'll call Ready and Set, then fire the cannon. Okay?"

"Okay!" everybody chorused. Max and the grown-ups eased themselves off the dock and into the water. (Nonswimmers don't start with a dive, obviously.)

"Ready! Set!" cried Cap'n Teddy. Then he fired the cannon. *Bang!* They were off.

It's hard to watch the doggie paddle race without totally cracking up. I'm sure everybody laughed when *I* was in that race years ago. Not that I'd have noticed. I was probably totally focused on keeping my head above water.

Max started out strong and stayed in front all the way out to the boat. He churned his hands under his chin and kicked randomly, propelling himself along at a surprisingly good speed. Rita Carson was close behind him, her red roses bobbing as she motored through the water. Mr. Wallbridge and Mrs. Green were hopelessly behind in seconds.

Out at the boat, Max reached a hand up to slap its side. "Look at me, Helena!" he yelled. "Viola, watch." He gurgled a little on that last word, as his chin dipped below the water. But he kicked a few times and got himself above water again, then started making his way back to the dock.

I'll spare you the suspense: It was neck and neck the whole way, but Max was victorious in the end. He ran right past his mother's open arms and into Viola's, then made her and Helena come with him as he went up to receive his trophy from Cap'n Teddy.

The trophies are recycled from year to year, and most of them aren't even real swimming trophies. The only one I ever won, when I was ten, was a bowling trophy with a statue of a woman in a little skirt, holding up a bowling ball. But boy, was I proud. I got to go to the common house every day and see that trophy on display, next to a little card with my name on it.

The next race was for eight- to twelve-year-olds. Helena entered, Viola didn't. The twins are very different that way: Viola is so not into athletic competition, while Helena eats it up. Sally Wallbridge entered, too, and so did Juliet.

Rinker brought the motorboat in and tied it up, since the next race went all the way out to the floating raft. Cap'n Teddy checked to see if everyone was ready. In a few moments, *boom*! The cannon went off again and the swimmers thrashed through the water. Helena was doing the butterfly stroke, which she does really well. (I've never been able to do it without looking like an uncoordinated dodo bird.) Sally and Juliet were both doing the crawl. The race was close as they headed out to the raft, but on the return leg Sally fell behind a little, leaving Helena and Juliet to fight it out.

In the end, Helena won by a nose. Max was ecstatic.

Sam, Amanda, and I were the only ones in the thirteen-to-fifteen category. I knew I didn't have a chance. Sam spends the entire summer at Paradise and swims like a fish, and Amanda is on her school's swim team. I wasn't even going to enter, but they talked me into it.

When the cannon went off, I did my best. Unfortunately, I've never totally gotten the breathing thing down, so I can't do the crawl all that well. I have to switch off between styles, starting out with the crawl, changing to the backstroke, then doing the breaststroke for a while in order to catch my breath. I was concentrating on making it out to the raft and was a little more than halfway there when I saw Sam steaming back toward me. Where was

Amanda? She was ahead of me, I knew that. But way behind Sam. Then I spotted her, stopping in midstroke to tug at her bikini bottoms.

I could have told her that bathing suit was a mistake. I knew she had a perfectly good Speedo with her; I'd seen it when we unpacked. But no, she had to wear the bikini because Patrick was going to be watching.

I honestly think she could have won. But Sam was the winner by a mile. No contest. She grinned as Cap'n Teddy gave her a big hug and handed her a trophy (with a statue of a boy swinging a baseball bat).

Amanda wrung out her hair. She didn't seem too upset about her big loss. "Good luck, Patrick," she said, walking over to watch as Patrick warmed up, swinging his arms and stretching his calf muscles.

"I may need it," Patrick said, glancing at Tessa. I followed his glance. Tessa sure did look ready to race, limbering up on the other side of the dock. She'd left her towel and dry clothes in a neat pile.

"Are the sixteen- to eighteen-year-olds ready?" Cap'n Teddy called. These racers had to do two laps: out to the raft and back, then out again and back once more.

"Ready!" answered Derek, who had just jogged

up onto the dock and pulled off his warm-up pants.

Hmm. Speaking of ready to race, Derek looked surprisingly fit for a computer guy. I saw Tessa checking him out, a tiny frown on her face. Like the rest of us, she probably hadn't thought she had any competition other than Patrick.

Cap'n Teddy got his cannon loaded.

The swimmers were poised to go.

"Ready! Set! Go!" yelled Cap'n Teddy. The cannon boomed, and the three swimmers started to knife through the water.

"Check out Derek!" Juliet said.

He took the lead right away, streaking along like an Olympic swimmer. Tessa and Patrick were working hard to stay near him.

Derek stayed in front all the way to the raft, and even for a while on the return trip. But then he must have run out of steam. He fell back, and Tessa and Patrick passed him, Patrick a little bit ahead.

The second lap of the race was a total nail-biter. First, Tessa would be ahead. Then Patrick would sprint for a while, catch up, and pass her. Then Tessa would pass Patrick again.

Amanda could barely watch. She kept squinching her eyes shut, covering them with her hands.

“I can’t watch!” she’d say. “Is he winning?” Then she’d peek through her hands. “Yes!” she’d cry, if Patrick was in the lead, or “Go, Patrick!” if he wasn’t.

I was rooting for Tessa myself. I’ve always liked her. She’s never acted better than me, just because she’s older.

In the end, it was nearly a tie.

Nearly.

Tessa won, by about a centimeter. Her hand slapped the dock first; I was right there, and I saw it. So did Cap’n Teddy. As soon as all three racers were standing on the dock, he handed her the biggest trophy yet. It had a hockey player on it. Everybody there started clapping and whistling for Tessa. “Congratulations,” he said, pumping her hand. Then he turned to Patrick. “You did well, son,” he said in a quieter voice. “Tried your best. Good job.”

Patrick just grunted. He didn’t look happy. When Amanda tried to hand him a towel, he brushed past her without a word and left the dock. Sam went after him.

Derek, meanwhile, was beaming. “Did you see me?” he asked his dad. “I was out front for a long time!”

Cap’n Teddy called for a ten-minute break before the adult race. Rinker headed toward the common house, probably to refill his pipe or something. Some other people drifted that way, too, until there were only a few of us left on the dock: me, Helena, Max, Rita Carson, and Susan Buxton. Max kept patting Helena's trophy and telling her how beautiful it was.

In a few minutes Cap'n Teddy called for all the adult racers to assemble. Jeremy Wilson was the first to be ready.

"I talked to him this morning," Tessa whispered to me. "Turns out he was a star on his college swim team. I think he's going to blow everybody away."

The rest of the adults lined up more slowly: Jack Carson, Steve Green (Tessa's dad), Susan Buxton, and (surprise!) my own mom were all going to race.

I have to say that out of that crew, Jeremy and Susan were the only ones who looked as if they had a chance. Mom is no athlete, even though she did play basketball back when she was in college. Jack has quite a potbelly. And Steve Green pretty much looks like your basic couch potato.

Cap'n Teddy pushed back his hat and took a look at the racers. "Everybody ready?" he asked. "You'll be racing to the raft and back."

"Ready!" they said.

"Okay, then." Cap'n Teddy bent to check his cannon. "Ready! Set!"

"Fire!" someone yelled from back on shore.

Cap'n Teddy looked confused for a second. That wasn't what came next.

"FIRE!" The person shouted it louder this time.

I turned to look back at the shore. Then I saw it. A column of black smoke, rising from behind a grove of trees.

# Chapter Eight

There really was a fire.

We all took off running toward the smoke.

It was Windswept.

And, by the time we got there, it was obvious that there was no point in calling the fire department. There wasn't anything anyone could do. The cottage was totally engulfed in flames, and it was burning down more quickly than you can imagine.

We stood there watching. Nobody spoke. I could feel the hot breath of the fire on my face and hear the crackling as it gobbled up the little house. Mom, who'd ended up near me, put her hand on my shoulder as we stood there, waiting for it to be over. It didn't take long. The roof fell in, the cottage collapsed, and the flames began to die down.

Quickly, Cap'n Teddy and Rinker organized a bucket brigade. We made a line of people from the lake to the cottage and handed buckets full of water from person to person. The first person scooped water, and the last one poured it on the flames.

Before long, the fire was almost out. Wet, blackened timbers sent stinky smoke into the air, but there were no more flames.

I stood there, staring at the rubble.

And thinking.

# Chapter Nine

"Well," said Cap'n Teddy. "Well." He stood looking at the mess that was once Windswept. His face was smeared with black soot; everybody's was. He shook his head. I'd never seen him look so down. He turned to face us. "I guess that's it for the day, folks," he said. "Thanks for your help. We'll postpone that last race. Somehow my heart's just not in it now."

Sam stood between her gramps and Duchess. I could tell she was fighting back tears, but she stood straight and tall, holding her grandmother's hand. Duchess looked very sad and suddenly years older.

"Can't blame you," said Jack Carson, who was standing on Cap'n Teddy's other side. He put a hand on his friend's shoulder. "Come on, I'll buy you an ice-cream sandwich."

The two of them walked off, followed first by Rinker and then by the rest of us. I saw Mom counting heads, making sure that Helena, Viola, Juliet, Amanda, and I were all there. Then she gave me a little wave and headed down the path. Juliet and Sally took off toward the dock. I turned to Sam as we left the clearing where Windswept once sat. "This is serious," I whispered to her. "We have to figure out who's doing this stuff."

"No kidding. I *hate* seeing Gramps so sad," she said fiercely.

We grabbed Helena and Viola as they walked by. "Time for a meeting," I told them. "Coming, Amanda?"

Surprisingly, Amanda had been a big help with the bucket brigade. For a few minutes, she'd seemed more like the old Amanda, the one who was always ready to get involved in whatever was going on.

"You're not going to play detective again, are you?" she asked, wrinkling her nose. "I'll catch you later. Right now, all I want is a shower. Anyway, I have to see how Patrick is doing and all."

Old Amanda had disappeared again, and Valley Amanda had taken her place once more.

What could I say? "Later," I told her. She walked off toward our cottage.

That left four of us. "Okay," I said, facing the others. "Here's the deal. We have to figure out who could have set that fire. And we have to do it soon. Right now is the time to question everybody. It's our best chance to catch the perp."

"Perp?" Helena asked.

"Perpetrator," I explained. "The person who committed the crime. That's what they always call them on the cop shows."

Helena shrugged. "Okay," she said. "If you say so."

"I have a plan," I went on. "We divide the cottages up between us. Then we fan out and question everybody. When we're done, we meet up again and try to put it all together."

"What are we questioning them about, exactly?" Viola asked.

"Their whereabouts. Where they were during the races."

"But everybody was down at the dock!" said Sam. "I mean, I was there the whole time. Well, except for when Patrick and I went back to our cottage, just after his race. But we were together then. We were together the whole day."

"I'm not asking *you* for an alibi," I told her. "But that's exactly the kind of information we need about every resident of Paradise. *Were* they at the races? If so, were they there the whole time? If they weren't there, or weren't there the whole time, we need to account for where they were. And it's best if there's some way we can verify what they're saying. Like, the way you said that you and Patrick were together. You can vouch for each other."

Viola was nodding. "I get it," she said. "Then, maybe once we have all the information, we can make a chart or something."

I beamed at her. "Exactly what I was thinking!" I said. "Okay. I'll take our cottage, because I have to go back there anyway for a notebook and pen. And I'll do Dunrovin' and Dunworkin'. Helena, you take Dew Drop Inn and Happy Hideaway. Viola, Seventh Heaven and Bide-A-Wee. Sam, Shangri-La and Sleepy Hollow. How does that sound?"

Sam shrugged. "Fine with me," she said.

The twins nodded, too.

"Let's meet at the Poppa Bear rock in half an hour," I suggested.

We were off. I headed straight for our cottage. Mom was sitting out on the porch, so as soon as I'd found my notebook (I always have one around in case I hear a new word I have to write down) I decided to question her first. I sat down next to her and clicked my pen.

*Beverly Parker*, I wrote at the top of a clean page in my notebook. "So, Mom," I asked, trying to sound casual, "did you see all the races?"

"Every one," she answered, without really looking up from the watercolor she was working on. "You did very well, honey."

"Are you sure you saw my race?" Nobody who

watched that pathetic performance could say I'd done well at all.

Then she did look up. She smiled at me. "I know you didn't win," she said. "But you tried hard. That's what counts."

Right. That's what everybody always says. But it's not really so true. From what I've seen of most sports, what counts is winning. I let it go. "So, you were down at the dock all morning, right?" I asked.

She nodded. "All morning," she agreed. "Up until the fire, that is." Her face changed, thinking of that terrible fire. "I feel so bad for the Drysdales. Wasn't that awful? Anyway, after I helped out with the buckets, I came back here to wash up."

*At dock for all races,* I wrote. *Helped with fire.* "Well, I guess you want to get back to your painting," I said. "It's good. The pine trees look real."

She sighed. "Thanks. But I'm not concentrating all that well, to tell you the truth. That fire really shook me up."

"Me, too," I told her. We sat in silence for a few moments. Then I glanced down at my notebook. If I wanted to get all my questioning done, I had to get going.

Before I left Whispering Pines, I talked to Poppy and Juliet. They checked out perfectly: Both of them were on the dock the whole time, except when they headed up to the common house together during the break because Poppy wanted some pretzels.

*David Parker: On dock all morning. Common house. Alibi supported by Juliet Parker.*

*Juliet Parker: Ditto. Supported by David Parker.*

Amanda was in the shower, so I couldn't talk to her, but I didn't have to. She'd been pretty much in my eyesight the whole time.

That did it for Whispering Pines. On to Dunrovin' and Dunworkin'.

I passed Dunworkin' first, so I stopped to talk to the Carsons. They were on their porch, sipping iced tea and talking quietly.

"Hi!" I said. "I'm Ophelia Parker, from Whispering Pines. Sam's friend?"

"Sure, honey," said Rita. "We haven't been formally introduced, but we know who you are. We're Rita and Jack." She'd changed out of her bathing suit and was now dressed in a lilac sweatsuit. "Come sit for a spell and have some tea."

It seemed like a good way to ease into the questioning thing, so I accepted, even though I don't love iced tea. "Were you really a safecracker?" I asked Jack when he handed me a frosty glass he'd brought from the kitchen.

He laughed. "Teddy's been telling tales again," he said.

That wasn't exactly a denial. I was itching to

make a note in my notebook, but I thought I'd wait until I left. I sat and chatted with them for a while, mostly about the fire and how awful it was, and managed to get a pretty good idea of their whereabouts that morning. Finally, I took the last few sips of tea, thanked them, and headed off down the path. As soon as I was out of their sight, I stopped to make some notes.

*Jack Carson: Watched wife's race. Then spent some time on porch doing crosswords, until he heard someone yell "Fire!"*

*Rita Carson: On dock for most of morning. Returned to cottage to change clothes. Was in shower and did not hear of fire until Jack returned from bucket brigade.*

Next stop: Dunrovin'. The Drysdales. I felt a little awkward about barging in on them, since I knew they must be very upset about the fire. And it seemed obvious that neither of *them* could be a suspect. Why would they destroy their own property? But I thought it was a good idea to hear what they had to say about the fire, anyway.

I didn't get a chance to talk to Cap'n Teddy. He was down at the common house, Duchess told me, handing out free snacks to everyone who had helped on the bucket brigade. Duchess herself was very upset. "The summerhouse was bad enough," she said. "I hated to lose it. But then a boat is stolen, and now this! Can it really be a coincidence?" She paced around, clutching Brinkley tightly against her chest. As usual, she was beautifully dressed in white pants, a navy-blue blouse, and a single string of pearls. Brinkley's collar was navy blue that day, too, I noticed. I wondered if they always matched.

"Are you going to call the police?" I asked.

She shook her head. "Teddy doesn't want to," she said. "He feels it would be bad publicity for Paradise Cottages. And that's the last thing we —" She stopped herself. "Nobody needs bad publicity," she finished.

I nodded. "Of course not." I wanted to tell her not to worry, that we'd find out who had set the fires and stolen the boat. But could I really promise that? After all, I didn't really have a single clue yet, unless you counted the gas-can lid or the bent matches.

I figured I should at least ask her the same question I asked everyone else. "Were you down at the dock all morning?" I asked.

She nodded. "Oh, yes, dear," she said. "I love to watch the races." She thought for a moment. "On second thought, I wasn't there the *whole* time. I missed the second race, because I came back here for a hat. I remember, because I saw Rinker talking to Mike Buxton, over by the old summerhouse site. I believe Rinker was asking for some professional advice on rebuilding."

Interesting. That meant that neither Mike Buxton nor Rinker had been down at the dock at that point.

I talked with Duchess a little longer. Then I glanced at my watch and realized it was time to meet the others. I said my good-byes and raced over to the Poppa Bear rock. Helena and Sam were already there, and Viola joined us a few minutes later.

I took a second to write down what Duchess had told me:

*Duchess Drysdale: At dock, except for walk to get hat. Saw Rinker and Mike Buxton.*

Then I asked the others what they'd found out. And suddenly, I began to realize how complicated this was going to be. There weren't that many people at Paradise Cottages, but they sure did move around a lot.

Derek Wallbridge slept late and barely made it on time for his race.

Carl Moscowitz napped with the twins, then took them for a walk in their stroller. Both of them spit up and needed their clothes changed.

Sally Wallbridge went back to Happy Hideaway after her race because she'd forgotten a towel.

Susan Buxton was doing yoga on her back porch until it was time for her race.

Rinker wouldn't answer any questions. Said he was too busy for such nonsense.

And Jeremy Wilson borrowed a canoe for an early-morning paddle, then changed and showed up in time for his race.

I tried to make a chart. But when it was done, it was just a confusing mishmash of lines intersecting all over the place. The only people we could definitely clear, it seemed, were the ones who really *were* on the dock the whole time: ourselves and Cap'n Teddy.

We weren't exactly narrowing in on a suspect.

# Chapter Ten

Frustrated, we all trooped down to the dock for a swim. I figured it wouldn't hurt to get our minds off the situation. All that cerebration[9] was exhausting. Besides, this *was* still my vacation! I wasn't about to let the investigation take over everything.

Amanda, now with clean, shining hair, was lying on the dock sunning herself. When she heard us coming, she turned over and yawned, adjusting the strap of her bikini. "Hey, Nancy Drew. Caught the desperate criminal yet?" she asked. I stripped down to my bathing suit and plopped down next to her, while the twins and Sam jumped into the water. I wanted to get a little warmer before I went swimming. I love the feeling of cooling off after I've been roasting in the sun.

"Ha-ha," I said. "You won't think it's so funny if *our* cottage burns down." I'd been thinking about that. So far, the person had set fire only to buildings that had fallen into desuetude[10]. But who was to say what the firebug would do next? I knew I wouldn't be sleeping all that well for the next few nights.

[9]cerebration: mental activity

[10]desuetude: disuse

"Patrick says it's probably just coincidence," Amanda reported.

Great. Now I was going to have to hear *Patrick's* opinion on everything. "But what would *Daniel* think?" I said. It was a little mean, but I couldn't help myself.

"Daniel?" she asked, looking blank.

"Yes, Daniel," I said. "Remember? Your boyfriend?"

"Like, why would he have anything to say about this?" she asked. She didn't get it.

"Never mind," I said. "But what *about* Daniel? I mean, it's like you've forgotten all about him. If you and Patrick — if anything happens between you two, isn't that cheating?"

She sat up and shook back her hair. "It's totally *not*," she said, very serious all of a sudden. "Ophelia, everybody knows that summer flings don't count. They're just, like, for fun."

"That's ridiculous!" I burst out.

She looked hurt.

"I'm sorry," I told her. "But isn't it? I mean, either you want Daniel or you want Patrick. You have to choose one or the other. Don't you?"

She shrugged. "Daniel will never know. And what he doesn't know can't, like, hurt him. I wouldn't care if *he* had a summer fling."

I didn't believe her, but I didn't want to get into

a fight. What did *I* know about this stuff? I've never even had one boyfriend, much less the prospect of two. Still, even if it was okay with Daniel, I was worried about another thing: Amanda getting hurt. Patrick's a nice guy, but I already had the feeling that Amanda liked him more than he liked her. He seemed happy to pay attention to her when it suited him, but when he wasn't in the mood — like after he lost the race — he ignored her. "Okay," I said. "Well, just be careful."

"Careful?" she asked, raising an eyebrow. "Of *what*, exactly?"

I dipped a foot into the water to see how cold it was, avoiding Amanda's eyes. "I just wouldn't want you to get hurt," I mumbled.

She made a face. "Hurt? What, you think he doesn't like me as much as I like him?"

"No, I —" It was *exactly* what I thought, but how could I say so?

"Well, for your information, he *does* like me," Amanda said. "In fact, he promised to take me out to the island later on and show me the Indian footprints."

If she'd been ten years younger, she would have added, "So there," and stuck out her tongue.

"*I* wanted to show you!" I cried, feeling ten years younger myself. The Indian footprints are one of the coolest things at Paradise. They're carved into a rocky cliff out on the island. Just the outline of footprints, six of them, walking up the rock. Some people say they're hundreds of years old and were carved by American Indians who passed through the area. (Other people say they appeared in the seventies and were carved by teenagers, but what do they know?) I really *had* been looking forward to showing them to Amanda.

Amanda just shrugged and lay back again, closing her eyes. "You never mentioned it."

Oh, well. What could I say? She wanted to go with Patrick. I looked at Amanda, lying there in the sun with her hair so shiny. "Panda?" I asked, using a nickname from way back when her dad used to call her Amanda-Panda.

She opened her eyes. "What?"

"Is everything okay? Like, with your parents and stuff?" I thought it was really weird that she wasn't talking about that at all. I mean, if you could see her e-mails. That's *all* she writes about.

She closed her eyes again. "Yeah. It's fine."

There was no mistaking her tone. She didn't want any more questions. In fact, she probably didn't want to talk anymore at all. "Well," I said, getting to my feet. "That's good." Then I walked to the edge of the dock and dove into the cold, clear water.

# Chapter Eleven

"Got any real suspects yet?"

"Huh?" I shaded my eyes, looking up at the porch of Bide-A-Wee. Jeremy Wilson was sitting there, his feet up on the railing and an upside-down book on the arm of his chair. Sam was walking me back to Whispering Pines, where I was planning to do some reading myself. Amanda and the twins were still back at the dock.

"I had the feeling you girls were investigating our recent crime wave. Am I wrong?" Jeremy smiled.

"Well," I said, feeling strangely shy about it, "I guess not."

"Why?" asked Sam. "Do you have any leads?"

"Come on up," said Jeremy. "Who's your friend, Sam?"

"This is Ophelia," Sam answered. "Her family has been coming here for years."

"The Parkers," he said, nodding. "I met your dad. That's quite a kayak he built."

"He says *your* kayak was pretty nice," I told him. "I'm sorry it was stolen."

"Me, too. I'd like to know where it went!"

"It would make a good mystery story," said Sam. "A boat-stealing firebug on the loose in Vacationland."

Jeremy nodded without smiling. "It *would* make a good mystery," he agreed. "If only I knew how it ended." He paused. "I'm not convinced that the boat thief and the firebug are one and the same, though," he said.

"What do you mean?" I asked.

Jeremy gave Sam a quick glance, then turned back to me. "I've been thinking. What if the fires were set on purpose? What if they were actually arson?"

"Arson?" I kind of knew what it meant, but I wasn't sure.

"Like, what if those buildings were burned down for a reason? For example, so the Drysdales could collect the insurance money?"

Sam sat up stiffly. "What?" She turned an angry face toward Jeremy. "Are you accusing my gramps of setting fires?"

"No!" said Jeremy. "I mean, not exactly. But what if he *hired* someone to set the fires? Or what if somebody took it upon themselves to set the fires, to help him out?"

"You're crazy!" Sam stood up and faced him, her hands on her hips. "I'm not going to hang around and listen to you talk about my grandparents that way!" She stomped down the porch stairs and ran off toward the common house.

I knew I should follow her. But I was incredibly curious about what Jeremy might have to say next. So I stayed right where I was, sitting on the steps of Bide-A-Wee. "I still don't get it," I said to Jeremy. "Why would they do that?"

"To get the insurance money," he repeated. "Haven't you noticed how run-down this place is? And I know I'm paying more than you folks used to. They must have had to raise the rents because they're in financial trouble."

"Cap'n Teddy and Duchess?" I asked, thinking of Duchess's jewels. "But they're rich!"

"They *live* like they're rich," Jeremy corrected me. "I'm not so sure they really are."

"Anyway," I said, "Sam's right. It's crazy to think that Cap'n Teddy would burn down his own property!"

He shrugged. "Maybe he wouldn't," he said. "But — could you imagine Rinker doing it for him?"

I pictured Rinker's lanky form, his habit of appearing where you least expected him, the way he always did whatever Cap'n Teddy asked him to do. Plus, he had access to the boathouse, where the gas was stored. "Well . . ."

"Or what about that Carson fellow?" Jeremy asked. "I hear he has a shady past."

I'd forgotten about Jack Carson supposedly being a safecracker. "That's just a story!" I said.

"Maybe, maybe not."

I had a sudden image of Jack Carson with a red gas can. Sure, he needed gas for his boat. But what *else* was he using it for?

Jeremy Wilson was definitely getting a kick out of all of this. I could see why he might make a good mystery writer. "Any other suspects?" I asked, figuring I might as well hear everything he had to say.

He smiled. "The grandson," he said.

I gulped. "Patrick?"

He nodded. "The boy's a minor. He wouldn't be prosecuted the same way as an adult would. Maybe the grandparents talked him into it." He paused. "Or maybe he just likes setting fires. Some people do, you know."

Wow. Good thing Sam wasn't there to hear that. She would have flipped out if she heard Jeremy accusing Patrick. I didn't like it, either. I've known Patrick for a long time, and I don't think he's the criminal type. But still, I filed away what Jeremy was saying. It would be silly to ignore any possibilities this early in the investigation. And Patrick probably had access to the boathouse, too. "It's like —" I said. "Like you could think of a reason for *anybody* to do it."

"Almost." Jeremy laughed a little. "Although I can't quite figure out a motive for the Moscowitzes."

I laughed, too, thinking of those two squirmy babies and their busy parents.

Then Jeremy got serious. "Mike Buxton, now there's a different case," he said. "I find it interesting that a contractor is sniffing around like that. Especially one whose brother is one of the biggest builders in the area. They could be checking out the possibilities. Thinking about developing Paradise Cottages *their* way. After they drive the present owners away, of course."

"Whoa!" This guy had *all* the angles figured out. "You must have read a *lot* of mysteries," I said.

He laughed again. "When I'm not reading city council reports," he said. "That's my usual beat for the paper. *Bor*-ing. I read mysteries to keep my mind alert."

I could see what he meant. This conversation had definitely made *my* mind alert. By the time I said good-bye and headed on toward Whispering Pines, my head was spinning with new ideas.

# Chapter Twelve

"Grab your sleeping bag! Let's go!" Sam leaped up the stairs and onto the porch of Whispering Pines. She hoisted herself onto the railing and sat there, kicking her heels.

"Go? Where?" I asked, a little groggily. I was reading a Sherlock Holmes mystery, and I was lost in a world of foggy London streets.

"The island!" Sam jumped back down off the railing. "Patrick's taking Amanda there. I figured, why not go, too, and make this the night we camp out?" She was hopping from one foot to the other, all full of energy and excitement. She seemed almost nervous.

But her enthusiasm was contagious. I put my book down and started to think out loud. "We'll need more than sleeping bags," I said. "The tent, and food for dinner tonight and breakfast tomorrow —"

"I already started packing," Sam told me. "All that stuff is taken care of. I'm telling you, all you need is your sleeping bag." Now she was actually wringing her hands. I had the feeling she really needed to get away for a bit, away from the fires and from worrying about her grandparents.

"And maybe a towel, and some warm clothes." I was still thinking. It can get chilly at night out on the island.

"Patrick said he wants to head out soon, like in half an hour," Sam urged me on. "And I'm dying to get going. Amanda's on her way back here to pack. We're meeting at the dock at four."

"My parents —"

"They'll say yes," Sam said. "You know they will. We always spend a night out there. If they let us do it when we were nine, they'll let us do it now."

She had a point. And it turned out she was right.

"Sure," said Mom when I asked.

"*Cuidado,*" said Poppy. (That means "be careful.")

I threw some things into a backpack. Amanda showed up just as I was squishing my sleeping bag into its stuff sack. She'd brought one, too, so we squished together. Then she grabbed a few things, and we were off.

Patrick and Sam were waiting on the dock, next to *Serenity*, which was packed to the gunwales[11] with boxes and duffel bags. We tossed our stuff in,

[11]gunwales (pronounced "gunnels"): the upper edges of a ship's sides

too, then climbed aboard. Patrick started the motor and we took off.

"Yay!" cried Sam, flinging out her arms. It was good to see her so happy.

Amanda smiled into the breeze, arranging herself so her hair flew back like a model's.

Patrick looked straight out at the island, steering carefully across the smooth water.

Paradise isn't a huge lake. It took only a few minutes for us to get to the island. Patrick circled it once, just to show Amanda the whole shoreline, then turned off the engine and rowed in toward some rocks that make a natural docking spot, on the side facing Paradise Village.

Sam jumped off to tie up the boat. Then we unloaded all the stuff onto the beach. "I'll take that one," Sam said when I tried to lift a big box. She's bigger and stronger than I am, so I let her wrestle it off the boat.

"Are we going to set up the tent right here?" Amanda wanted to know.

"No," Sam said. "There are better spots over near the hut."

"Hut?" Amanda looked confused.

"There's a building on the island," I explained. "Sort of a little cabin. We're allowed to stay in it if the weather's bad, and we usually cook our meals in there. It has a stove and a sink."

"Who owns it?" Amanda asked. "Is it part of Paradise Cottages?"

"No," Sam said. "My grandparents don't own the hut or the island. They both belong to a businessman over in the village. But he lets people use them."

"Cool." Amanda went to pick up her backpack, but Patrick grabbed it first. "I'll carry that," he said. "Come on, I'll show you the hut. Then we'll check out the Indian footprints."

They took off ahead of us. Sam made a little gagging face at me, then picked up the heavy box. "She's perfectly capable of carrying her own backpack," she pointed out.

"I know," I said. "Hey, do you smell gas?"

Sam sniffed the air. "A little," she answered. "Must be the boat. Come on, let's get going!" She was still full of energy.

I guess that gas smell sort of got stuck in my nose, because I kept smelling it all the way to the hut. We made a couple of trips, until all our stuff was stowed away. Then we set up the tent and unrolled our sleeping bags inside it. We put a flashlight inside, too, so we were all set for dark. Then we set out on our usual trip around the island, checking out all the familiar spots, like the rocky place where blueberries grow and the rope swing that hangs from a tree leaning out over the water.

We decided to take a swim later, and headed for the Indian footprints.

Amanda and Patrick were there when we arrived in the little clearing, staring at the cliff. "Aren't they cool?" I asked, coming over to find the footprints and trace their outlines.

"Patrick says they're, like, really old," Amanda reported.

Like, big news.

It was hard to be annoyed at Amanda, because she seemed really happy to be getting Patrick's attention. I knew the last couple of years had been hard for her, and she deserved some good times. So I did my best to be happy for her. But it wasn't always easy that night out on the island.

After Patrick left (saying he'd be back the next morning to pick us up), she couldn't seem to talk about anything but him. She gushed about what a great swimmer he was, how good he was at driving the boat, how elegant his dive off the rope swing had been. I could tell that Sam just tuned her out after a while; in fact, Sam headed off to the hut to get dinner started and left me to listen to Amanda. I think it was just too much for her to have to listen to Amanda gush about her brother.

"And," Amanda confided in me when we were alone, "check this out. He asked me on a date!"

"A date?" I asked. "What kind of date can you

have around here?" I pictured the two of them arriving at the common house together for one of the movies Cap'n Teddy shows on an old black-and-white TV.

"We're going out for pizza," Amanda said. "On the Fourth. In Paradise Village." She kind of hugged herself, closing her eyes tight. I figured she was imagining the scene.

I wondered if she knew that the pizza place, Ozzie's, was pretty basic, with fluorescent lights, rickety tables, and a couple of stools at a high counter. "That's great," I said.

Over dinner (mac and cheese, chocolate chip cookies out of the bag), I tried to steer the conversation in another direction. "Jeremy Wilson sure had some interesting ideas for our investigation," I said.

Sam's face darkened. "Yeah, right. What does *he* know? Like, my gramps is so *not* setting those fires." She obviously thought Jeremy was guilty of ultracrepidarianism[12].

I didn't want her to get all mad again, so I skipped Jeremy's theory about Patrick. "You should have stuck around," I told her. "He had some other suspects. Like Mike Buxton." I thought she'd be surprised, but she wasn't.

[12]ultracrepidarianism: the habit of talking about things you know nothing about

"I have my eye on him," she told me.

"Patrick says —" Amanda began, but I interrupted her. I'd heard enough about Patrick for one night, and I knew Sam sure had.

"Anybody else?" I asked Sam.

Sam nodded. "I suspect Jeremy Wilson himself."

That *was* a surprise. "What?"

She smiled. "He could be desperate for a good story. For one of his books, or even for the newspaper. So he's *creating* it. See what I mean?"

"Wow." I tried to take it in. Suddenly, I saw what she meant. Jeremy had been really into this whole mystery. Maybe that was because he was its author!

We cleaned up the dinner stuff, debated whether to make a bonfire or not (*not*, we decided, since we were too tired), and snuggled down into our sleeping bags. I fell asleep almost immediately and didn't wake up until early the next morning.

*Very* early. It was barely light out when my eyes popped open. What had woken me up? I lay there for a minute, wondering. Then I heard it. A rustling noise — coming from the bushes nearby!

## Chapter Thirteen

I peeked over at Amanda, who was sleeping on my left. She was still fast asleep, a little smile on her face. Dreaming of Patrick, no doubt.

I checked Sam, on my right. Also snoozing. One of her braids was lying over her face, so I moved it carefully. Then, slowly, I sat up and peeked out of the little screened window in the tent. I couldn't see a thing.

But I could hear something. There was definitely something — or somebody — rustling around in the bushes nearby. A bear? No, not on the island. Maybe it was just a squirrel. It rustled again. No, definitely not a squirrel. It was something bigger than that. Much bigger.

I wanted to lie back down, pull my sleeping bag up around my ears, and go back to sleep. But I knew there was no way that was going to happen. For one thing, I'd never get back to sleep now. For another, I had to pee.

Slowly, as quietly as possible, I unzipped the tent and slipped out into the misty morning air. There was a pink glow in the sky over Paradise Village; the sun was about to rise. I listened again.

No more rustling. I figured it was safe to walk over to the outhouse near the hut.

I padded along quietly, checking over my shoulder once in a while and peering around trees to see if I could spot whatever it was that was making that noise.

Whatever it was, it had stopped.

I entered the clearing near the hut and headed straight for the outhouse, a little wooden building around back.

And that's when I nearly ran into her.

Tessa Green.

"Aahh!" I cried when she came around the corner.

"Eeehh!" she cried when she spotted me.

I don't know which of us was more surprised. Tessa was in her bathing suit, and her hair was dripping wet. "Out training again?" I asked.

She nodded. "That's right. Training." She didn't meet my eyes. I wasn't sure why, but she seemed nervous.

"You're dedicated," I said. "I mean, the race is over."

"Well." She stood on one foot and then the other, hugging herself a little to try to keep warm. "Sure. But I'm a swimmer."

"So, you're just taking a break here?" I asked. "You swam out from the cottages?"

"That's right," she said again. "From the cottages."

"How long does that take?" I was impressed that she could swim so far.

She shrugged. "I don't know. Half an hour? Anyway, I better get going. My folks'll be wondering where I am."

I doubted that they'd even be up yet, but I didn't say anything. I just waved good-bye and watched her wade into the water and swim off in her indefatigable[13] way, with strong, sure strokes. Then I headed for the outhouse.

Afterward, I walked down a path and sat on a rock near the shore to watch the sunrise. It was pretty spectacular, all orange and red and pink. The sky changed constantly as the glowing ball of the sun popped over the trees that lined the lake, and all the colors were reflected in the little waves that lapped against the shore.

I was so hypnotized by what I was watching that I nearly jumped out of my skin when a canoe appeared, slipping silently through the water. I stood up fast.

"Whoa!" It was Patrick. "Caught me! I thought I could sneak up on you guys."

He was smiling, but he seemed truly surprised

[13]indefatigable: untiring

to see me. I couldn't help remembering what Jeremy had said about him. Was he up to something suspicious? Or — was he just hoping to catch a glimpse of Amanda in her pj's?

"Did you come to get us already?" I asked.

He shook his head as he climbed out of the canoe and pulled it up onto shore. "No way. The canoe isn't big enough for all your gear. Rinker's coming out later with the boat. But I thought Amanda might like to go for an early-morning paddle."

"I don't think she's up yet," I told him. "She and Sam were both totally out of it when I got up. But we can go check."

We walked back toward the hut. Sam was there, rummaging through one of the boxes we'd brought. She jumped a little when she saw us (seems like everyone was sneaking up on everyone that morning), but then she smiled.

"Pretty early for breakfast," said Patrick. "Don't you usually sleep until eleven or so?"

"Must be the island air," Sam said, closing the box and moving away from it. "I woke up hungry."

"Were you getting out the food?" I asked. "I think that's the wrong box. The bacon is in this one." I opened another box and started pulling out bacon, eggs, and bread.

By the time we had breakfast started, Amanda showed up, rubbing her eyes. She perked right up when she saw Patrick. The two of them went off for a short ride in the canoe, then came back to feast with us on slightly burnt bacon and scrambled eggs.

We were just cleaning up when Rinker arrived to ferry us back to the cottages. I couldn't believe our night on the island was already over! But we couldn't hang around much longer — not if we wanted to make it to Regatta Day.

# Chapter Fourteen

"Go, Ophelia! Row! Row harder!"

That was Helena, cheering me on from the dock as I threw myself against the oars, rowing as hard as I could. Mom and Amanda, my passengers, were cheering, too. My lungs were screaming, my shoulders were crying out for mercy, and I could feel the blisters forming on my hands.

Ahh, Regatta Day.

Mention the word *regatta* to most people, and they'll picture big, beautiful white yachts sailing gracefully around a harbor. Or maybe they'll have an image of speedy, trim sailboats racing through whitecapped waters.

I think Cap'n Teddy had those pictures in mind when he organized the first Regatta Day at Paradise. But the reality here at our little lake is a bit different.

Here, Regatta Day is basically just an excuse for all of us to spend the day on the water, in whatever craft we choose. I've been known to spend Regatta Day on a rubber raft, paddling about happily, surrounded by boats of every type. Oh, there are races. That's what the word *regatta* really means: boat race. But I think the races are mostly another excuse for Cap'n Teddy to load up his cannon and fire away.

Anyway, this year I'd decided to enter the row-boat race. I was using a leaky old dinghy that belonged to the Drysdales. It was blue, or at least it used to be before most of the paint flaked off. I had to bail out four inches of water before I even got started. And the oars seemed guaranteed to give me splinters. But how could I resist the chance to win a race as skipper of the mighty *QE II*? Yes, that was the boat's name. My humble little rowboat was named after one of the biggest, most luxurious ocean liners to ever sail the high seas, the *Queen Elizabeth*.

What a laugh.

And what a gas.

The boat races are always pretty competitive, just like the swimming races. But the boat races are open not only to Paradise Cottages people but to citizens of Paradise Village as well. (Cap'n Teddy figures we go to their Fourth of July parade, so it's only polite to invite them to our Regatta Day.)

I was competing against two other rowers. Derek Wallbridge was one of them. The other was a girl from the village who looked about ten years old. Like mine, each of their boats had two passengers; it's one of Cap'n Teddy's weird rules. I was worried about Derek, but figured the girl was no threat.

Boy, was I wrong. From the moment the cannon boomed, that girl was way out in front. I could see that Derek was working as hard as I was to keep up. And he had his own cheering squad: Tessa was screaming for him to pick up the pace.

He tried.

I tried, too.

But in the end, the little girl won by at least two lengths. I'd never seen her before, and I haven't seen her since, but I'll never forget how strong she was. She deserved the trophy that day, no question.

"You did your best," said Mom as she climbed out onto the dock.

"Nice try, Ophers," said Amanda, using a nickname I hadn't heard in about five years. As she helped me tie up the boat, I saw her glance toward a row of kayaks lined up next to the dock, looking for Patrick.

Amanda had been hoping to be in the canoe races with Patrick, but at the last minute he'd switched to the kayak race. It turned out that Tessa was going to be in that race (she said it would be her first time in a kayak!), and he couldn't resist the opportunity to compete against her again. That's why Amanda ended up as my passenger.

Oh! Speaking of the kayak race: big news. Jeremy Wilson's kayak had been returned! A guy from the village had towed it over that morning behind his motorboat. The kayak had turned up at his dock one morning, and he had no idea where it came from until he saw one of Jeremy's signs (MISSING KAYAK!) at the creemee stand. Jeremy was so happy that he tried to give the man a reward, but he wouldn't accept it. When Amanda, Sam, and I pulled into the dock after our night on the island, we found Jeremy standing there, staring happily down at his trim little boat. The only damage he could find was a streak of red paint where the boat must have bumped hard against something. Naturally, he was planning to enter the kayak race, too.

Almost everybody at the Cottages was out on the water that afternoon. Dad was going to be in the kayak race, of course. So was Sam. Juliet and Sally were racing the Wallbridges' sailboat. And the twins had been talked into the canoe race; they'd be riding with Susan Buxton and Max. (Mike wasn't feeling well; according to Susan he was napping back at Seventh Heaven.)

Cap'n Teddy and Duchess were aboard their big motorboat, along with Brinkley and the cannon, and the Carsons were aboard theirs.

It was quite a scene when you looked around. The lake was full of boats, and some people had put some effort into decorating their craft with red, white, and blue crepe paper or gold streamers. There was definitely a holiday feel in the air, even though it was only July third.

"Canoe racers! At the starting line, please!" boomed Cap'n Teddy through the old-fashioned megaphone he always uses on Regatta Day.

Amanda and Mom and I rowed out toward the finish line (an imaginary line between the Drysdales' boat and the Carsons') to watch the twins compete. They were the only Cottage people in the race; the two other canoes had come from the village. One was a solo canoe, piloted by a guy who looked about Patrick's age; the other was an authentic-looking birchbark canoe paddled by a woman in a fringed buckskin dress. I've seen her before, riding a palomino in the village's Fourth of July parade.

The cannon boomed and the racers were off. The twins tried their hardest, Viola in the stern, steering, and Helena in the bow, paddling like mad. But their canoe was overloaded compared to the other two, and they didn't have a chance. The guy in the solo canoe sailed ahead and won easily. And here's the weird thing: As he crossed the finish line, he blew a kiss back toward the cottage dock!

"What was *that* about?" I asked Amanda. She just shrugged.

"Looks like the kayak race is getting under way," Mom said. "Let's row back to the dock and give Poppy some encouragement."

I let her take the oars, since my hands were still a little sore, and she rowed back toward the dock.

Poppy was joking with Tessa as he explained the basics of kayak paddling. "It's easy," he said. "The hard part is getting in and out." He showed her how to get in by straddling the cockpit and inserting one leg at a time, all the while keeping the kayak balanced. "Oops!" he hollered as the kayak tipped and sent him splashing into knee-deep water. "See what I mean?"

Tessa laughed. "I think I do," she said. She straddled her own kayak (one of the three that Cap'n Teddy keeps for customers) and gracefully stuck her legs inside.

You'd never have known it was her first time. I guess Tessa is just a natural athlete.

So, I'm not going to go into the gory details of the kayak race. I'll just tell you that Poppy didn't have a chance, but he did have a great time. Tessa and Patrick fought for the lead most of the time.

But, in the end, Jeremy won the race — and everybody was glad. It seemed fitting, since he had just gotten his boat back.

Once the races were over, my favorite part of Regatta Day began. That's when everybody pulls their boats into a big circle (usually it's just cottage people by then) and we settle in for some serious eating. Everyone has packed picnic baskets full of awesome food, and there's lots of sharing from boat to boat. You know, "I'll trade some chicken salad for some of that great-looking coleslaw." Like that. We eat until we're totally stuffed. Then we eat some more. Finally, Duchess always passes out these incredible brownies she bakes.

Then, to work off our meal, we all paddle around some more until the sun starts to go down and the stars start to pop out. That's one of my favorite times to be out on the lake. The wind dies down completely so that the surface of the water is completely calm, reflecting the stars. Everything is very quiet, except for the loons calling and the sound of soft conversation from other boats. The sky turns a deep blue, and you can just barely make out the silhouette of the trees along the shore. I always feel very content and peaceful when I'm on the lake at twilight.

Once it's dark, Cap'n Teddy calls us all back and hands out little toy boats made from a hunk of wood with a tiny sail attached. Each one has a little candle on it. We light them, make a wish, and put them in the water to sail away. It's *such* a beautiful moment. I always feel like crying.

"What did you wish?" I asked Amanda as she gave her boat a little push that night. She and I were out in a canoe together; Patrick had gone off alone in a kayak, so I guess I was her next best choice for a dinner date.

"I'm not telling!" she said. "Then it won't come true."

"That's only for birthday candles," I told her. "You're allowed to tell your boat wish."

She shook her head. "I'm still not telling."

It probably had something to do with Patrick.

My wish? Simple. I always wish the same thing. That I get to come back to Paradise *next* summer.

I looked around at the others, wondering what they wished. Poppy probably wished to go to Spain or Mexico, to try out his Spanish. And I bet Helena wished to be goalie on the soccer team this year. No doubt Mrs. Moscowitz was wishing that the twins would grow up to be strong and healthy, and —

*Boom!*

There was a huge explosion. I felt it down in my stomach.

I looked over at the Drysdales' boat. Was it the

cannon going off by mistake? Nope. I could barely make out Cap'n Teddy's face, but I could see enough to know he looked as surprised as the rest of us.

*Boom! Boom! Boom-boom-BOOM!* The tonitruous[14] sound echoed all over the lake.

Now there was light, too. It was like a thunderstorm without the wind and rain. Flashes of bright light lit up the sky as the explosions continued.

"It's my fireworks!" Cap'n Teddy yelled. "Oh, no!"

Fireworks?

"They were a surprise," I heard him tell Duchess. "I got them months ago and hid them in the hut on the island."

The hut! The island! My stomach clenched up. This was not good.

In fact, it was very, very bad.

Within moments, the worst had come true.

The island was on fire.

[14]tonitruous: like thunder

# Chapter Fifteen

Flames shot into the air, mirrored by the still water of the lake. It was like a dream — no, a nightmare. How could this conflagration[15] be happening?

"Head for shore!" yelled Cap'n Teddy. "Head for safety!" He started his motor. Everybody started paddling and rowing for the main dock.

This fire was big. Much, much bigger than when Windswept burned down. The entire island was burning up, and there wasn't a thing I could do to stop it. I paddled as hard as I could, looking back now and then at the burning island as I pulled for shore. The flames grew higher and higher. I could hear the crackling of the fire and occasional loud explosions — more fireworks? The fire grew so quickly. By the time we got to the dock, even the tallest trees on the island were engulfed by flame.

"We need a head count!" shouted Cap'n Teddy. "Who's here? Who's missing?"

Oh, my God! I never even thought of that. Was everybody safe? I looked around. Amanda was

[15]conflagration: huge fire

with me. I spotted Poppy's kayak across the dock; he was just climbing out of it. I saw Mike Buxton run up the dock, coming from shore, to look for his wife and Max. He spotted their canoe just as I did. Helena and Viola and Mom were paddling hard, just coming in to the dock in our canoe. Sally and Juliet were already there. Quickly, I counted some other cottage people: Derek and his parents, Jeremy Wilson, Tessa and her parents. The Carsons pulled up in their motorboat. And the Moscowitzes were probably back at Shangri-La.

Rinker strode up the dock. "I called the village fire department," he yelled to Cap'n Teddy. "They'll do what they can."

I didn't see how they could do much. I know they have a special boat that's equipped with hoses, but I could tell just by looking at the island that it was too late.

"Where's Patrick?" cried Duchess. "Has anybody seen Patrick?"

"Patrick!" yelled Amanda. "Oh, my God! Where is he?" She stood up in the canoe, nearly tipping us over.

"And where's Sam?" I asked, suddenly realizing that I hadn't seen her, either.

We all stared into the darkness. The bright flames made it hard to see, but finally, there they were, paddling toward us in their kayaks. Patrick came first, and Sam came paddling after. As she drew closer, I could see that tears were running down her face.

"We — we were on the other side of the island," she told me, joining me on the dock after running to her gramps and gram for a hug. "It's awful! Horrible!" She was still sobbing. "Our beautiful island. The hut. Gone!"

"I know," I said, reaching out to hug her. "How could somebody do that?"

She stiffened. "Somebody? You think somebody did it on purpose?"

"I don't want to think that," I told her, "but how could all these fires be coincidental?"

She didn't answer. She just hugged me back as we stood watching the flames destroy a place we both loved.

# Chapter Sixteen

I slept late the next morning. I guess I was just really, really tired.

When I woke up, the sun was streaming in through the window. Amanda's bed was empty, but otherwise everything seemed normal.

Then I remembered.

It was like being punched in the stomach.

The island was gone. Every tree, every blueberry bush, every board in the hut. Gone.

I took a deep, shaky breath — and that's when I smelled it. The smoke still hung in the air. Usually, the smell of a fire makes me feel all cozy and nostalgic; it reminds me of campfires and marshmallows and warm, fuzzy sweaters. But this time, the smell almost made me sick.

I could picture the flames leaping into the air. I could picture the way they were reflected in the water. I could picture the special fire-fighting boat that came roaring over the lake to try to put out the fire, even though it was hopeless by then.

And I could picture Sam's face, streaked with tears.

Poor Sam. I think that island meant even more

to her than it did to me! I wondered how she was feeling this morning.

I got out of bed and threw on jeans and a shirt. I had to go find Sam and see how she was doing. But when I got downstairs, I found Poppy and Mom in the kitchen, eating cereal and talking very seriously.

In Spanish.

Poppy had to keep stopping to consult his dictionary and textbook, so the conversation wasn't going so well. But I caught enough of it to know what they were discussing.

*"Es demasiado peligroso,"* said Mom. (It's too dangerous.)

*"Quizá debemos ir a casa,"* Poppy said. (Something about going home.)

"No!" I cried. "We can't go home! We just *got* here."

Poppy looked at me. "Ophelia," he began. Then he flipped open his dictionary and started looking something up. After a second, he flipped it closed again. "Forget it," he said in English. "It's too complicated. Look, your mother and I have been talking. We're thinking that maybe we should just pack up and go home."

"But Poppy —" I began. "Who said you had plenipotentiary[16] authority to make that decision?"

[16]plenipotentiary: having full power

He held up a hand. Usually, Poppy gets a kick out of it when I use big words. This time, he ignored me. "Don't you realize, Ophelia? You could have been *on* that island when the fire started."

That's when it hit me. I know it sounds crazy, but somehow, I had managed to avoid thinking about that. I had focused all my energy on feeling terrible about the island burning up. But I had never once thought of the danger. I had never once thought of the fact that the fire took place less than twelve hours after we'd left the island. And we were out there without a boat, no way to escape. "Oh, my God!" I said, covering my mouth with my hands. I sat down, hard. "Oh, my God!" I said again.

Mom got up and came over to hug me. "It's okay, sweetie," she said soothingly. "It's okay."

But it wasn't. It was awful! Was it possible — was it possible that somebody *knew* that Sam and I were investigating the fires? Was it possible that somebody wanted to scare us, or even hurt us? I shivered a little, thinking about it. Mom held me closer.

"That's okay, sweetie. We'll just go home and be safe."

Go home? Back to Cloverdale? No way! I pulled away from her. "Mom, that's not what I want."

"This isn't necessarily *about* what you want," Poppy said quietly.

I gulped. "But I'm sure the twins and Juliet want to stay, too," I said. "And Amanda. Where are they all, anyway?" I was beginning to have the feeling that there was some convincing to do, and I needed reinforcements.

"Amanda went down to the common house," Mom said. "Juliet and Sally went for an early-morning sail. And the twins are watching Max this morning so Mike and Susan Buxton can have some time to themselves."

Great. So I was on my own. I thought quickly. Arguing with parents can be a special art. If you really want something, you have to know how to go about asking for it. "What about the parade?" I asked, trying not to sound whiny. They hate whining. "Today's the Fourth. We've never missed the parade before!"

Poppy, frankly, didn't look as if he cared much. But Mom's more sentimental. I could tell that got her thinking.

"And wouldn't it be kind of rude to the Drysdales?" I tried another tack[17]. "I mean, if everybody just ditches this place on them? They'd feel terrible if everybody left."

Poppy nodded, considering that. I saw him exchange a glance with Mom.

[17]tack: a course of action, especially one in a series of different approaches. It's a word from the sailing world. Juliet taught me what tacking means; it's when you go back and forth trying to get the most wind in your sails.

What I didn't say, but what I was thinking, was this: *And I haven't even had a chance yet to catch the person setting the fires!*

It was time to finish up. (I've found that it's best to keep it to three points at a time. More than that and you lose track of your argument.) "Anyway, it's not like any of the fires have been set in places where people are actually *living*. I mean, first it was the summerhouse. Then Windswept, which was empty. I bet last night's fire wouldn't have been set if anyone was on the island."

I knew it was sort of a long shot, trying to convince them that we weren't actually in danger. For all I knew, our cottage could be next. But it did seem unlikely. I tried to put my own fears away. I *hated* the thought of leaving. I hadn't done any of the stuff I love to do every summer with Sam, other than sleep on the island. I didn't want to miss my whole Paradise vacation just because of some stupid firebug.

After that last argument I kept my mouth shut and watched as Mom and Poppy had one of their silent conversations, the kind they're great at. They don't say a word. It's all just eye contact and facial expressions. I guess you learn to communicate like that when you've been married as long as they have.

Finally, Poppy nodded, as if they'd come to an

agreement. Mom nodded, too. Then Poppy turned to me. "Okay," he said. "We'll stay for the parade, at least. We can all go over there together this afternoon. It doesn't seem fair to make you miss that. But after that —"

I didn't even let him finish. I just jumped up and kissed them both. "Thanks!" I said. "Thanks, thanks, thanks." Then I grabbed a bagel from the counter. "I'm going to find the others," I said as I headed out the door. Little did my sisters and Amanda know how close we had come to packing up the van. I couldn't wait to tell them how I'd saved the day.

"The parade's at four!" Poppy called after me. "Meet us at the common house at three, okay? We'll figure out who's going in which boat."

I found them all down at the main dock. Sam was sitting at the end, her arms wrapped around her knees. She was staring out at the island. It looked horrible that morning; all the trees were blackened stumps, and there were still gray feathers of smoke rising from a few spots.

Patrick and Amanda sat next to each other on the other side of the dock, kicking their feet in the water. Just as I got there, Patrick scooped up a handful of water and splashed her playfully, and Amanda shrieked and giggled. I knew she didn't really mind; it was already so hot out that the water must have felt great.

Meanwhile, Helena and Viola were playing with Max in the shallow water, wading around trying to catch minnows in an old mayonnaise jar. I remembered doing that for hours at a time when I was little. Max was totally into it, yelling, "Here, little fishies! Come here!" as he chased them around.

I went up to the end of the dock and sat with Sam. I tried to be quiet, since I could see that her eyes were still red from crying. It was like being around somebody who just had a death in the family. In a way, I guess that's exactly how Sam felt, like the island was part of her family.

But after a few minutes of respectful silence, I just had to speak up. "Sam," I said, "we have to figure out who's doing this."

She nodded bleakly.

Just then, Helena waded over and hauled herself up onto the dock. "Ophelia," she said urgently. "I have to tell you something." She glanced back at Max and Viola, who were still engrossed in the minnow game. "It's something Max said this morning."

I nodded. Of course, I had told my whole detective team about everything Jeremy Wilson and I had talked about, and I'd told the twins to keep a special eye on Mike Buxton. "Go on," I told her.

"He said that his daddy told his mommy that he

had his checkbook and his hammer ready," reported Helena. Then she giggled. "Actually, Max didn't say 'checkbook.' He said 'bookcheck.' But Viola and I figured out what he meant."

"Wow," I said. "Did you hear that, Sam?"

But Sam didn't really seem to be listening.

I turned back to Helena. "So, you think that means he's all ready to buy this place and fix it up?" I asked. That would make me extremely suspicious. Naturally, he'd be trying to get Paradise Cottages for the lowest price possible. Wouldn't the fires make it worth less? "Listen," I told her. "Just keep a very, very close eye on Mike, okay? And keep listening to everything Max says. Let's meet up again later. When are you done baby-sitting?"

"We're supposed to meet Susan and Mike for lunch. After that, we're free. So, one o'clock?"

"One it is," I said. "Meanwhile, Sam and I will poke around some more. And we're supposed to meet Mom and Poppy at the common house at three, to figure out how we're all getting over to the parade." Later, I'd tell Helena and Viola how lucky we were to even be there that day.

I nudged Sam. It was time to get her moving. She couldn't sit and stare at that island all day. "Let's go look around," I said. "Maybe we can find some clues." I got up and held out a hand. Reluctantly, she took it and let me pull her up.

I looked over at Amanda, wondering if she'd want to come with us. But she didn't even seem to see me, she was so focused on Patrick.

"Forget it," Sam said, following my gaze. "I have something to tell you, anyway."

"What?" That sounded very mysterious.

"Not here," she said. "Let's go up by Poppa Bear." She took off at a fast pace. After one last guilty glance back at Amanda (she was my guest, after all, and we'd hardly spent any time together), I followed her.

"So, what's up?" I asked, panting a little, as we leaned against Poppa Bear a few minutes later. The rock felt cool against my skin, and the blasting sun didn't penetrate through the thick trees surrounding us.

"I didn't want to scare everybody," Sam said in this very serious way, "but I think you should know. I was out early this morning, and I saw a guy."

"A guy?" What was she talking about?

"In the woods. He had a beard, and he was wearing these old, filthy clothes. I think he, like, *lives* in the woods or something." Sam nodded. "I think he's, like, a drifter."

"What are you saying, Sam?" I asked. "Do you think this guy might have set the fires?"

She shrugged. "He looked kind of suspicious,

that's all. And he could only have gotten here by coming through the woods. Why would he bother? Maybe he was living in the summerhouse and thought he was about to be discovered, so he burned it down. And then he moved to Windswept —"

"Right." It sounded a little far-fetched to me, but if there was some stranger in the woods we should definitely tell somebody. "Shouldn't we tell Cap'n Teddy?" I asked.

She shook her head. "Not yet. Let's look around and see if we can figure out where he's living," she said. "Then the police will have more to go on."

That made me a little nervous. The guy could be dangerous. But the sun was shining and I was dying to do *some* kind of investigating, so I let Sam talk me into it. We roamed around in the woods all morning, looking for footprints or snapped branches, but we didn't find a thing. We just got hot and sweaty and scratched up from pushing through the undergrowth.

Finally, we popped out of the woods near Windswept, only to find Rinker poking around in the ruins of the cottage. He looked up when he saw us, startled.

"Uh, just figuring out how much work it's going to take to rebuild this place," he offered, even though neither of us had asked. He tapped the dead ashes out of his pipe, filled it up again, and lit it. I saw him blow the match out carefully and grind it into the dirt with his boot.

Suddenly, I knew Rinker was probably not the firebug, even though he *did* act suspicious sometimes. For one thing, the way he ground out that match proved that it wasn't his "carelessness" that had burned down the summerhouse, as Duchess had thought. For another, he lit the match as if he'd been lighting matches all his life.

That little pile of matches I'd found? They were all bent, and some of them hadn't ever lit. To me, that was the mark of somebody who wasn't used to lighting matches.

In my mind, I put a light line through Rinker's name on the suspect list. I hadn't *proved* him innocent, but he didn't seem guilty.

Later, I crossed Jack Carson off, too. Sam and I spotted him acting suspiciously near the equipment shed, and at first I thought he was using his safecracker skills to break in and steal more gas. But it turned out he was using a key, and that while he was "borrowing" some gas from the Drysdales, it was just to fill up his boat so he could bring people over to the village for the parade.

That's when Sam and I gave up and went for a swim. It was too hot to think anymore.

Later, when we met up with the twins, they had nothing new to report, either. Max hadn't dropped any more clues, and from what they'd seen of Mike that day, he seemed like a normal, vacationing dad who was enjoying his time off. Also, as Viola pointed out, he had been on shore at the time the island went up in flames. It would have been difficult, if not impossible, for him to have set that fire.

Our investigation was going nowhere fast.

And if we didn't figure out something soon, we'd be headed back to Cloverdale even faster.

## Chapter Seventeen

"But I want to go with Cap'n Teddy!" Helena said. "He said I could steer the boat."

"All right, then," Mom said patiently, "so you and Viola can go with the Drysdales, and Amanda and Ophelia can come with me in the canoe."

Amanda gave me an imploring[18] look. I knew what *that* meant. Patrick would be riding with the Drysdales, and Amanda couldn't stand not to be in that boat, too.

"Um, I think Amanda would like to go with the Drysdales, too," I said. "And Sam asked me to paddle over in her canoe. How about if you and Viola take the canoe, Poppy takes his kayak, Juliet sails with Sally, and Helena and Amanda ride in the motorboat?"

It was ridiculous how hard it was to figure out who was going in which boat. Everybody at Paradise Cottages was heading to the village for the parade and fireworks. Some people had already headed off, like Jeremy, who'd gone in his kayak, and Tessa, who had decided to swim. She'd dived

[18]imploring: pleading

off the dock, leaving her clothes and a towel in a neat pile on the dock so her parents could bring them over when they came in their canoe. Poppy was already sitting in his kayak, and the Moscowitzes had piled into a canoe and were halfway across the lake.

Jack Carson was just starting up his boat. He and his wife had invited the Buxtons to ride along, and Max was perched in the bow, waving goodbye to Helena and Viola even though the boat was still sitting at the dock. Mr. and Mrs. Wallbridge were riding in the *QE II*, with Rinker at the oars, while Derek paddled a kayak.

What a crew!

I smiled to myself as our little flotilla made its way to the village. Going to the parade is one of my favorite summer traditions. Sam always asks if I want to be on the Paradise Cottages float, but I always say no. I like to pick out a good spot along the parade route and just watch as everyone goes by.

Anyway, there isn't much room on the Paradise Cottages float. It's just an old dollhouse they've fixed up to look like one of the cottages, set on the back of a pickup. Cap'n Teddy, dressed in full yachting gear, waves to the crowds while Duchess, Sam, and Patrick throw candy for little kids to scramble for. WELCOME TO PARADISE, says a big sign hung on the bumper of the truck. It's the same every year. This year, the only difference would be that Amanda would be on the float, since Patrick had asked her.

Paradise Village was already bustling by the time Sam and I pulled into the village dock. The floats were lining up behind the fire station, and people in costume — I saw Uncle Sam, a duck on stilts (?!), and a dairymaid — were running around trying to figure out where they belonged. The members of the kazoo band were already assembled, all wearing bright purple T-shirts with PARADISE KAZOOSTERS on the back in yellow script. They were warming up with a painfully off-key version of "The Star-Spangled Banner."

I said good-bye to Sam and walked off on my own, scouting out the perfect spot to watch the parade. Last year I sat on top of a picnic table out in front of the creemee stand, but that spot was already taken by a big family. I didn't mind. It was too hot to sit in the sun anyway. I was looking for some shade.

A few minutes later, I found the perfect spot on a little hill near the church. A towering maple tree cast a huge cool circle of shade, big enough for all the people who had already gathered beneath it. I squeezed in between a mom with a very tiny baby and a grandfatherly guy who was wearing a red-white-and-blue top hat and carrying a little flag.

"They're about to start," he told me. "Want a flag to wave?"

"Sure." I accepted the little flag he handed me. He seemed to be carrying a whole bunch of them. He gave one to the mom next to me, too, and one each to a bunch of little boys who were running around playing tag.

"Here we go!" said the mom, pointing down the street.

Sure enough, the parade was coming our way. The first thing we could hear was the kazoo band, a little more in tune now, humming "America the Beautiful."

We cheered and waved our flags as they marched past. Behind them came a whole bunch of tractors, sputtering and backfiring as their drivers inched them along. Most of them had obviously been washed and polished for the parade, and some of them were decorated with red-white-and-blue crepe paper.

Behind the tractors came the fire truck, and after the fire truck were a bunch of floats: the Little League Champs, the Paradise Dog Club, the 4-H kids on a float made to look like a haystack, and — Paradise Cottages. "Whoo! All right, Paradise Cottages!" I yelled, waving at Sam, Patrick, and Amanda. Sam was standing between her grandparents, a protective arm around each of them.

Everyone waved back, and Amanda tossed a big handful of candy as hard as she could, right in my direction. I managed to catch one Tootsie Roll, but the little boys got the rest.

After those floats, there were a few marching groups: the Veterans of Foreign Wars, old men in their clean, pressed uniforms; the Paradise High School marching band, which was pretty small, but made up for it by playing as loudly as possible; and the Paradise Preschool, each older kid pulling a wagon carrying a younger kid.

After them came some antique cars, three horseback riders dressed in full cowboy gear, and Ella Cates, the town clerk of Paradise, riding in a red Mustang convertible and waving at everybody as if she were royalty.

Next up? The kazoo band — again! The Paradise parade always goes two times around the parade route, just to make a little parade seem bigger. This time the Kazoosters were playing the theme from *Star Wars*.

I decided it was time to walk around a little. I got up, holding my flag, and headed down the sidewalk, threading my way through the spectators as I walked in the opposite direction from the paraders. I was watching for the Paradise Cottages float to come by again when I bumped right into someone I knew: Tessa Green.

She was standing near Ozzie's, the pizza place, holding hands with a cute guy who looked very familiar. He wasn't from the Cottages, though.

"Hey, Tessa!" I said, yelling a little to be heard over the marching band, which was just going by.

She turned and saw me, and I saw her face go pale. She dropped the guy's hand. "Ophelia!" she said.

Why did she look so guilty?

# Chapter Eighteen

"Hi, Tessa," I said. I looked her right in the eye. "Aren't you going to introduce me to your friend?"

She was obviously hiding something. Was this guy connected with the fires? Was she trying to protect him? *Why* did he look so familiar?

"Have you seen my parents?" she asked, ignoring my question.

"Not since we left the Cottages," I told her. "Why?"

She let out a breath. "Because, if they see me with Kurt, they'll kill me," she said. She turned to the guy. "Kurt, this is Ophelia. Ophelia, this is Kurt."

That's when I realized who he was. "You won the canoe race!" I said. This must be the boyfriend Sam had told me about, the one Tessa's parents didn't like. Suddenly, it all came together. I remembered seeing him blow a kiss when he crossed the finish line. It must have been aimed at Tessa! "Do you live in the village?" I asked. He didn't look like such a bad guy. In fact, he seemed really nice. I liked the way he looked at Tessa, like he couldn't take his eyes off her.

He nodded. "At the house with the red dock," he said. "I grew up there."

I knew that house. It was in a little cove, just across from the island. "You must have hated seeing the island burn," I said, watching his face closely. Could he be the arsonist? I still felt like he and Tessa were hiding something.

He shook his head sadly. "That was the worst," he said. "I've been going to that island since I was two and my mom took me to pick blueberries."

He looked a little choked up, and I decided he wasn't a suspect.

Tessa was glancing around nervously, looking for her parents, I guess.

"That guy must have been pretty glad to get his boat back, huh?" Kurt asked me.

Tessa swung around and glared at him. "Kurt!" she said.

Something in the way she looked at him got my brain working. I thought of the red dock at Kurt's house, and the red mark on Jeremy's kayak. I thought of the way there *was* no neat pile of clothes waiting on the dock that first early morning when I saw Tessa swimming. And I thought of how she almost won the kayak race, even though she said she'd never paddled one before. And suddenly, I figured it out. "You took it!" I said to Tessa. "You took Jeremy's boat so you could visit Kurt, didn't you?"

She took a step back. "Whoa!" she said, holding up her hands.

"When I saw you that morning, before he knew his boat was missing, you had just swum all the way back across the lake from Kurt's place!"

She stared at me, openmouthed. "Wow. Not bad, Ophelia." Then she grinned. "Busted, I guess. Yep, I borrowed the boat and paddled it over to see Kurt. But when I was ready to come back, the sun was up and I knew I'd get caught and my parents would be furious. So I swam back instead. I figured we'd get the boat back to Jeremy somehow."

"And ever since then you've been swimming all the way across and back," I said, picturing that morning I'd seen her on the village side of the island.

She nodded. "It's good training." She shot a smile at Kurt. "Hey, you won't tell on me, will you?" she asked me.

"Well, no," I said, "I guess not. Jeremy has his boat back. Anyway, I'm really glad to know that you're not the arsonist. At first I thought *that's* what you were feeling guilty about."

She closed her eyes for a second.

"What, Tessa?" I asked, suddenly a little afraid. "You're *not* the arsonist, are you?"

She shook her head. Then she opened her eyes. "But I think I might know who is," she said.

# Chapter Nineteen

"WHO?" I nearly shouted. Then I realized people were staring at us. "Who?" I asked again, quieter this time.

She'd turned away from me. Now she was staring at the floats going by. At that moment, the Paradise Cottages float appeared. She nodded toward it. "Patrick," she said.

"What? *Patrick?* Why him?" I watched Patrick glide by, riding on the float. He smiled as he tossed candy to a bunch of little girls who were chasing after the float. I remembered what Jeremy Wilson had said about Patrick. *The boy's a minor. He wouldn't be prosecuted the same way as an adult would. Maybe the grandparents talked him into it. Or maybe he just likes setting fires. Some people do, you know.*

"That morning I saw you on the dock? I had just swum by Windswept. And I saw something — some*body* — walking around. Somebody in a yellow hooded slicker. At the time, I didn't think anything of it. But later, when Windswept burned down, I remembered. And Patrick was wearing that very same jacket, just before the swimming races."

I couldn't think of a thing to say. I remembered the way he'd appeared out of the dusk the night the island burned down, just ahead of Sam. And the smell of gas when we unloaded the boat, the day before. He must have been preparing to set the hut on fire!

Did Sam know? Was she covering for him?

It looked bad — really bad — for Patrick.

# Chapter Twenty

"I — I have to go," I said to Tessa. I nodded at her and Kurt and drifted away, walking back down the parade route in the same direction the Paradise Cottages float had just gone. I was actually feeling a little dizzy. Maybe it was just the heat; it was truly sweltering by then and very humid. I felt as if I couldn't breathe. Or maybe it was the shock of what she'd told me. I didn't want to believe it. How could it be true, anyway? Patrick had an alibi; he'd been with Sam right before both of the last two fires. Plus he was *Patrick*, the same boy I'd known practically all my life. How could he have turned into somebody who would burn down the island? The island didn't even belong to the Drysdales, so he couldn't have done *that* for the insurance money. Maybe he *did* just enjoy setting fires, as Jeremy had said.

"Ophelia! *Ophelia!*"

My brain felt all foggy, but finally I realized that someone was calling me. I looked up and saw Olivia and Miranda across the road. They were both waving like maniacs. "Over here, Ophelia!"

yelled Olivia. Her frizzy hair was wilder than ever, with all the humidity.

I waved back. The Paradise Preschool was just passing by. I waited for the little gap between them and the antique cars and dashed across the road. I threw myself into Olivia's arms. "I am *so* happy to see you guys," I said.

Olivia looked surprised. "Well, we missed you, too. Why do you think we drove all the way up from Burlington on the hottest day of the year?"

"It's not so much that I missed you," I began. No, that didn't sound right. Of *course* I'd missed them. I love Miranda, and Olivia's not only my favorite sister but one of my favorite people in the universe. "I mean, I *did* miss you. But it's also all this awful stuff that's going on."

"You mean the fire on the island?" Miranda asked. "I heard about that at the station. I was so upset!"

"Me, too," Olivia said. She hefted the big bag over her shoulder. "I brought my camera up. I bet there are some amazing images there, with the burnt trees and all. I'm hoping Mom will paddle me out in the canoe."

Olivia's a photographer. A really good one. She's studying photography in college, and she's already had a few of her pictures published in the paper.

"I don't think you're going out in a canoe anytime soon," Miranda told her, pointing to the sky.

I looked up and was surprised to see huge dark clouds gathering right overhead. I'd been so spaced out that I hadn't even noticed!

Just then, there was a rumble of thunder.

"Uh-oh," said Olivia.

"Let's head for the Rec Center," Miranda said. "We can get shelter there and talk some more."

We started walking, but before we'd even gone two steps it started raining: huge, fat drops splashing down out of the sky. Right away, there was that special smell of rain on a summer day: the mixture of fresh water and dust kicked from the streets that just tickles your nose.

A second later, the fat drops changed to windblown sheets of rain, driving down hard enough to hurt a little if you turned up your face. We started running as fast as we could; so did everybody else along the parade route. The marchers scattered, too, running for shelter.

The Rec Center was pretty crowded when we got there, but we pushed in and found some space under one of the baskets in the gym. We were soaking wet, but it was warm and cozy inside. People were laughing and talking as they wrung out their hair, cleaned their glasses, and squeezed water out of their clothes. The gym felt as steamy as a jungle. The windows rattled as thunder cracked and rolled outside, and flashes of lightning streaked past the high windows.

"Listen, you guys," I said as soon as we were a little less sopping, "it's not just the fire on the island. There have been other fires, too. The summerhouse, and one of the cottages."

"Wow! Which one?" Olivia asked.

"Windswept."

Her mouth fell open. "I always *loved* Windswept. I thought it had the most romantic name. And I liked the way it sat out there all by itself."

"Exactly what might have made it attractive to an arsonist," said Miranda, thinking out loud. She wants to be a detective on the force someday; I know she'll be a great one. "So, who are the suspects?"

She knows me. Since I love mysteries, she figured I was already on the case. "Just about everybody at the Cottages!" I said. "But I haven't had any really strong suspects until —" I looked around. "I just heard something," I said in a lower voice. "There's some evidence — just hearsay[19] so far — that Patrick might be involved."

"Patrick?" Miranda asked. "Little Pat Drysdale? But isn't he only, like, seven?"

[19]hearsay: a report from someone else

I shook my head. "Patrick's sixteen," I told her. She might remember him as a little kid, but Patrick was plenty old enough to be starting fires.

"I can't imagine Patrick being dangerous," said Olivia.

I couldn't, either. But suddenly, I realized that he might be. And he had a date, that very day, with Amanda! For all I knew, the two of them were already at Ozzie's, ordering pizza. "You know what?" I said. "I think I should find Amanda and Sam and let them know about this."

Miranda nodded. "That's fine," she said. "We'll come with you. Looks like the rain stopped, anyway." She waved at the window. Sure enough, the sun was already out again. Summer-afternoon storms in Vermont can be intense but very short. "While we're looking, you can tell me about the other suspects. I'll make a list and call the station to see if any of them have records." She pulled a notebook out of her pocket and flipped it open. Miranda is always prepared, even when she's off duty.

We headed down the street. Water was still running down the sides, but the hot sun was making steam rise from the asphalt. As we walked, Olivia took pictures of the crowd and I told Miranda about Jeremy Wilson's ideas — and about Sam's ideas about Jeremy Wilson. I mentioned Jack Carson and Mike Buxton and Sam's drifter and Rinker.

"Rinker?" she asked. "We never *did* figure out whether that was his first or last name, did we?"

That cracked us all up. We were still laughing when we ran into Sam and Amanda, who had just stepped out of the firehouse. Amanda was trying desperately to fluff up her wet, flattened hair, while Sam squished along in her waterlogged clothes.

"Hey, Miranda! Hey, Olivia!" Amanda was happy to see both of them. They were like older sisters to her, too, when we were growing up. Sam knows them, too, of course, but not as well. After everybody had said hi, I sat my friends down on a bench for a minute and told them what Tessa had told me. I didn't tell them about Tessa taking Jeremy's boat; I'd promised to keep that a secret. I just said she'd been out swimming early one morning, and —

"*Patrick?*" Sam asked, her voice rising. "Are you crazy? I don't know why you want to make him a suspect. First you listen to what that stupid Jeremy Wilson says, and now this." She was furious. "Why don't you listen to *me*? I *told* you it's that drifter guy. I *told* you Patrick and I were together, both times."

"Sam, I'm not saying he's guilty. I'm not even saying I believe he's a suspect. But we can't rule anything out!" I felt like I was pleading with her. I couldn't stand seeing her so mad at me. I knew it must be upsetting to hear something like that about her brother, but detectives have to be objective. You can't let emotions get in your way, if you want to solve a case.

Amanda still hadn't said anything. She was just standing there, looking shocked. Then she turned on me. "I don't believe you!" she shouted. Her face was red, and her tangled wet hair shook as she yelled. "You're making it up, aren't you? Just because you don't want me to like him. You've been against us getting together the whole time!" She spun around and stalked off. Then she spun around again. "I have to go," she said, pronouncing every word very carefully. "I have a date."

# Chapter Twenty-one

I watched her go. If our friendship wasn't already in trouble, this would have done it. As it was, I wondered if we'd ever be able to patch things up. "Amanda," I said, just whispering the word as she disappeared around the corner.

"She's seeing Patrick?" Miranda asked. She'd put two and two together pretty quickly.

I nodded. "They're having pizza at Ozzie's," I said. "At least, that was the plan."

"Well, why don't *we* go grab a slice, too?" Miranda was already walking that way, following Amanda.

"I'm not hungry," Sam said, crossing her arms. She sat on the bench, unmoving. "You just want to watch Patrick, see if you can catch him lighting matches or something."

"It's not that," I said. But it was, sort of. Also, I couldn't help being the tiniest bit worried about Amanda. If Patrick really was setting the fires, maybe he was a little unbalanced. She shouldn't be left alone with him, should she?

"Come on, Sam," said Olivia. "I'm buying. How does extra cheese and pepperoni sound?"

"Please, Sam?" I asked.

"Oh, all right." She got up slowly and stuck her hands in her pockets. "But if I catch you treating him like a criminal —"

"We *won't*, Sam," I promised. "I just want to be there. Anyway, aren't you kind of curious? We'll be able to spy on Patrick and Amanda's first real date."

"Oh, yeah," she said sarcastically. "Like, I'm so fascinated." But she came.

The three of us caught up to Miranda just as she was walking into Ozzie's. The place was packed, which wasn't surprising. There aren't too many places in Paradise to get something to eat, and Ozzie's makes really good pizza. Still, most people just go straight to the counter to order a slice, and then take it back outside to eat. You can usually find a seat at a table, if you're patient.

I spotted Amanda and Patrick as soon as we came in. They were sitting at a tiny table near the counter, staring into each other's eyes. Somehow, Amanda had managed to fix up her hair since I'd last seen her; she'd lost that drowned-rat look, anyway.

The smell of tomato sauce and garlic made my mouth water, and I suddenly realized that I was starving. My stomach rumbled as I looked around the room, trying to find a table we could grab.

“Over there!” said Miranda, pointing at a family that was just getting up from a table near Amanda and Patrick’s.

“I’ll grab it,” said Olivia. “You guys order.” She went over to claim the table, and the rest of us went to wait in line at the counter.

By the time it was our turn, I was hungrier than ever.

“Hi, can I help you?” The girl behind the counter was smiling at me.

“Definitely,” I said. I couldn’t help smiling back. She was pretty, with long dark wavy hair and striking blue eyes. Her diastema[20] only made her even more interesting-looking. “I’d like a slice with extra cheese and, um, mushrooms.”

“Got it,” she said, making a note on an order pad. “Who’s next? Oh, hi, Sam!”

“Diana!” Sam said. “I haven’t seen you all summer.”

“I’ve been working hard,” said the girl. “Hey, let me ask you something. Who’s that girl with Patrick?” She cut her eyes toward Patrick and Amanda.

“That’s Amanda. She’s staying at the Cottages,” Sam said. “With Ophelia.” She gestured at me. “Ophelia, this is Diana.”

[20]diastema: a gap between teeth

Diana smiled at me again, but her eyes weren't smiling this time. Just her mouth. "So, your friend Amanda," she asked me. "Is she —"

Just then, a woman behind us in line cleared her throat. "People are waiting, you know," she said.

"Oops," said Diana, ducking her head. She picked up her pen again. "What'll it be, Sam?" she asked.

Sam ordered a slice with pepperoni, and so did Olivia. Miranda got the veggie special. Diana gave our order to the guy behind her. "Talk to you later," she whispered to Sam. Then she turned to the next customer. We got sodas out of the cooler and went back to our table to wait for our slices. They came a minute later, all piping hot and greasy and gooey. Yum. I took a huge bite. "Ow! Hot!" I said, fanning my mouth. I put the slice down to cool for a second.

Patrick and Amanda were still deep in conversation. She was gazing into his eyes, but I noticed that his gaze was shifting. He was seated facing the counter; Amanda was facing away from it. Patrick would look at Amanda for a little while, then flick his eyes over to Diana behind the counter. Amanda didn't seem to notice.

Then I saw Diana, between customers, look back at Patrick. The expression on her face was unmistakable. She was hurt. And jealous.

"Sam." I nudged her. "Who *is* that girl, Diana?"

She shrugged. "Just a girl from the village," she said. "Patrick and she —" Suddenly, she put down her slice and covered her mouth. "Oh, my God."

"What?" I leaned forward, and so did Miranda and Olivia.

"I am *so* dense," she said. "I can't believe I didn't figure this out before."

"*What?*" Olivia asked this time.

"Patrick's just *using* Amanda," said Sam. "He wants to make Diana jealous. They've liked each other forever. But last year she barely talked to him. She had this other boyfriend. So now he's trying to get back at her. He's still crazy about her, I can tell. They're always playing games like this. Ever since they were little, they've been torturing each other." She watched Patrick, who, it was now totally obvious, was watching Diana's every move.

I knew in an instant that Sam was telling the truth. Suddenly, my pizza didn't look so appetizing anymore. Poor Amanda! Patrick had been working up to this pizza date the whole time. Did he really like her at *all*? I couldn't believe he'd be such a jerk.

Of course, I didn't want to believe he would go around setting fires, either.

But he might have.

I took a few more bites of my pizza, which wasn't quite so molten anymore, and looked over at Patrick and Amanda again. One more time, I saw his eyes go to Diana. This time, he actually winked!

And this time, Amanda saw it. How could she not?

Her mouth fell open. She turned in her seat and saw Diana, who couldn't hide the smile that wink had produced. Then she turned back to stare at Patrick. She knew. I saw it in her eyes. Amanda might have been *acting* like a dope lately, but she is anything but stupid.

Her face turned red. She balled up her napkin and threw it at Patrick. Then she jumped up and marched right out of Ozzie's.

# Chapter Twenty-two

"Amanda!" I left my pizza and soda on the table and ran out of Ozzie's, shooting a nasty glance at Patrick as I passed by him. "Wait up!" I called.

Amanda was striding down the street, threading her way through the crowds that still lingered on the sidewalk. Nobody had left town; they were waiting for dusk, when there'd be fireworks.

I ran to catch up with her. "Come on, Amanda," I said, panting a little, when I was right behind her. "Talk to me."

She turned to face me. Her eyes were full of tears. "Oh, Ophelia," she said, "I feel like such a jerk."

I held out my arms, and she let me hug her. I felt her shoulders shaking. "It's okay," I said. I patted her hair. "It's okay, Panda."

She stepped back and shook her head. "No, it's not," she said. "I was an idiot. I can't believe I actually thought he liked me. How could I be so stupid?"

"First of all, I think he *does* actually like you," I said. I'd seen them together, laughing and talking. I really couldn't believe it was all a fake on Patrick's part. After all, Amanda was pretty and smart and fun to be with. "You're pretty, and smart, and fun to be with," I said out loud. "You can't help it if you're not Diana. He's obsessed with her. Always has been, according to Sam."

"That's her name?" Amanda asked, sniffling a little. "Diana?"

"Yup." I smiled at her. "And second of all, you're *not* stupid. Or an idiot. You just — wanted to be liked."

She nodded, sniffling some more. "Still," she said. "He *was* a total jerk. Using me that way."

I couldn't disagree.

"And if he did that," she said, "maybe he *is* capable of setting a bunch of fires. I mean, he can't *prove* he was in the common house when that cottage burned down." She turned to me, and I saw that she'd stopped crying. "Ophelia, if he *is* the one, I want us to catch him. I want him to *pay* for what he's done."

I wasn't sure whether she meant the fires or breaking her heart, but it almost didn't matter. There were two other things I knew for sure: I had my friend Amanda back. And she had joined my team.

# Chapter Twenty-three

Speaking of which, it was about time for a team meeting. It was getting late by then; dusk would be falling any minute, and as soon as it was dark the fireworks would begin. Would the firebug use the opportunity to set another fire? I had a creepy feeling that we hadn't seen the end of the destruction — unless we could catch the criminal before he (or she) acted again.

"Let's find the others," I told Amanda. "We have to make a plan."

We headed back to Ozzie's. Amanda wouldn't go in, but I stepped inside just far enough to wave to Miranda, Olivia, and Sam and give them the signal to meet us outside. Patrick was leaning against the counter, chatting with Diana. I was glad Amanda didn't see that.

"What's up?" asked Sam when she and my sisters came out of Ozzie's.

"Time for a meeting," I said. "We have to crack this case *now*, before there's another fire."

Sam nodded. "Where are Helena and Viola?" she asked. "We'll need them, too."

"I bet they're already up on the hill," said Olivia.

"They always like to get a good spot for watching the fireworks."

I knew she was right. The hillside in back of the Paradise Elementary School always started filling up around this time, since it was the best viewing spot. The fireworks would be set off from a raft floating on the lake, by the village beach. We headed to the school, hoping to find the twins.

I spotted them as soon as we crossed the baseball diamond. They'd grabbed an excellent spot, on the highest part of the hill. Fortunately, Mom and Poppy were there, too. They could save the spot for all of us. I waved to Juliet and Sally, who were sitting off by themselves.

"Did you eat?" Mom asked when she saw us. She held up a covered container that I knew was filled with her famous potato salad. I was still a little hungry, but there was no time to eat right then.

"We had pizza," I answered. Then I turned to Helena and Viola. "Want to walk around a little before the fireworks?" I asked them. "We're having a meeting," I added in a whisper.

"Save our spot!" Helena told Mom and Poppy as she and Viola got up to follow us back down the hill.

We gathered near the swings in the playground.

"Okay, everybody," I said. "This is it. It's time to get serious about figuring out who's setting the fires. We need to check out all our prime suspects *now*, since there's a good chance the firebug is all set to act again. So, who wants to do what?"

Helena was nodding. "Viola and I can keep an eye on Mike Buxton," she offered. "I saw him go by just a little while ago. We'll find him and follow him."

"Good," I said. "Sam?"

"I've been meaning to tell you," she said. "I think I saw that guy — the drifter? He was over by the library when the parade went by. I spotted him from the float, but I couldn't exactly get off and follow him. I'll see if I can find him now."

Miranda nodded. "Good idea," she said. "I'll make that call to the station to see if any of the suspects have records."

"I'll prowl around with my camera," Olivia suggested. "Maybe I can catch someone in the act. A picture would be the proof we need."

Then Amanda spoke up. "I'll follow Patrick," she said.

"Oh, no, you won't," I told her. "You're way too emotionally involved. How can you be objective when you're so mad at him?"

Sam was nodding. "Ophelia's right. That wouldn't be fair. Anyway, nobody has to follow Patrick. He's innocent, and I know it."

I reached out to touch her shoulder. "I know you

believe he's innocent," I said. "And you're probably right. But we still need to check him out, after what Tessa told me."

"Whatever," she said, shrugging off my hand. She was mad at me, I could tell. But I knew I was doing the right thing.

I turned back to Amanda. "I'll follow Patrick. Why don't you try to find Jack Carson?" I suggested. "We still need to keep an eye on him. And maybe Jeremy Wilson, too."

"Whatever," she said, echoing Sam. She was mad at me, too. How did *that* happen? I never set out to make my two best friends angry. All I was trying to do was solve this case.

By the time we split up, the sun was starting to set. Fireflies were flying by, blinking their greenish lights off and on, and little kids were running around with light sticks in luminous red, yellow, and blue. The Kazoosters were still at it, performing a medley of patriotic songs for the gathering crowd. On any other Fourth of July, I would have been sitting high on the hill, eating Mom's potato salad and anticipating the fireworks. But this year, I had a job to do. "Okay, everybody. Check back here in" — I pushed the button that lights up my watch — "half an hour?"

When we split up, I headed back to Ozzie's, hoping Patrick would still be there. I was in luck!

Just as I came up the street to the restaurant, Patrick and Diana stepped outside. She must have just finished work.

I ducked into a doorway so they wouldn't see me, then peeked out to see which way they were walking. They were moving away from me, so I followed them, sticking close to the buildings so I could hide again if they happened to turn around.

Patrick had his arm around Diana, and she was looking up at him and laughing as they walked. I guess they had a truce on "torturing each other," at least for a little while.

I kept following them as they walked up Main Street. They were walking in the opposite direction from everybody else on the street; most people were headed up to the hill for the fireworks.

Main Street pretty much ends in the lake. The dock there is the one where Patrick had met us just a few days earlier. So much had happened since then! I was thinking about all of it when I suddenly realized that Patrick and Diana had stopped, about a half a block from the lake. There weren't any more stores at that end of Main Street, just houses with big, overgrown yards. They were standing underneath a tree, and it looked as if they were saying good-bye. I got as close as I could, ducking from bush to bush. I strained to hear what they were saying, but I caught only a few words.

". . . only take a few minutes," Patrick was saying.

"I'll find us a place," Diana told him. I figured he had an errand to do, so they were arranging to meet on the hill. It all seemed totally innocent so far. I was beginning to wonder if I was wasting my time. Maybe I should be helping Sam find the drifter instead. But I decided to stick it out. My legs were cramping a little from staying in one position, so I shifted a bit, hoping my bush wouldn't rustle and give me away. Then I settled in to listen some more.

I didn't hear anything for a while. Then Diana's voice rose in a question, and I could hear only two words of Patrick's answer. But I heard those loud and clear. "Whispering Pines," he said.

The name of our cottage.

My blood ran cold. (*Love* that expression. It may be melodramatic, but it really does describe what happens when you get a shock like that one.) Was *that* Patrick's "errand"? To burn down Whispering Pines? Was Diana in on the whole thing?

# Chapter Twenty-four

It was nearly dark by then. The sun had set in a blaze of gold and red and pink, but I'd hardly noticed; I was too busy watching and listening.

I followed Patrick as he headed straight for the dock.

I saw him walk out to where *Duchess* (the boat, not the person!) was tied up. He threw a leg over the side, grabbed something from a spot near the motor, and jumped back out onto the dock, carrying it.

I took one step closer, squinting. What was he holding?

Then he turned to walk back toward me, and suddenly there was no question.

It was a red gas can.

# Chapter Twenty-five

I didn't stop to think.

Now that I look back, I realize that it was stupid, what I did.

You don't confront a criminal on your own.

At the end of a dark street.

But, at the time, I didn't even think about it. I just stepped out of the shadows and spoke up. "What do you think you're doing?"

Patrick looked around and saw me. "Hey, Ophelia," he said, smiling. "What are you doing down here?"

"I could ask *you* the same question," I said, putting my hands on my hips.

He laughed. "I guess you could. And I'd tell you that I just came down to get this gas can. I told Gramps I'd fill it up, and I almost forgot. Fontaine's is going to close in a few minutes."

Fontaine's is the one gas station in the village.

I kept my hands on my hips. "Look, Patrick," I said. "Forget the gas. It's all over. I know what you've been doing."

He gave me a quizzical look. "What I've been doing?" he repeated.

"I understand that you're trying to help your grandparents," I said. "But if you think you can't get in trouble, you're wrong. What you're doing is a crime."

He held up the gas can. "Getting gas?" he asked. "How is that a crime?"

"It's a crime," I said, taking another step toward him, "when you're using the gas to start fires." I glanced over my shoulder, hoping against hope to see Miranda, or Olivia, or *anyone* who could back me up. That was the point when I began to realize that what I was doing was maybe not so brilliant. "And when you're about to burn down *my* family's cottage."

Patrick shook his head. "I haven't set any fires," he said. "What are you talking about?" He seemed more confused than angry.

"I'm talking about the summerhouse," I told him. "And Windswept. And the island. And then you just said something to Diana about Whispering Pines. Is our place next?"

He shook his head again. "Look, Ophelia. I was just telling Diana where you — and Amanda — are staying. I don't know how you can think I —"

"Tessa saw you!" I burst out. "In your yellow raincoat, early that morning. When you were out preparing Windswept for being burned to the ground."

There was a momentary silence. Patrick was staring at me. "That wasn't me," he said slowly. "I was home in bed that morning. I slept late on purpose, because I had the race later on."

There was something in his voice. Something strange.

"So who —" I began.

Then I stopped speaking. We stared at each other. Patrick's eyes were wide.

And I answered my own question.

# Chapter Twenty-six

"It can't be *Sam,*" I said at the same moment as I realized that it probably was.

Patrick sat down suddenly, the gas can at his side. He put his head in his hands and let out a little moan. "I wondered," he said. "She's been acting strange lately. She'll hardly talk to me. She says I don't care about Gramps and Gram."

"Let me ask you something," I said. I had just remembered something Amanda had mentioned, about how Patrick had been at the common house when Windswept caught fire. That didn't jibe with what Sam had told me that day. "Where were you when the cottage burned down?"

"At the common house," he said. "I remember, because I had just grabbed an ice-cream sandwich. My race was over, and I was starving because I was too nervous to eat before it."

I nodded. So he wasn't back at the cottage with Sam, as she had said. Her alibi, which covered both of them, had been a lie. "And what about when the island burned down?" I asked.

He looked down at his shoes. "I was here," he said finally. "During dinnertime, I paddled over to visit Diana for a few minutes. Then I was going to paddle right back for the candle ceremony. Only that's when the island —" His voice cracked. "Anyway, I was paddling back as fast as I could, after those first explosions. That's when I caught up to Sam. She was on the village side of the island. We paddled together the rest of the way."

Once again, the alibi Sam had supplied for both of them contained a lacuna[21]. "One last question," I said as gently as I could. Patrick still had his head in his hands. "Does Sam ever borrow your yellow raincoat?"

He took his hands away from his face and turned to look at me. "All the time," he said softly. "All the time."

[21]lacuna: a missing part, a gap

# Chapter Twenty-seven

Patrick came with me to find Sam.

We walked through the dark streets of the village, watching for her in the crowds that surged toward the hill.

I wondered about Sam's drifter. Was he completely chimerical[22]? I groaned. I couldn't stand the thought that Sam had set the fires.

Sam.

My best summer friend. The one I thought I knew so well. Suddenly, it seemed as if I didn't know her at all. How could the Sam I knew, the one who skipped rocks and picked blueberries until her fingers were purple, how could *that* Sam light the match that would burn down the island we both loved so much? All this time, I had thought she was covering for Patrick. But she wasn't. She was covering for herself.

The more I thought about it, the more I became convinced I was right. I remembered the bent matches: Sam never *could* light a campfire out on the island. And the way she was so defensive

[22]chimerical: imaginary

about her grandparents, like a mother bear protecting her cubs. Then there was that gas smell when we unloaded the box on the island — and the way she had insisted on carrying one certain box herself. Not to mention the way she'd jumped when Patrick and I walked into the hut that morning as she was unpacking that same box. How could I *not* have seen it all? How could I have been so blind?

"There she is!" Patrick said, pointing into the crowd.

I spotted Sam's braids. I gulped. How was I going to find out the truth?

"Hey!" she said, waving when she saw us. "I saw the drifter! He's walking around looking really, really suspicious. But I just lost him in the crowd."

"Sam," Patrick said.

She didn't seem to notice. "He's all furtive and stuff," she went on. "Like, he's checking all the time to see if somebody's following him. I had to stay back so he wouldn't —"

"Sam," Patrick said again. "Ophelia and I —"

"We have something to ask you," I broke in.

Sam stopped talking. She looked from Patrick's face to mine. Even though it was almost completely dark by then, I could tell that her face had turned pale. "What?" she asked.

Just then, there was a loud *BOOM!* as the first of

the fireworks went off. I glanced up to see a trail of blue stars flickering overhead.

"It was you, wasn't it?" I asked. "Why, Sam? Why did you do it? *How* could you do it? The island?" I wasn't making any sense, and I knew it. I had meant to present my case in an organized way, confront her with the evidence: the borrowed raincoat, the bent matches, the false alibis. But it all flew out of my mind when I was standing there near her. Near my friend.

Sam's shoulders collapsed. She looked down at the ground. And when she looked up, I could see that she was crying. "I didn't mean to!" she said. "I didn't *mean* to burn down the whole island!"

"Oh, Sam," I said, stepping forward to hug her. Another *BOOM!* shook the air around us as she cried into my shoulder. Patrick looked on helplessly.

"I just wanted to help Gram and Gramps," she said after a little while. "That's all." She wiped her face with her sleeve. "So I set the summerhouse on fire. It was about to fall down anyway. I thought they could get the insurance money, and it would help save the Cottages. They're going bankrupt, you know," she told me.

Patrick nodded in agreement.

"I didn't know," I said softly, stroking her shoulder. Fireworks were going off one after the other now, first a shower of red, then green, then blue and sparkly white. But I barely heard the booms. I was listening to Sam.

She sniffed. "But then I realized it wasn't enough. The insurance money wouldn't even begin to pay for everything we needed to do. So I burned Windswept. I hated doing that! I *hated* it! Windswept was always the coolest cottage. But it was falling down, too. They were never going to have the money to fix it." She drew a long breath.

"And the island?" I asked as gently as I could.

She started crying again. "It was like I *had* to do it," she sobbed. "Everybody was talking about how Gram and Gramps were probably burning down their own property to get the insurance money. So I thought, if there was a fire at the hut, that would prove it wasn't them. 'Cause the hut's not their property. You know?" She gave me a pleading look.

What could I say? It made some kind of crazy sense. "I know, Sam."

"I brought the gas can out when we stayed there. Then I snuck back to light the fire, after the boat races. But then everything went out of control," she said. "I didn't know the fireworks were in there. I ran for my boat — there was nothing I could do — I was so scared!" She started sobbing again, and I hugged her close. Patrick stepped in, too, and started rubbing Sam's back.

Miranda got there just in time to hear Sam's last few sentences. Just then, the grand finale went off. Gigantic, glittering flowers bloomed overhead, lighting our faces with their shimmering brilliance, and the booms were like continuous thunder. I held Sam tight and met Miranda's eyes in the light cast by a silvery shower of sparks. There was a question in hers. I nodded slightly, to give her an answer. We had caught our firebug.

# Chapter Twenty-eight

"And how would you like your burger, young lady? Medium? Well done? I've got a perfect medium-rare, just waiting for someone!"

Cap'n Teddy beamed at me. He was dressed in a white apron that said, in big cartoony red letters, KING OF THE GRILL. And he'd traded his yachting cap for one of those floppy white chef's hats. It was the next day. He and Rinker had set up a huge grill out in front of the common house and invited everyone at the Cottages to a picnic.

I smiled back. I knew his happy-host act was just that, an act. I knew he was incredibly upset about what Sam had done — and about what would happen to her. Earlier that day, he'd stopped me as I was walking past the common house. He thanked me for helping to figure out who'd been setting the fires, and for being a good friend to Sam. He was pretty choked up and emotional then. But now he was back to being Cap'n Teddy, jovial host of Paradise Cottages. It's what he does best.

"Medium-rare would be great," I said, holding out my plate. I'd already grabbed a bun, some coleslaw, and a deviled egg. Duchess and Sam had spent the whole day in the kitchen, cooking up a storm.

Sam? Yes, Sam was at the Cottages. Miranda and I had gone with her to the Paradise police, and Sam had turned herself in. After they'd gone through the whole arrest procedure — she even got fingerprinted! — the police released her into the care of her grandparents. Miranda's best guess was that Sam would end up getting put on probation and sent for counseling. I was so glad that she didn't have to go to jail. I guess Sam was glad, too, but it was hard to know. She wasn't talking much, or even making eye contact. I think she was feeling totally overwhelmed. I sensed that she was mostly just relieved the whole thing was over. "No more fires, Ophelia," she said to me as we rode back across the lake that night in the Drysdales' boat. "No more fires." She looked very, very tired.

Speaking of friends, Amanda joined me just then. She had a plate full of food, too. "Let's go eat on the dock," she suggested. "It's too nice out to sit inside." Most of the grown-ups were seated at tables in the common room, but Amanda was right. It was a gorgeous evening, the kind I always picture when I think of Paradise. The sky was sapphire blue, and the first stars were just beginning to twinkle. A crescent moon shone in their midst, just a tiny fingernail of silvery light. There was a soft breeze, perfumed with the scents of lake water and pine trees, and you could hear little waves lapping on the shore.

Too perfect.

It had been a beautiful day, too. Hot, but not as muggy as the day before. Just a crystal-clear blue sky and lots and lots of sun. Amanda and I had spent the whole day doing "Paradise things." She hadn't said a word about Patrick, or Daniel, or any other boy, and she hadn't used the words "hottie" or "as if!" all day. It was like being with the old Amanda. We dove off the dock and swam to the raft. We picked blueberries and brought them home to Mom, who'd made a pie to bring to the picnic. We walked through the woods, and I showed her all the old familiar landmarks. We built fairy castles, tiny palaces made out of moss and twigs and leaves. It was a perfect Paradise day, only Sam wasn't there with me.

Amanda even talked a little about her parents and the divorce. That was hard, since I hate seeing her sad. But it was good, too. For one thing, it made me see that her whole Valley Amanda act was just that, an act. Something to distract her from having to think about the real pain in her real life.

I thought about that. If I'd learned anything from this week on the lake, I'd learned this: Things are not always what they seem.

Anyway, that day at Paradise, Amanda's problems seemed far away. She seemed really happy.

"Patrick apologized to me," she told me now as we ate our burgers out at the end of the dock. She'd taken off her sneakers and she was letting her feet dangle in the cool water. "Just now, when I was getting a soda."

"What did he say?"

She shrugged. "He just said he was really sorry he'd hurt me, and that I didn't deserve to be treated the way he'd treated me." She kicked the water, sending up a little splash. "And he said that I was wrong if I thought it meant he didn't really like me. He said I was one of the nicest, prettiest girls he'd met in a long time, and that if it weren't for Diana . . ." She looked over at me with a little smile.

"Yay, Patrick," I said. "I knew he wasn't a total loser."

"Hey, you guys!" Helena was yelling at us from the shore end of the dock. "Come to the common house! Cap'n Teddy says he has an announcement to make, and he's handing out free ice-cream sandwiches!"

I popped the last bite of burger into my mouth. "Sounds good to me," I said. Amanda and I jumped up and headed for the common house.

When we got there, just about everybody staying at the Cottages was already seated. I saw Annette and Carl Moscowitz, each holding a baby, sitting next to Tessa and her parents. Jeremy Wilson was roaming around with a half-eaten ice-cream sandwich in his hand, looking for a seat. The Buxtons were sitting near my family, probably because Max insisted on being with Viola and Helena. Juliet and Sally were hanging out near the back of the room, while Derek sat with his parents near the door. Jack and Rita Carson were up front with Duchess and Patrick and Sam, and Rinker was pulling more folding chairs off a cart and opening them up so everyone could have a seat.

Cap'n Teddy stood on the little raised platform at one end of the room and cleared his throat. He was wearing his yachting cap again. He held out his arms. "Welcome, everybody. Hope you enjoyed your dinner!"

We all burst into applause. "*Olé!*" I heard Poppy call.

"Did everybody get an ice-cream sandwich?" he asked. "If not, come on up and get one. Don't be shy." He gestured toward the freezer. Then he cleared his throat again. "This isn't easy to say," he began, looking a lot more serious than the Cap'n Teddy I was used to.

"As some of you may have guessed, Paradise Cottages is in financial trouble." He stopped and cleared his throat. "For a while there, we even thought we might have to give up the place, sell out to a developer."

I glanced at Mike Buxton. He was listening to every word.

"But I'm pleased to report tonight that we'll be in business for the rest of this summer, and for next summer, and — hopefully — for every summer after that!" Cap'n Teddy nodded and smiled. "Duchess and I have always felt that everyone who comes here is family. Now we know that's true. Dave Parker, could you come up here?"

Poppy! What did he have to do with this?

Poppy worked his way to the front of the room, and Cap'n Teddy threw an arm around him. "David and his family have been coming to the Cottages for — how long, Dave?"

Poppy beamed. "Twelve wonderful years," he reported.

I looked over at Mom and saw her smiling up at Poppy. She seemed to know what was going on. In fact, a lot of people in the room were smiling. What was up?

Cap'n Teddy explained it all. "This morning,"

he said, "Dave and a couple of others came to see me. They'd come up with a plan — a plan to save Paradise." He gave Poppy a little shove forward. "Tell them about it, Dave," he said.

Poppy looked a little sheepish. He ducked his head. "It's nothing fancy," he said. "Just that we all agreed that we'd like to help out, be even more a part of this place. From now on, all the regular tenants of Paradise will be part owners, too. Just a tiny part — the Drysdales will still be the main owners. But the rest of us will have a stake, too. And that means we'll be helping out. Rebuilding buildings that have" — he faltered a little, obviously not wanting to mention the fires just then — "been destroyed. Painting a little here, doing a little landscaping there. Just routine maintenance, really. To keep Paradise alive. To keep it the heavenly place that we all know and love." He stepped back a little, and people started to clap. Then he stepped up again and held up his hands. "I just want to acknowledge Mike Buxton as one of the folks who came up with this plan. He came to me this morning and said he was ready with his checkbook and hammer. Said he'd been saying so to his wife all along, since they've come to love this place as much as the rest of us do. So, thanks, Mike! We'll depend on your expertise as we go along!"

He stepped back again, and everybody started

clapping and whistling and yelling. I glanced over at Helena and Viola. They were grinning back at me. So much for Mike Buxton plotting to take over the Cottages!

The fact was, we were *all* going to take over the place. With any luck, I'll be bringing *my* kids here someday. I can't wait to show them all the things I love. I can't wait to welcome them to Paradise.

# About the Author

**Ellen Miles** lives in a small house in Vermont with her large dog, Django, who can eat a maple creemee in the time it takes to say "maple creemee." She has one brother and one sister, both older, and while she loves her siblings, she always thought it might be fun to have many more of them. One of her all-time favorite books is *Harriet the Spy*. She loves to ride her bike in the summer and ski in the winter, so Vermont is the perfect place for her to live.

# The Mystery
## of the Missing Tiger

Laura E. Williams

*For Sheryl, John, Matt, and Josh*



A Roundtable Press Book

For Roundtable Press, Inc.:
Directors: Julie Merberg, Marsha Melnick, Susan E. Meyer
Project Editor: Meredith Wolf Schizer
Computer Production: Carrie Glidden
Designer: Elissa Stein
Illustrator: Laura Maestro

ISBN 0-439-21728-8



12 11 10 9 8 7 6 5 4 3 2 1 1 2 3 4 5 6/0

Printed in the U.S.A.
First Scholastic printing, March 2001

# Contents

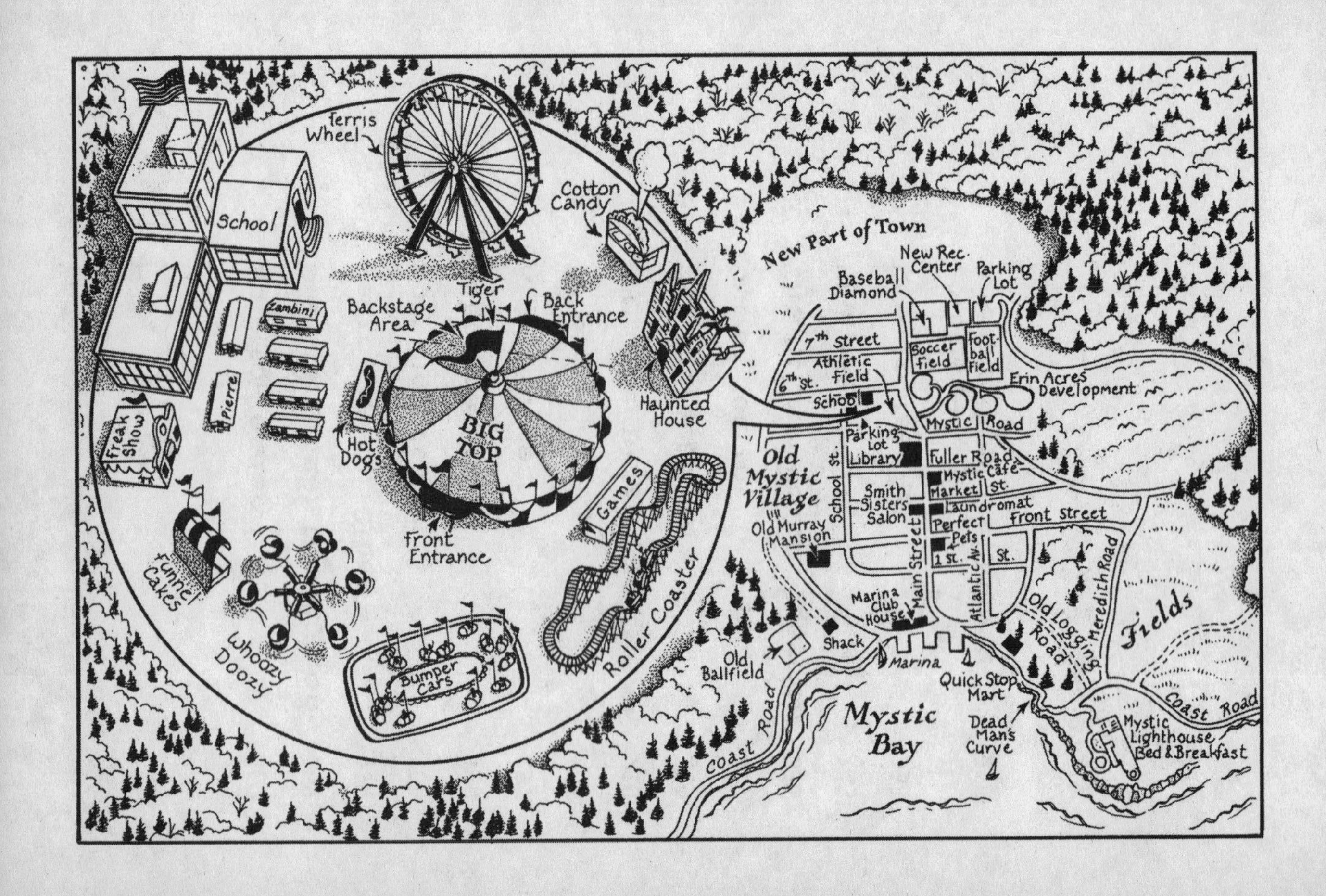
Ferris Wheel
School
Cotton Candy
New Part of Town
Zambini
Pierre
Freak Show
Tiger
Backstage Area
Back Entrance
Haunted House
Hot Dogs
BIG TOP
Front Entrance
Games
Funnel Cakes
Whoozy Doozy
Bumper Cars
Roller Coaster
Baseball Diamond
New Rec. Center
Parking Lot
7th Street
Soccer field
Foot ball field
Athletic Field
6th St.
School
Erin Acres Development
Mystic Road
Parking Lot
Library
Fuller Road
Mystic Café
Market St.
Old Mystic Village
School St.
Smith Sisters Salon
Laundromat
Perfect Pets
Front Street
Old Murray Mansion
Main Street
1 St.
Atlantic Av.
St.
Meredith Road
Marina Club House
Old Logging Road
Fields
Shack
Old Ballfield
Marina
Quick Stop Mart
Coast Road
Mystic Bay
Dead Man's Curve
Mystic Lighthouse Bed & Breakfast
Coast Road

# Note to Reader

Welcome to *The Mystery of the Missing Tiger,* where YOU solve the mystery. As you read, look for clues pointing to the guilty person. There is a blank suspect sheet in the back of this book. You can copy it to keep track of the clues you find throughout the story. It is the same as the suspect sheets that Jen and Zeke will use later in the story when they try to solve the mystery. Can you solve *The Mystery of the Missing Tiger* before they do?

Good luck!

# 1 Disaster Under the Big Top

"This is so cool!" Jen exclaimed, nudging her best friend Stacey in the ribs. She'd never been to a circus before and didn't know where to look first. Fresh Maine air wafted through the open flaps of the red-and-white-striped big-top tent. Sitting in the fifth row with her twin brother, Zeke, and their best friends Stacey and Tommy, Jen had a great view of the dusty ring in the center of the tent.

Zeke checked his watch. The show wouldn't start for another ten minutes. "Good thing we got here early," he commented as more and more laughing people crowded into the big top. He saw groups of kids from school and waved. Little kids ran in, their faces buried in big pink puffs of cotton candy. Their parents hurried in after them.

Jen nodded. "We lucked out getting the circus

right here at Mystic Middle School. I'll bet all the high school kids are bummed that they had to rush over after school from the other side of town!"

Stacey stood up to stretch out her leg.

"What's wrong?" Jen asked.

Stacey grimaced and leaned down to massage her plump calf. Her short, curly blond hair fell forward. "I think I pulled a muscle at yesterday's game when I jumped up to block that ball."

"It was a great save," Jen said. "We won because of you." Now their soccer team, the Mystic Monsters, would go on to the playoffs.

Stacey sat down and tenderly rubbed her leg. "I just hope I can play by next week. I don't want to miss the first game at the new field." Yesterday's game was the last that would be played at the old recreational field. From now on, all the teams would get to play at the brand-new ballfield. The awesome new clubhouse even had showers and an indoor pool. The old field only had a beat-up old shack that barely protected the equipment from rain.

"Just think, we've lost our last ball to the Atlantic Ocean," Jen added, remembering how she had kicked the soccer ball over the fence yesterday, sending it rolling over the cliff and down to the ocean below.

"And now we'll be able to hear Coach Riley's

instructions!" Stacey said, her light blue eyes sparkling.

Jen laughed. The only thing louder than Coach Riley's voice was the sound of the ocean crashing right near the old field. You couldn't hear anything on days when the ocean was whipped into a frenzy by a coming storm or an especially strong wind. It was about time the Mystic recreation department built a new field and clubhouse.

Zeke leaned forward and pointed toward the ring. "Look, they're gonna start."

The crowd cheered as three clowns tumbled into the ring, pushing each other and then somersaulting out of each other's way.

"That one looks like a kid," Jen said, pointing to the shortest clown. He wore a blue-and-green polka-dotted clown suit, and his bright green hair stuck out in tufts all over his head. A huge smile was painted on his face, and his nose was covered by a red-and-blue ball.

The boy clown jumped forward onto his hands and walked around the entire ring while the other clowns playfully somersaulted and cartwheeled in his way. When he stood up again, the audience clapped wildly.

Five jugglers ran into the ring, their bright yellow-and-black costumes making them look like buzzing bees. They were tossing fluorescent pink balls around and around and back and forth at a dizzying rate.

"And I thought *I* was good with a soccer ball," Jen said with a sigh of admiration. She could keep a ball in the air for a long time, bouncing it with her head, knees, and ankles, but these jugglers were truly amazing. "I guess I can't join the circus."

Zeke laughed. "Don't feel bad," he said. "Aunt Bee would never let you go, anyway. Who would help me clean the bed and breakfast?"

Jen smiled. They had been living with Aunt Bee ever since their parents' death when the twins were just two years old. Aunt Bee, their grandmother's sister, had become like a parent to them. Living in the Mystic Lighthouse B&B was perfect. The twins got to live in the remodeled lighthouse tower, and they ate very well, since Aunt Bee was the best cook in town.

Suddenly, the crowd hushed. A tall, bald man with an enormous, glossy black handlebar mustache marched into the spotlight.

"Welcome! Welcome! WELCOME!" he said as he turned in a full circle. "I am Pierre the Magnificent, and I welcome you to my circus—the Most Amazing Show on Earth!" He lowered his voice. "Or at least in Maine," he added in a loud whisper.

The crowd laughed.

"We have a fabulous show for you this afternoon.

Sights you have never imagined! Animals that behave like humans! The Great Zambinis, who fly through the air with the greatest of ease!" He held up his hands to stop the applause. "But you must all come back on Friday night . . ." He paused. "To see Terra the tiger trainer in action with our new, our very own, very special, and very rare Siberian tiger!"

A golden-haired woman wearing a black leotard and sparkling tights ran into the ring. She was as tall as Pierre and very thin. When she bowed in their direction, Jen noticed she had catlike eyes. Terra clawed the air with her bloodred fingernails, and her mouth pulled back into a snarl.

"She looks even more fierce than a tiger," Stacey whispered to Jen.

Jen nodded. She wouldn't want to mess with the Siberian tiger . . . or its trainer!

As soon as Terra took her bows and ran out of the ring, Pierre announced the first act. "Please welcome Patti's Prancing Ponies!"

Everyone cheered as six adorable, ginger-colored ponies circled the ring, tossing the bells on their fluffy manes in time to the music. Jen didn't know where the next hour went. One after another, varied acts impressed and amused the crowd. After the ponies came trumpeting elephants, ostriches that flipped large green balls back and forth over a net, and then acrobats who made a human tower that was ten men high. Between the acts, the clowns entertained the audience with their silliness. There were at least seven different clowns, and two of them were obviously kids around Jen and Zeke's age.

Jen looked around at the audience. The crowd was enthralled—laughing and clapping and pointing to things all over the ring. About five rows behind her, Jen noticed Mrs. Watson—Jen and Zeke's science teacher at Mystic Middle School—with her plastic pocketbook in her lap. Everyone knew Mrs. Watson was a strict vegetarian, and she used no animal products. She had once told Jen that even her hair dye was all natural and had never been tested on animals—which is why the color didn't always come out as planned. Right now it looked sort of greenish.

Jen waved, trying to get her teacher's attention. But Mrs. Watson sat stiffly, staring down into the ring with her face set as still as stone into a fierce frown. This was unusual—Mrs. Watson was good at telling jokes, and she liked to have a good time. She made science class fun by creating all kinds of neat experiments. Jen gave up trying to get her teacher's attention, but wondered why Mrs. Watson was the only person in the audience who wasn't having fun.

A drumroll sounded. Pierre the Magnificent moved to the center of the ring and held out his hands for quiet. When he finally got it, he announced, "And now the finale . . . the Greeeeeaaat Zambini Family!"

Spotlights focused on two poles at opposite sides of the ring that reached nearly to the top of the tent. A man and a teenage boy climbed up the pole on one side of the ring, while a woman and a girl who looked slightly younger than the boy climbed up on the other.

"I'm getting dizzy just watching them. I hope no one falls," Stacey whispered.

"They're trained for this," Jen said, craning her neck to watch the trapeze artists. She barely noticed that a safety net was spread across the ring in case one of them did fall. The Zambinis arranged themselves on the tiny platforms at the top of each pole. The father and mother simultaneously untied trapezes that had been secured near the platforms with ropes. The man handed the tiny swing—really just a bar suspended between two long ropes—to the teenage boy by his side, while the woman passed her trapeze over to the girl.

The drumroll stopped abruptly and was replaced by gentle, melodic music over the loudspeakers. The girl and the boy swung back and forth. The boy hung upside down and hooked his legs over the bar. Jen gasped as the girl let go of her bar in mid-swing, twirled through the air, and caught the boy's outstretched arms. It looked almost effortless, but Jen couldn't breathe again until each of them was standing on a platform, bowing to the wildly excited audience below them.

Mr. Zambini grabbed a different swing and swung out over the center of the ring. He locked his legs and ankles over the bar and pumped his arms so he went higher and higher with each swing.

The next thing happened so fast that Zeke wasn't sure he was seeing correctly. Then he heard a loud cry from everyone around him. One of Mr. Zambini's ropes had broken and he was plunging to the ground!

# 2 Searching for Clues

Zeke jumped to his feet and watched, horrified, as Mr. Zambini fell into the net below.

"Oh no!" Jen gasped, trying to see over the heads of everyone standing up in front of her. "Is he hurt?"

Pierre rushed into the ring, along with several of the clowns. They helped Mr. Zambini off the net and onto his feet. The crowd erupted into applause when Mr. Zambini waved to the fans and limped out of the ring. Pierre remained behind to announce that tonight's circus would be canceled, but reminded everyone to return for Friday's show. "In the meantime, enjoy the rides outside!"

"Mr. Zambini could have been killed if that net hadn't been there," Tommy said after Pierre hurried out of the ring. He ran a hand over his buzzed brown hair. "I can't believe he didn't break an arm or leg."

"Or his head," Zeke added. "That was a really lucky fall."

Jen tightened her lips. "Or unlucky, depending on how you look at it."

The twins glanced at each other. They had seen enough strange occurrences before to wonder if this accident had anything to do with luck at all.

"Let's go see if Mr. Zambini is okay," Zeke suggested casually.

Tommy lifted his eyebrows at his friend. "You can't fool me, Dale," he said, using the twins' last name. "You're snooping. Well, I hate to disappoint you, but this was obviously just an accident. No mystery here."

Zeke shrugged. "You're probably right." Then he grinned. "But it can't hurt to look, right?"

Tommy rolled his brown eyes. "I'm not wasting my time looking for nonexistent clues. I'm hungry. Anyone want to go eat?"

The twins shook their heads, and Stacey said, "I have to get a story about the Zambini family for the school paper. This will definitely make the front page." She started down the bleachers. "I'll find you when I'm done," she called over her shoulder.

With a wave, Tommy joined the crowd heading

out of the tent. Jen and Zeke hopped over the seats to the ground level and headed backstage.

The area behind the ring was chaotic with performers milling around in their glitzy costumes, mixing with several people who looked as out of place as Jen and Zeke felt.

Jen caught sight of Stacey trying to push through the crowd surrounding the Zambinis, her notebook and pen in hand.

Zeke pulled Jen back as she started to follow her friend. "Let's wait till the crowd dies down a bit."

Jen nodded. They backed out of the way until they came up against some metal bars. Jen turned around to see what had stopped their backward progress and almost screamed. Instead, she caught her breath and grabbed Zeke's arm.

Zeke felt the alarm in Jen's grip and turned to look behind him. They were face-to-face with the huge head of the white Siberian tiger! The tiger was absolutely enormous.

"Good kitty," he mumbled, taking a hasty step away. "Good kitty!"

The tiger opened its mouth as if to yawn, but suddenly a tremendous roar bellowed out from deep in its chest. Jen stumbled back in shock. The tiger licked its lips, blinked twice, then took three turns around the cage. Its muscles rippled gracefully with each step. Jen knew it could take her head off with one bite if given the chance. She shivered. Thank goodness it was behind steel bars!

Terra rushed over, her green eyes flashing. "Lady," she crooned. "Hush, Lady." She stuck her arm between the bars and scratched the tiger's massive head.

Jen and Zeke hurried away. When they were a safe distance from the cage, Zeke felt calmer. "I think I'd be a pretty good tiger trainer," he told his sister.

Jen lifted one eyebrow, something she had been practicing for months now. "Oh, really? Maybe after your knees stopped shaking."

Pierre's loud voice cut through the noise of the crowd. The twins turned to look. "Get out of here," the circus owner barked at a woman, his bald head wrinkled and red with anger.

Jen thought she recognized the odd, green cast to the woman's hair. Sure enough, when she turned, Jen saw it was their science teacher, Mrs. Watson. What was she doing back here, and why was Pierre so upset about it? Before Jen had a chance to find out, Mrs. Watson ducked out of sight.

Zeke pulled Jen behind another cage, grateful to see it wasn't filled with anything kid-eating, just two chattering monkeys. "Don't let Pierre see you," he warned. "We don't want to get kicked out of here before we have a chance to look around."

They watched Pierre head toward the tiger cage, where he confronted Terra about something. The twins were too far away to hear their conversation clearly over all the commotion backstage. Zeke edged forward, trying to stay partially hidden at the same time.

"You have to trust me," Terra said, a sharp edge to her voice. Her greenish cat eyes narrowed. "Trust me."

Pierre tugged nervously on one side of his mustache. "But everything depends on you. You have to pull this off, especially after what happened tonight, or we'll be ruined."

Terra scowled, looking fiercer than ever. "Don't worry, I've got it all planned. You'll get your money."

"I'd better!" With that, Pierre hurried away.

"What was that all about?" Jen asked Zeke when they had wormed their way through the crowd to avoid being seen by Pierre.

Zeke shrugged. "It sure didn't sound good, that's all I know."

Now that the crowd was thinning, Stacey had finally gotten through to the trapeze artists. Jen and Zeke heard Stacey's high, clear voice over the sounds of all the rides and amusements outside.

"Mr. Zambini, are you all right?" Stacey asked.

Jen and Zeke craned their necks to watch their friend in action.

Mr. Zambini nodded. "No problem," he said. He had a slightly foreign accent. "My leg is a little sore, but I'll go to the doctor tomorrow and everything will be fine."

Stacey scribbled something on her pad. Then she looked up again. "What happened to the rope?"

Mr. Zambini looked rueful. "I did not check it as I should have. It must have been frayed from overuse. I am just thankful that my dear wife and children were not injured." He hugged his wife to his side.

Stacey continued her questions. "How do you feel about Terra and her tiger taking over the spotlight of the show?"

Mr. Zambini's face turned red and for a split second contorted into an angry mask. But he regained control of himself and smiled thinly. "That is also no problem. The Great Zambinis are just that—great! Nothing can be greater! No more questions."

By now, the worried onlookers had left, and the backstage area was almost deserted. A couple of clowns were still chatting off to the side, and Zeke noticed a portly man standing in the shadows. He couldn't be sure, but it looked as if the man was wearing a fancy suit with a vest and watch chain over his rounded belly. When he raised his right hand to shoo away a bug, Zeke saw a flash of glittering diamonds on his pinky.

"Come on," Jen said, distracting Zeke for a second. When he looked back, the stranger was gone.

Zeke headed toward the exit, managing to pass as close to the Zambini family as possible.

"When William hears about this, he'll be worried," Mrs. Zambini fretted, her eyes red and her long, thin nose sniffling back tears. The two children had their mother's nose and their father's pointy chin.

Mr. Zambini put a hand on his wife's shoulder. "Call him, then, if it makes you feel better." He lowered his voice. "And tell him not to worry about the tuition money."

Jen poked Zeke in the back and urged him along faster. As they shuffled toward the exit, they caught sight of Mrs. Watson, who seemed to be trying to linger in the shadows without being seen while edging toward the tiger cage.

"What's she doing?" Jen asked Zeke.

"Let's go ask her," he suggested.

But at that moment, Mrs. Watson looked over at the twins. She frowned and disappeared behind several cartons of corn kernels that were obviously being stored there for the popcorn machine.

"Why is she avoiding us?" Jen said, about to head after their science teacher.

Zeke held her back and motioned behind them with his head. "Maybe she was looking at him, not us."

Jen turned and gulped. Pierre was headed right for them, a dark scowl on his face.

# 3 Nothing but Air!

The twins didn't wait for Pierre to reach them; they scurried out of sight as quickly as possible, ignoring Pierre's shouts commanding them to stop. Out of breath, they finally edged out of the big top. The sun had set, and the lights from the rides and games sparkled and shimmered.

"There's Mrs. Watson," Jen said, pointing. "Let's see what she was doing."

They followed her, trying to catch up, but the crowds kept getting in the way. When they reached a large circle of people watching an informal clown act near the cotton candy booth, they lost her for good.

"We'll have to ask her tomorrow in class," Jen said. "She was probably nosing around like we were." Then she smiled. "Or maybe she wants to join the circus."

Zeke laughed, but shook his head. "I don't think

so. Anyway, we haven't figured out what happened to Mr. Zambini's rope yet. I don't believe it was an accident."

"Let's go back into the ring," Jen suggested. "Maybe there's a clue there."

They sneaked around to the front entrance of the big top, afraid Pierre would jump out at them any second and demand to know what they were doing.

"The coast is clear," Zeke whispered.

The twins ducked into the big tent. The deserted ring looked a bit spooky now that the spotlight was off and the other lights had been dimmed. High above them, the trapeze towers disappeared into the darkness.

The large blue flap covering the entrance to the backstage area fluttered occasionally, but no one came through as Zeke and Jen quietly made their way into the ring. The sawdust covering the ground muffled their footsteps. They went around the ring in opposite directions, scouting around for clues. Jen found a tassel from one of the prancing ponies, and one of the jugglers' pink balls, but that was all.

"Find anything?" Jen whispered when she and Zeke met up on the other side of the ring.

Zeke shook his head. "Something that might have been elephant droppings," he whispered with a slight scowl, "but that's it. Seems like this is a waste of time. We may as well enjoy a couple of rides before Aunt Bee picks us up."

Jen shook her head, looking up. "I have an idea."

Zeke followed her over to one of the trapeze towers. "What are you doing?"

Jen put her hand on the first rung of the ladder-like steps that ran right up the pole. "If I go up there, I might be able to inspect the rope."

"Are you crazy?" Zeke exclaimed, forgetting to keep his voice down. Just looking up the pole made him dizzy. "Just because you can climb a tree like a monkey doesn't mean you can climb this. You could get killed."

Jen didn't answer. The next thing Zeke knew, she was at least ten feet above him and climbing steadily. His hands were slick with sweat, watching her nervously from below. He wanted to shout, "Get down from there!" but he was afraid that any loud noise would startle her. There was no net on this side of the trapeze tower.

Jen tried not to think about how far away the ground was. "Hand, foot, hand, foot," she kept repeating. She kept her eyes straight ahead. If she looked down, she knew she would be doomed.

Luckily she was in great condition from all the

hours spent on the soccer and softball fields. But her nerves were eating away at her energy. She was worried that if she didn't make it to the top soon, her legs might give way.

Just as she was tempted to give up and head back down, her hand hit the platform. She carefully scrambled over the edge and rested for a long moment on her hands and knees.

"Are you okay?" Zeke's voice floated up to her.

She took a deep breath and peeked over the edge of the narrow platform. "I'm fine," she replied. Zeke was just a dark shadow about a million miles below her. She closed her eyes. *Don't look down*, she reminded herself.

Trying to calm her nerves, she slowly stood up. All the trapeze ropes had been gathered and tied together and attached to the pole. Keeping one hand on the small handle jutting out from the post, she leaned forward and grabbed the ropes, trying to tug them closer to her. They swung a little, but not close enough for her to examine them. She realized she'd have to let go of her handhold.

Was the post swaying, or was that her imagination? *Get a grip*, she told herself firmly. She edged closer to the ropes, reluctantly letting go of the pole. Gingerly, she grabbed hold of the broken rope and

examined it closely. This was no accident—the rope had been cut!

"Hey!" someone shouted from below.

Jen jumped in alarm. Her foot slipped. She lunged wildly for the ropes, the post, anything to grab onto, but all she felt was air rushing past all around her!

# Sabotage

Jen tried to scream, but the sound got stuck in her throat. She tumbled through the air, falling . . . falling. . . . Instinctively she twisted and curled into a ball just in time. She landed on the net, which felt like a very large trampoline. When she stopped bouncing, she scrambled to the edge of the net, leaned over and grabbed the underside, then flipped over and off of it, landing gracefully on solid ground.

Zeke grabbed her in a bear hug. “I thought you were a pancake.”

Jen hugged him back. “So did I,” she admitted with a shaky laugh. “Who was the jerk who yelled?”

“I was,” said a boy clown wearing a polka-dotted suit, with a big smile still painted on his face. But Jen could see that under his makeup, he was frowning.

"What do you think you were doing up there?" the boy demanded.

Jen felt her spine stiffen. "I was just checking something out. Who are you, anyway?"

The clown boy narrowed his eyes. "Checking something out?" he asked doubtfully. "Not trying to cut the ropes?"

"No way!" Jen exclaimed.

"We'd never do that," Zeke said before his twin could say something she'd regret later. She had a bad habit of putting her foot in her mouth. "We just want to know what's going on."

The clown relaxed and he grinned. "Sorry about that," he apologized. "I guess I'm kind of upset about Mr. Zambini's accident." The clown turned to Jen. "I'm really sorry for scaring you. I thought maybe someone was up to no good. I'm glad you're okay. Oh, and my name's Mitchell, by the way."

The twins introduced themselves, both wondering if Mitchell could be trusted.

"I thought maybe the rope was cut or something because some strange stuff has been happening lately," Mitchell admitted. "When I saw you up there, the first thing that ran through my head was that the jerk who did it was back. I'm really sorry."

Jen waved away his apology. "Don't worry about it. You were just trying to protect the circus." She looked at Zeke and he nodded. "And you were right about the vandalism. Before I fell I saw the rope. Someone cut through it with a knife. Only a little edge of it was frayed. Also, I noticed some masking tape on the rope, as though whoever had cut the rope left a little still attached, then covered their work with the tape to disguise it."

"So none of the Zambinis would have noticed it when they got up there," Zeke added.

Jen nodded. "Exactly. And they were so involved with the audience, they obviously wouldn't notice it later, either. Not until it was too late."

Mitchell shuddered, his big blue-and-red nose wobbling on his face. "Who would want to ruin our show like that?"

"That's exactly what we want to find out," Zeke answered. "Do you know anyone who would want to hurt the Zambinis?"

"But it's not only the Zambinis," Mitchell said quickly. With crossed eyes, he pointed to his nose. "Look at this. It used to be red, but right before the show someone splattered blue paint over all the clown noses in the dressing room."

"That's not exactly as bad as cutting a trapeze

rope," Jen pointed out.

Mitchell frowned. "It may not seem like much to you, but clowns are very particular about their noses. And costumes have disappeared. Also, the other day the ostrich trainer found a metal spike in the ostrich cage. Luckily none of the birds got hurt."

"Someone is definitely trying to damage the circus," Zeke said thoughtfully. "We didn't find any clues here, but maybe we should check out the dressing room. You said stuff has been happening there, too."

"Sure," Mitchell said, leading the way. "I'll show you. I've worked and traveled with the circus all my life. My parents are two of the jugglers. I don't know what we'd do if Pierre closed down the show."

"Maybe we'll be able to help," Jen said. She didn't tell Mitchell that they had successfully solved other mysteries. She didn't want to raise his hopes, just in case.

The clowns' dressing room was a long trailer that had been painted on the outside with giant, smiling clown faces. Inside, it smelled like greasepaint, sweat, and dirty socks. All of the clowns were still in costume out on the grounds. Mitchell told them it was part of their job to entertain the crowds after a show until closing time. When the rides stopped at eleven P.M., there would be a mad rush in here with all seven clowns trying to remove their makeup at the same time. He waved his hands as he spoke, pointing out the dressing area and the brightly lit, mirrored makeup tables.

"What do you do about school?" Zeke asked.

Mitchell wrinkled his nose. "Don't worry, I can't get out of that. Pierre hired a teacher who travels with us and teaches all the kids. There are fourteen of us who live with the circus."

"Neat," Jen exclaimed.

Mitchell shrugged. "I guess it's pretty cool. But sometimes I wouldn't mind staying in one place longer than a week or a weekend. I'd like to live in a house for a month and see what it feels like."

"I guess that isn't so neat, after all," Jen said, changing her mind. She couldn't imagine not living at the B&B with Zeke and Aunt Bee.

"Anyway," Zeke interrupted, "where do you keep your noses?"

Mitchell pointed out the counter. Whoever had vandalized the noses had gotten blue paint on the countertop as well. "And we keep our costumes on this rack." He pointed. "We each have about four or five costumes because we sweat a lot in them and it's not good to wear the same one night after night." He swung a few hangers out to show them. "These are mine. I was the first to notice that one was missing. When we searched, we found several were gone. Everyone else thought the missing costumes were getting washed. But when we asked Jack, the man in charge of all the laundry, he said that he didn't have them."

"Who would want clown outfits?" Jen asked, amazed. Then she hastily added to Mitchell, "No offense."

Mitchell grinned. "You mean you wouldn't want to wear this to school?" He held out a red, white, and blue puffy one-piece suit and tapped his oversized shoe in pretend annoyance.

"Uh, it's very patriotic," Jen laughed. "Honestly, you wouldn't catch me dead in that—unless, of course, I was a clown."

Mitchell laughed, too. "Sometimes I do wear this to school . . . clown school!"

The twins warmed up to Mitchell, who straightened the rack of clothes. "These are old costumes," he said, pointing to several shoes and outfits at the end of the rack. "We wear out our costumes pretty quickly from jumping and rolling around, but sometimes it's hard to get rid of a favorite."

Jen nodded. “I have T-shirts like that. I can’t bear to get rid of them, but Aunt Bee won’t let me wear them anymore.”

“None of this helps solve the mystery of who is trying to sabotage the circus,” Zeke pointed out. “If we don’t figure this out soon, the next accident could be even worse!”

# 5
## A New Suspect

The next morning, Jen stuffed her books into her backpack. After the circus the night before, Aunt Bee had picked them up and driven them home. Jen and Zeke had spent the rest of the evening doing homework.

"Why can't teachers cancel homework when there's something this exciting going on in Mystic?" she asked Slinky, her Maine coon cat. Slinky just yawned.

"Thanks a lot," Jen said with a laugh. "You're sure a big help."

"Ready?" Zeke asked, peeking in her door.

Jen hoisted her backpack over her shoulder and followed her brother down to the kitchen where they each grabbed a homemade cranberry-almond muffin.

"We're riding our bikes to school," Jen reminded Aunt Bee.

Aunt Bee nodded, sipping her cinnamon tea. Her long gray hair wasn't in its usual braid, but hung loosely down her back. "Have a great day," she said with a smile.

Zeke jumped up and exclaimed, "Of course we will. Today's Friday!"

"Shhh," Aunt Bee hissed. "Mr. Richards, the guest who checked in yesterday, is on the parlor phone and he asked not to be disturbed. He was quite upset that the guest rooms didn't have phones in them."

"He doesn't have a cell phone?"

Aunt Bee shrugged. "Apparently not. But take a look at his car as you leave," she said with a twinkle in her blue eyes. "Just tiptoe out."

Zeke motioned for Jen to follow him. They could have left through the back door in the kitchen, but he wanted to get a glimpse of Mr. Richards.

They crept by the parlor, but all they saw was Mr. Richards's slicked-back, glossy black hair and his back.

"That's right," Mr. Richards said. "Buy all five of them. Can never have too many bucks."

The twins moved on. "He must be a banker," Jen whispered.

They went outside and around the side of the

B&B. Zeke whistled in amazement. "He's got lots of bucks all right," he said, pointing to a small green sports car in the parking lot. "That must have cost him a fortune."

"It looks like an insect," Jen remarked, mystified. "What is it?"

"It's a Lamborghini, and it's worth hundreds of thousands of dollars!"

The twins raced down the B&B's long driveway. Then they pedaled on the side of the road that led into town. A few cars sped by them. They had ridden for about five minutes when Jen spotted a large, white truck with a black triangle painted on the side that had pulled over to the side of the road. The truck was very clean. The front hood was up and a man was peering at the engine.

Zeke braked to a stop. "Need any help?" he asked.

The man looked up and smiled, showing off a gold front tooth. "I sure do, kid. Know anything about truck engines?"

Zeke shook his head. "I don't, but my friend's uncle does. He owns a garage down the road. We're going right by there and could tell him you need help."

The stranger nodded and glanced at his watch. "That would be great, kid. I really appreciate it. I'm already late."

Zeke smiled. "No problem."

Jen waved to the man as they headed off. As soon as they got to the garage owned by Tommy's uncle, they pulled in and Zeke relayed the message as promised.

Tommy's uncle, Burt, was a gruff man who wore oil-stained coveralls. He thanked them with a nod of his balding head. Jen knew he didn't like kids hanging around the garage, and she urged Zeke away as fast as she could. She knew that even though Tommy loved his uncle, he didn't get in Burt's way, either.

At last they pedaled onto the school grounds. The circus was already bustling with workers feeding animals, and jugglers in normal clothes practicing their moves. Zeke noticed that one clown was already in costume and walking with a slight limp. He saw that the tiger cage was completely covered by a gold cloth with tassels on the edges. He wondered if Mitchell was in school with his circus friends and the teacher Pierre had hired.

The bike rack stood near the front entrance of the school. Zeke parked his bike, not bothering to lock it up. Detective Wilson, a great friend and a retired police detective, had told them that in all the years he worked on the Mystic police force, not even one bicycle had ever been stolen.

Jen parked her bike next to Zeke's. "I wonder what's going on over there," she said, looking toward a cluster of trailers where circus workers had gathered.

"Someone's mad about something," Zeke said, hearing an angry voice. "Let's check it out before the bell rings."

They hurried through the gathering crowd until they stood in front of one of the trailers. From the outside, everything looked fine. But Pierre stood in the doorway, shouting angrily, his mustache jerking up and down with each word. Jen stared at the circus owner. He was covered with splotches of blue paint.

"It's ruined," Pierre shouted. "Everything in my trailer is ruined! Blue paint everywhere! When I catch the vandal, he will pay!"

Jen learned from the bearded woman standing next to her that Pierre had left his trailer early that morning, but when he'd gone back to get something, he'd found the destruction. "So many things are going wrong," the woman murmured, shaking her head.

Not able to help herself, Jen blurted out, "Is your beard real?"

The woman took a step forward. "Of course it is. Wanna pull it?"

"Uh, no thanks." With that, Jen tugged Zeke

aside and told him what the woman had said about the paint in the trailer. "It's definitely part of the mystery," Jen said. "And her beard is real. I asked her."

Zeke rolled his eyes. When would she learn to keep her mouth shut? "At least this wasn't a dangerous accident," Zeke said in reference to the vandalism. "But it sure made Pierre mad." Then he cocked his head to one side and Jen could practically see his sensitive ears perk up. "Oops, there's the bell. We'd better get to homeroom."

They rushed into the building, then split up to head for their different homerooms. Jen hustled and made it to her seat just as the late bell shrilled.

"Where were you?" Stacey asked, leaning toward her. "You weren't on the bus."

"Bikes," Jen said, catching her breath.

The morning announcements came over the loudspeaker; Jen sorted through her books, only half listening as a student talked about next week's lunch menu, the boy's baseball team, and the math team championships. As soon as the announcements ended, Jen stood up, ready to head to first period, but then the principal's voice clicked on.

"One more announcement," she said. "As a special treat, today will be a half-day for students and teachers. Classes will last only twenty minutes each and no lunch will be served. Have fun at the circus this afternoon!"

A cheer erupted in homeroom. Jen looked at Stacey, her mouth in a silent O. "I should tell Aunt Bee it's only a half-day. She knows we're staying after school for the rides, but I should let her know school's getting out early."

On the way to first period, she stopped in the office and borrowed the phone, but the B&B line was busy. It was busy after first period, too. And after second, and third, and fourth. Finally, at eleven o'clock, she got through.

"Who's been on the phone?" Jen exclaimed. "I've been calling you forever!"

Aunt Bee sighed. "It was Mr. Richards. He must have talked to every country on this planet at least twice."

Jen shook her head. "Jeez, if I spent that much time on the phone, you'd have it disconnected."

Aunt Bee laughed. "You've got that right. Now what's so urgent?"

Jen told her aunt about the shortened day, and Aunt Bee asked if they had enough money to buy lunch and still go on all the rides.

"Don't worry, I've got twenty bucks," Jen said, using Mr. Richards's term. She hung up and ran to science class.

Mrs. Watson nodded to her when Jen entered. Stacey had already told her that Jen was trying to call her aunt.

"As I was saying," Mrs. Watson continued, "it is horrible the way they have those poor circus animals locked up and trained to do those silly tricks."

"But they're fun to watch," someone piped up.

Mrs. Watson ran her fingers through her oddly colored hair. Today it had a bit of an orange tinge to it. "It's not fun, it's . . . it's agonizing."

None of the students said anything.

"Especially that poor Siberian tiger, trapped in a cage like that. It's supposed to be a wild animal. It should be free. In fact, I'd do anything to put it back into its own environment. Anything!"

Jen glanced back at her brother, who sat two rows behind her. They raised their dark eyebrows at each other. It wasn't unusual for one of them to know what the other was thinking—it was a twin thing, they'd decided long ago.

*Anything?* they both thought.

# 6
## Escape!

When the bell rang at 12:16, everyone cheered. Jen and Stacey met Zeke and Tommy, and they made their way toward the rides and games along with every other middle schooler.

"Sheesh," Stacey grumbled, shaking her blond curls. "Are there enough people here?"

"Let's try the Ferris wheel," Jen suggested. "The line isn't very long."

Before they knew it, Jen and Stacey were sitting on a swaying bench, heading up into the big, blue sky. At first the ride kept stopping and starting as the other passengers got off and on. Finally, it smoothed out.

"Yikes," Stacey said, gripping the bar across her lap. "I didn't know this went so high."

Jen laughed. "But look at the view." They gazed in all directions. Mystic Village spread out at their feet.

Beyond the buildings they could see the fields and the dark forest. To the east they followed Main Street down to the Mystic Marina and Mystic Bay. The Atlantic looked calm and sparkly in the sunlight.

"Hey, there's the B&B," Jen said, pointing toward the lighthouse.

"And there's the old ballfield," Stacey said, nodding south. "It looks so lonely and deserted."

Jen looked around for the new town field and recreation center, pointing it out when she spotted it.

By the time the ride had stopped, the girls had found all the major landmarks. They got off the Ferris wheel before the boys, so they waited for Zeke and Tommy to join them.

"That was cool," Tommy said. "We could see everything."

But Zeke didn't want to stand around talking. "Come on," he said. "Something's wrong."

Jen looked around. "Where?"

"The big top," Zeke called over his shoulder, already heading in that direction. "I saw it from the Ferris wheel."

Jen raced after her brother, Stacey and Tommy close at her heels.

When they entered the backstage area, Jen gulped. The gold covering had been pulled off the tiger cage, and the cage was empty!

"Where's the tiger?" Tommy asked, a nervous tremor in his voice.

"Lady is gone!" Terra said, as though she'd heard Tommy's question. She stood with a group of policemen near the cage. "But how did she get out?"

One of the officers said, "Someone must have stolen her."

"But that's impossible," Terra insisted, narrowing her cat eyes. "I checked on her very early this morning and I'm sure I locked the cage. No one could have gotten in there."

The policeman shrugged. "Does anyone else have the keys?"

"No. . . ." Terra bit her lip. "Well, actually, I misplaced my keys yesterday."

"Then how did you get in the cage this morning?"

"I have a spare set," Terra admitted.

"Someone probably stole your keys," the officer said grimly.

Terra shook her head in disbelief. "But who would want to steal Lady?"

At that moment Pierre charged up to the group. He took one look at the empty tiger cage and exploded. "Where's my star? Where's my tiger?"

A policeman tried to calm Pierre down. "Don't

worry. We'll find the cat. There aren't too many places to hide a tiger in Mystic."

Pierre fumed. He whirled on Terra, gripped her arm and yanked her aside. "This is all your fault," he hissed under his breath.

Zeke wondered if anyone else could hear them. He strained to hear the rest.

"If you don't find that cat, you won't have a job here or anywhere else. I'll make sure of it!"

Terra, who had looked upset before, now narrowed her eyes at Pierre and pulled her arm free. *She looks like Slinky when Slinky is mad*, Jen thought. Stacey and Tommy seemed to be more interested in watching the policemen as they talked into their radios to the rest of the force, who were out looking for Lady.

"You said I could trust you," Pierre went on. "Is this part of your plan? *Now* where will the money come from?"

Terra said something too soft to hear.

Pierre glared at the tiger trainer. "I'd better!" He let go of Terra and looked around. "Zambini. I need the Zambinis. They're all I've got left now. Where are they?" When Mr. Zambini didn't come forward, Pierre looked even angrier.

Finally, a voice called out, "I think my father is at the doctor's getting his leg checked." The girl who stepped forward was Mr. Zambini's daughter, the youngest of the trapeze artists.

"When will he be back?" Pierre demanded, tugging on his mustache.

The girl shrugged. "You said we weren't performing tonight because Terra and Lady were doing an extra-long show for the grand opening of their act."

Pierre stamped his foot. "Disaster!" he shouted, flinging his hands into the air and looking at the sky. "All of this is a disaster!" He marched away without looking back.

# 7

# A Clue in Blue

Stacey rushed off after Pierre, digging her notebook out of her bag at the same time. "I'm going to try to interview him," she shouted over her shoulder.

"Good luck," Tommy muttered. "I'd rather face a starving tiger than Pierre. Talking about starving, I'm really hungry. Food anyone?"

Jen and Zeke glanced at each other then shook their heads. "Not yet," Zeke said. "But you go eat. We'll find you later."

Tommy shrugged. "It's *your* stomachs." He jogged away toward a sign that read HOT DOGS, SOFT DRINKS, COTTON CANDY, FRIED BREAD.

"Or your stomachache," Jen added to herself. She liked junk food as much as the next person, but not if there was any chance of going on a fast ride after eating it.

A nearby policeman reported to Terra, "So far there's absolutely no sign of the tiger. No one's seen him—"

"Her," Terra corrected.

"Her, or heard her growl or anything. We have all of our staff on patrol, working overtime and extra duty. Don't worry, we'll find Lady. Now, if you don't mind coming down to the station with us, we'd like to fill out a report."

Terra looked nervous for a second, then she gave a small smile and agreed.

By now the crowd had dispersed. Jen and Zeke waited until no one was near the cage, then stepped cautiously inside it.

"I wonder who stole Terra's keys?" Jen asked.

Zeke frowned. "Do you think Terra really lost her keys, or was that just a cover-up? Remember how she told Pierre he would get the money last night? I wonder what that's all about?"

Jen scanned the inside of the cage, looking for clues. "It sure doesn't make her sound completely innocent. But then again, what money is Pierre talking about? If I wanted money from someone, I wouldn't go around yelling at her."

"Maybe it was just an act on Pierre's part," Zeke suggested. He squatted down to look more closely at the straw covering the bottom of the cage. "Jen! Come here!" he exclaimed, trying to keep his voice down.

Jen hurried over and bent low to look. "Blue paint! It's the same color as the clown noses."

"And the same color as the paint inside of Pierre's trailer," Zeke added. "It's definitely the same person behind all of this."

Jen tipped her head sideways. "Brush a little of that straw away."

Zeke brushed the straw away.

"Now brush that away over there," Jen continued. When Zeke did, they both gasped.

Zeke stood up for a better view. "Is that what I think it is?" he asked.

"If you're thinking it looks like the outline of a huge footprint, then you're thinking what I'm thinking."

Zeke nodded. "So either a giant did this, or someone else who wears big shoes."

"The clowns!"

"Exactly. Let's go find Mitchell."

The twins hurried through the fairgrounds to the trailer covered with clown faces. They knocked on the door and Mitchell opened it, already in costume.

"Hi, you guys," he said. He didn't look too happy.

"Is this a bad time?" Jen asked.

Mitchell shook his head. "Did you hear what happened to Lady?"

The twins nodded.

"Everyone's afraid that without his new star, Pierre will shut down the circus. We've been struggling for a

while, but Pierre was hoping the tiger would bring in new crowds."

Jen looked at Zeke. *So that explained the money he wanted. Or did it?*

Mitchell let them into the trailer. "He's actually just canceled tonight's performance because he can't find Mr. Zambini. His daughter said he's at the doctor's office. I guess he hurt his leg pretty bad when he fell last night." He slumped onto one of the dressing room chairs. "We're doomed."

"Not yet," Zeke said. "If Jen and I find the tiger, the circus will be okay, right?"

Mitchell looked back and forth at them. "Of course. But what can you two do?" he asked, waving his hands when he talked.

Jen grinned. "You mean, what *can't* we do!"

Mitchell seemed to catch on to their hopeful mood. "Can you walk around the ring on your hands?"

Jen's grin faded. "You got me on that one."

Laughing, Mitchell said, "Don't feel bad. It took lots of years and a whole bunch of knocks on the head to get the hang of it." Then he sobered. "But seriously, how do you think you'll find the tiger when the police haven't even found it yet?"

"We've already uncovered a clue that they missed," Zeke said. "We found a blue footprint in the straw that the police didn't see. We'll find out whose it was."

Mitchell scrunched his eyebrows together and waved his hand around. "How does that help?"

"The footprint was huge," Jen elaborated. "Like a clown's shoe. And the blue is the same color that was painted on your noses."

"So one of the clowns is trying to ruin the circus?" Mitchell asked. "I can't believe it."

"If we can find the shoe with blue paint on it, we'll know who is sabotaging everything and has the tiger," Jen said, already looking toward the lineup of clown shoes.

Mitchell jumped to his feet. The three of them turned over every pair of shoes.

"Here it is," Zeke crowed, holding up a large yellow shoe.

"That's weird," Mitchell said. As he shook his head, his green clown hair bounced back and forth.

"Weird?" Jen repeated. "Why?"

"No one wears those shoes anymore. It's like those costumes I showed you yesterday. Worn out, but not ready for the garbage. Those shoes used to belong to Petey, and he doesn't even work with this circus anymore."

Zeke frowned. "You're sure you haven't seen any

of the clowns wearing these shoes?"

"I'm sure." Mitchell's face fell. "So much for the clue."

"We may not know exactly who the person is," Jen said, trying to sound cheerful, "but we know it's someone who was wearing those clown shoes."

"I figure that the person first sabotaged Pierre's trailer and got paint on his—"

"Or her," Jen butted in.

"Shoe," Zeke continued, "then hurried to the tiger cage and stole Lady while everyone was distracted by Pierre's problem." He motioned to Jen. "We went over to Pierre's trailer before school, too, to see what had happened, remember? Someone could have been stealing the tiger and no one would have noticed."

Mitchell nodded thoughtfully. "It sure makes sense. So we have to be on the lookout for a clown who's not really a clown."

"Exactly," Jen agreed, realizing that this task sounded nearly impossible. But she refused to give up. Just then her stomach growled loudly. "Well, we missed lunch, and now it's almost dinnertime. We'd better hurry home or Aunt Bee will think we were eaten by the stolen tiger."

The twins said good-bye to Mitchell, retrieved their bikes, and headed home.

"Burt must have picked up that guy's broken-down truck," Zeke commented as they rode closer to the B&B.

"Yup, I noticed it at his garage when we passed it."

They pedaled on, panting heavily as they headed up the long hill to the B&B. The light was fading, and the sun lit up the top of the lighthouse tower. The rest of the B&B sat in shadows.

"Who's that?" Jen huffed, trying to talk and pedal uphill at the same time.

Zeke looked up, too out of breath to answer. Two figures were talking by the side door of the B&B. He couldn't tell who they were.

As they neared the door, Jen peered through the gathering dusk, trying to make out their faces. Something just didn't look right about them, as though they were trying to stay hidden. Just then one of the figures looked up and saw Jen and Zeke approaching. Jen felt certain it was a man. He slipped inside the B&B, leaving the other person alone.

The lone figure flashed them a quick grin as he hurried away on foot, heading down the driveway Jen and Zeke had just come up.

"That was the truck driver from this morning," Jen said when she'd caught her breath.

"Are you sure?" Zeke asked. He thought it was too

dark to be able to make out the guy's face.

"I'm positive," Jen said firmly. "I saw the flash of his gold tooth."

Zeke shook his head as he parked his bike. "What would the truck driver have to do with any of the guests at the B&B?" he wondered out loud.

"I don't know," Jen said, putting down her kickstand. "But they looked pretty suspicious."

# 8 The Perfect Plan

The twins hurried inside, hoping to catch a glimpse of the mysterious stranger, but when they got to the front foyer, a group of bird-watchers who were staying at the B&B were on their way out to dinner. It was impossible to tell who might have been outside a second ago.

Disappointed, they searched for Aunt Bee and found her in the parlor talking to a well-dressed man with shiny black hair. They recognized him from that morning as Mr. Richards. She beamed at them as they walked in.

"Children, this is Mr. Richards, one of our guests."

Mr. Richards stood up to shake hands with the twins. Zeke stared hard at the man. He'd seen Mr. Richards at the circus last night after Mr. Zambini's accident—the man in the fancy suit. Zeke checked out his pinky. Sure enough, Mr. Richards wore a diamond pinky ring that was in the shape of a pyramid.

"Good evening," Mr. Richards said pleasantly, patting his round stomach.

Jen almost felt like she was supposed to bow to this elegantly dressed man. She could tell his clothes were expensive. He sat down again and smiled.

"Mr. Richards was just telling me about fascinating places," Aunt Bee said. "He's traveled all over the world."

Jen noticed the man's briefcase at his feet for the first time. It was covered with travel stickers. It didn't exactly look like something a well-dressed businessman would carry around, but maybe he was eccentric. She peered closely at the stickers.

"You've been to all those places?" she asked. "South America," she read out loud, "Hawaii, the Amazon, Siberia, the Everglades, Africa." The rest of the stickers were partially covered or too small to read from a distance. "I've always wanted to go on a safari in Africa."

The man chuckled. "I've been on at least a dozen safaris there."

Jen was genuinely impressed. "Wow."

Zeke frowned. He couldn't imagine what this man

might be doing with a gold-toothed truck driver. But surely none of the bird-watchers had been talking to the truck driver. Zeke looked up as another man walked into the parlor.

"Is your room comfortable?" Aunt Bee asked the tall man.

Zeke was surprised to see Pierre the Magnificent.

"It's fine," Pierre grumbled. "Too many flowers for my taste," he added with a scowl as he saw the twins.

Jen hid a laugh. Her aunt was used to cranky guests and never got upset no matter how rude they were. "Well, your trailer will be cleaned in no time, and you'll be able to go back to it," said Aunt Bee soothingly.

"Just another added cost," he mumbled. "Had to cancel tonight's show. Do you know how much money I'm losing? Lots. Lots and lots," he stressed. "And now with Lady missing." He shook his head in disgust. "The star of our show gone." Suddenly, he brightened a little. "But thank goodness for the Big Top Insurance Company."

Jen and Zeke looked at each other.

"I'm hitting the hay," Pierre continued. "Circus life starts before the sun is up. G'night." Abruptly he turned away and stomped out of the parlor.

Aunt Bee shrugged. "The poor man is not having a very good time of it. I hope everything works out for him."

Mr. Richards nodded in agreement.

The twins excused themselves and Aunt Bee told them dinner would be ready in about a half hour. They headed up to Jen's room to talk. Each of the twins had a bedroom and a bathroom in the lighthouse tower. Aunt Bee's husband, Uncle Cliff, had renovated it, creating Jen's room on the second floor and Zeke's on the third. A spiral staircase ran from the lighthouse museum on the first floor, past the bedrooms, all the way up to the light itself. Unfortunately, Uncle Cliff died just before the grand opening two years ago, so he never got to see how successful the B&B would become.

Jen loved her partially round room. She had covered her walls with posters of sporting events and soccer stars, as well as a few cat pictures. Jen flopped on her bed, pulling Slinky close to her, and Zeke sat on the beanbag chair near the window.

"So who was talking to the truck driver?" Zeke asked once they were settled.

"I don't know, but I'll bet it was either Mr. Richards or Pierre."

Zeke nodded. "That makes sense, because I don't

think it was any of the bird-watchers. But what does his truck have to do with either of those men?"

"I can't figure that out," Jen admitted. "But if we're going to help the doomed circus in any way, we have to find out." She grinned. "And I have the perfect plan."

Zeke groaned.

Early Saturday morning, Jen tapped on Zeke's door. "Ready?" she asked when he opened it.

He yawned. "I guess so." He glanced at his clock. It was after seven, but it felt a lot earlier.

"I told Aunt Bee we'd be leaving early to go to the circus," Jen said. "She said she didn't need help with the breakfast buffet today."

They coasted down the hill on their bikes. The morning mist was cool and smelled like the ocean. Waves crashing against the cliffs sounded muffled, and early gulls were out looking for a bite to eat.

They pedaled silently. Not a single car passed them. At last they rounded the corner where Tommy's uncle's garage sat. It was still dark enough that the outside security lights were on. But as they watched, the lights flickered off automatically one by one.

They parked their bikes on a side street, then

crept silently back to the garage. They had to finish what they were going to do before Burt officially opened the garage at eight.

"There it is," Jen whispered, pointing to the white truck in the mist.

Zeke nodded. They headed for the truck. Jen climbed onto the step by the driver's door and tried the handle. The door was locked. She jumped down while Zeke tried the other side.

"Rats," Jen said when they met at the rear of the truck. "How can we check it out if we can't get in?"

"Didn't you figure the truck would be locked?" Zeke asked.

Jen glared at him. "No. I didn't."

Zeke shook his head. "I should have known this wasn't the perfect plan." Just as the words were out of his mouth, he heard a creaking noise. He turned to find Jen slowly lifting the back door of the truck.

She grinned at him. "They didn't lock the back! Part of my plan, you know."

"Yeah, right."

Whether it was part of the plan or not, they were able to slide under the rolling door. The inside of the truck was dark.

"Can you see anything?" Jen asked.

Zeke squinted. "Not really. What's this all over the floor?"

He heard some rustling, then Jen said, "I think it's straw or hay."

"Look over here," Zeke said. In the shadowed light, they could make out two large, empty plastic bowls. "What are these for?"

Jen peered at the bowls then ran a piece of straw between her fingers. "I'll bet this truck is for the tiger."

Zeke was about to protest, but the more he thought about it, the more perfect it sounded. "That's right, because we saw it the morning the tiger was stolen."

"But it broke down," Jen continued. "So it wasn't there to take the tiger away."

"Then the tiger must still be in Mystic somewhere."

"But where? Whoever stole it couldn't have taken it too far away. They could have used one of the circus vans to take it somewhere, but those vans would be too small to take Lady very far. I know I wouldn't want a frightened tiger sitting in my backseat."

"Shhhh," Zeke suddenly hissed.

Jen heard voices. She recognized the deep voice of Burt, Tommy's uncle.

"I told you," Burt said, somewhere close by, "the truck will get done when it gets done."

"But I need it *now.*"

"It's not ready *now,*" Burt said.

The other man sighed in frustration. "When, then?"

"Come back at five-thirty today."

"That late?"

"If you keep wasting my time," Burt growled, "it won't be ready till Monday. I'm closed tomorrow."

"It had better be ready by five-thirty," the man threatened. "Or else!"

# 9
# Out of Control

The voices faded away as Burt opened up his office.

"Let's get out of here," Jen said.

The twins slipped under the truck door and quietly lowered it. Crouching, they hustled across the parking lot, dodging behind cars and trucks that were waiting to be repaired. Out of breath, they ran around the corner and jumped on their bikes. They didn't slow down until they were on Main Street. Delicious smells were wafting out of the Mystic Café.

"Let's get something to eat," Jen suggested. "It's too early to go to the circus, anyway."

Zeke agreed eagerly. Aunt Bee might be the best cook in town, but the Mystic Café was known for its honey buns, and Aunt Bee didn't even try to compete with them.

Inside the café, the twins sat in a window booth

and ordered fresh orange juice, a double order of honey buns for Zeke, and a toasted sesame bagel with veggie cream cheese for Jen.

While they waited for their order, they talked, keeping their voices down. The café filled up every morning, and they didn't want to be overheard.

Jen leaned forward, her elbows on the table. "So, if the truck is finished at five-thirty, and if it really is to transport the tiger, we're running out of time." She glanced at her watch. It was barely eight.

Zeke nodded. "We have to solve this case—*fast*."

"We know who the truck driver is, but even if we tell the police our suspicions, they're not going to be able to arrest him without proof."

"That's right. We need to find evidence."

"What we need to find is Lady," Jen said somberly.

"Right," Zeke agreed. "We know it must have something to do with a guest at the B&B because we saw the driver talking to someone."

"It had to be either Pierre or Mr. Richards," Jen reasoned. "The rest of the guests are part of a bird-watching organization. I'm sure they wouldn't want a tiger."

"But why would Pierre want to steal his own tiger?"

"What would Mr. Richards do with one?"

Their food arrived at that moment, and for a

while they were too busy eating to talk. When they finished, they decided it was still too early to go to the circus, so they headed down to the Mystic Marina. Zeke loved sailing and he enjoyed inspecting the yachts and sailboats tied up at the docks.

Some time later, Jen was surprised when she looked at her watch to find it was already ten o'clock. She called to Zeke, who was talking to the skipper of a 60-foot sailboat called the *Rakassa*.

Zeke waved to show he'd heard her, and a few minutes later he trotted over to where she was sitting on a piling, waiting for him. "Joe said he'd give me a tour of the *Rakassa* later," he said, beaming.

Jen rolled her eyes. She didn't like sailing—it made her seasick. "What about the case?" she asked. "We only have until five-thirty to solve it. You don't have time for a tour."

Zeke knew his sister was right. The most important thing right now was to find Lady and figure out who had stolen her. He took one last wistful look back at the beautiful sailing yacht. He wished he could spend all day sailing.

"Come on," Jen said, pulling him away.

They rode up Main Street, took a left on Fuller Road and then a right on School Street. The colorful circus was already noisy with music and it looked like all the rides were running. Winding between the crowds, Jen and Zeke kept their eyes open for anything that looked suspicious.

"Hi," said a boy about their age. He wore a red-and-white T-shirt and red shorts, and his brown hair was slicked back as though it were still wet.

"Hi," the twins responded, staring at him blankly.

The boy smiled at them. "What are you two up to?" He gestured with his right hand and in his left he balanced a coffee cake that was wrapped in a plastic bag.

Jen and Zeke glanced at each other. *Who was this kid? Did they know him from school?*

"Uh," Zeke said, "we're just, you know, checking out the rides."

"You have to try the Whoozy Doozy," the boy urged. Again he waved his right hand.

Suddenly, Jen laughed. "Mitchell!" she exclaimed.

The boy's eyes widened. "Huh?"

Now Zeke caught on, too. "Mitchell, we didn't recognize you at first," he admitted. "You look totally different without your clown makeup on."

Mitchell grinned. "You mean you didn't even know it was me?"

Jen shook her head. "Not until I recognized the way you wave your hands around when you talk.

We've never seen you without your wig and costume and makeup on."

Mitchell laughed. "I forgot about that. Hey, I'm taking this coffee cake over to Mr. Zambini's trailer. My mom made it because she feels bad about his accident. Mrs. Zambini said he's in their trailer, resting. Want to come along?"

Zeke shrugged. "Sure."

They followed Mitchell behind a roped-off area that had a sign reading RESTRICTED—CIRCUS PERSONNEL ONLY. Mitchell led them to a cluster of trailers. "This is where we live," Mitchell explained. "Pierre's trailer is over there, but I guess you know that." He waved in another direction. "I live down that way, and here's the Zambinis' trailer."

It wasn't hard to miss. It was painted a dark purple and gold letters spelled out ZAMBINI across the side. Mitchell knocked on the door. No one answered.

"Maybe he fell asleep," Jen suggested.

"Maybe," Mitchell agreed. He tried the door handle. It turned. "Let's just leave this inside on the kitchen table. We don't have to wake him up."

They entered the trailer, tiptoeing and not speaking. Jen was amazed to see how much could fit into such a small space. There was a kitchen with a sink, refrigerator, stove, and oven, an eating area, and a living room with plush green carpeting on the floor. The bathroom door stood open, and two other doors farther down were open, too.

"The bedrooms are down there," Mitchell mouthed and pointed as he put the cake on the table.

Jen turned around and glanced down at the counter, which was covered with piles of opened letters. She noticed that the envelopes were holding what looked like bills. One pink sheet stuck out of an envelope and Jen could read the words "Final notice" written across the top in bold letters. Feeling guilty for spying, she moved toward the door.

Zeke stepped after her, then noticed the vase of flowers on the side table with a "Get well soon" card attached. One of the flowers in the arrangement was a lily. He tried to step away from the flowers as quickly as possible, but it was too late. His nose itched. Lilies always made him sneeze. He tried to squeeze his nostrils closed to stop the tickle, but it didn't work. A squeaky sneeze erupted. The three of them stared at one another, expecting Mr. Zambini to come groggily out of his bedroom at any second. But nothing happened.

"Either he's a deep sleeper," Zeke said with a sniffle, "or he's not here."

"Either way, we'd better get out of here," Jen said.

She led the way out of the trailer.

"I've got a while before I have to get into costume," Mitchell said. "Let's go on the Whoozy Doozy, my treat."

"Sure," Zeke said. One ride wouldn't hurt, but

then they had to get down to some serious sleuthing. Five-thirty would be here before they knew it.

Jen made a face. If sailboats made her feel ill, she could just imagine what the Whoozy Doozy would do.

The Whoozy Doozy line was long. The young man with the droopy blond mustache who was running the ride said that the regular ride operator was sick this morning and it had taken a while to find a replacement. He let Mitchell cut to the front of the line and they all got to ride for free. They strapped themselves into a small compartment just in time for the ride to start. The ride whirled slowly at first. Jen grinned. This wasn't so bad after all. But then the ride twirled faster and faster. Not only was the compartment going in circles, but the whole ride was turning as well. Jen began to feel green. She could see that Zeke and Mitchell were having the time of their lives, though. The ride continued spinning faster and faster. Jen closed her eyes, praying the ride would end soon. But it didn't. If anything, it seemed to turn even faster. And now it was bumping up and down, too.

She forced her eyes open and fear shot through her—not because Zeke was turning green, too, but because of the terrified look on Mitchell's face.

Something was definitely wrong!

"The ride is out of control!" Mitchell shouted.

# 10
# The Million Dollar Question

Jen knew she'd pass out if the ride didn't slow down. Along with the whirling and bumping, there was now a loud banging sound. *What if the operator couldn't* ever *stop the ride? They'd be twirling around forever!*

Even as these thoughts careened through her head, the noise and bumping abruptly stopped. Slowly, the spinning decreased, but it seemed like it took forever. As soon as the ride stopped, Mitchell released the strap that held them in place.

"I wonder what happened," he said, shaking his head to clear the dizziness.

Jen scrambled off the ride. Her legs wobbled and for a second she thought she'd fall flat on her face.

Zeke grabbed her arm to keep her on her feet. They passed the ride operator, who was inspecting the gears of the ride with two men in gray jumpsuits.

"Those are the circus mechanics," Mitchell told them as they walked by.

One of the mechanics scratched his head and said, "Looks like someone purposely jammed this gear."

Jen pulled Zeke aside. "Did you hear that?"

Zeke nodded. "Another act of sabotage."

Mitchell said he had to go put his clown makeup on and waved good-bye. As he trotted off, Jen and Zeke continued their conversation.

"But why would someone want to sabotage a ride?" Jen mused.

"So far there has been the Zambini accident," Zeke began, lifting one finger. He lifted another one. "And painting Pierre's trailer."

"Stealing Lady," Jen added. "And don't forget the clown noses and the stake in the ostrich cage."

"And now this ride." Zeke shook his head. "It doesn't seem to add up. Let's go home. I have a theory and there's something I want to look up on the Internet."

As soon as they got back to the B&B, the twins searched for Aunt Bee to tell her they were home.

As they neared the parlor, Zeke put his finger to

his lips. Jen heard someone talking—she recognized Mr. Richards's voice. The twins tiptoed so they wouldn't disturb him. Aunt Bee always reminded them that it was crucial to let the guests feel as if they were in their own homes and could talk on the phone without being disturbed, or even take a nap in the parlor if they wanted to.

Mr. Richards looked up at them and grinned. "Late this afternoon," he said into the receiver. "Don't worry." With that, he hung up, his diamond pinky ring flashing brilliantly. "What are you kids up to?"

Zeke shrugged. "Just looking for our aunt."

"Slinky, cut that out," Jen said as her Maine coon cat purred and rubbed against Mr. Richards's dark blue suit. She didn't normally warm up to the guests so quickly.

Mr. Richards laughed. "It's quite all right. I love cats and I miss all of mine." He rubbed Slinky's head and the cat purred even louder.

The three of them laughed.

"I think your aunt said she was going for a walk," Mr. Richards said.

Jen knew her aunt loved to walk along the bluff with the salty ocean breeze blowing her long gray hair. She could be gone for an hour or more. The twins excused themselves and hustled upstairs to

Zeke's room. He booted up his computer and signed onto the Web.

"What are you looking for?" Jen asked, flopping on a chair she had pulled up next to Zeke's. Her legs still felt a little wobbly from the ride.

"I memorized the license plate number on the truck. I just want to see if I can trace it."

Jen could hardly keep up with Zeke's fingers flashing over the keyboard and the way he flicked his mouse around. After ten minutes of investigating, Zeke sat back with a grin. "Check out this new Web site. It searches license plates for free, and it only takes seconds. . . ."

Jen leaned forward, anticipation tingling her fingers and toes. "So? Who does the truck belong to?"

Zeke put up his hand. "Just a sec. The computer is still searching."

They stared at the screen. Finally, a new image appeared. It listed the license plate number, the state in which it was registered, and the owner's name.

"The Pyramid Group?" Jen read out loud. "What's that?"

Zeke frowned. "It's the company that owns the truck. That must be why there's a black triangle painted on the side of it." His fingers flew over the keyboard again. He sat back in defeat. "The Pyramid Group must be the only company in the world that doesn't have a Web site. So we can't even find out anything about it or who the owners are."

Jen groaned. "A dead end."

"Hopefully not for Lady," Zeke said grimly, working at the keyboard again. "Let's look up the Big Top Insurance Company. I remember Pierre mentioning it."

They easily found the site and read the description of the company. "Insurance for all amusements, large and small. Put your trust in us. You lose, we pay!"

"It must be Pierre's insurance company," Jen said. "I wonder if he gets money for losing Lady?"

With Jen looking over his shoulder, he clicked on a policy information icon. They both read silently.

Then Zeke whistled. "The policy for rare animals covers up to a million dollars," he breathed.

Jen felt stunned. "That sure gives Pierre a motive for stealing Lady. It would take him months, if not years, of performing to make that much money from ticket sales. All he has to do is get rid of Lady and collect the insurance money and he's got it made."

Zeke thought for a moment and frowned. "But we still haven't figured out what all those other accidents and vandalism have to do with Lady's disappearance."

"Maybe he's trying to collect insurance on everything bad that happens?"

"That doesn't make sense. If he's trying to get the insurance company to pay for Lady, he wouldn't want to jeopardize that by having too many accidents happen or the insurance company might cancel the policy."

Jen nodded. Zeke had a point. "And it doesn't explain the clown footprint we found in the cage. When the tiger was stolen, Pierre was having a fit over his painted trailer."

They were both silent for a long moment, trying to sort out the clues.

"It'd be best if we could just find Lady," she said as she stood up. "Come on, we have to go look for her. If we find her we'll know who took her."

They hurried down the spiral staircase of the lighthouse tower, then stopped in the kitchen and grabbed sandwiches for lunch. Jen had one idea of where to look for Lady. She told Zeke about it once they were on their bikes and heading for town again.

"The old haunted house on Front Street would be the perfect place to hide a tiger," Jen insisted. "No one goes near that spooky place."

"But someone would hear if Lady roared."

"Well, it's worth a shot."

When they got to town, they headed for Front Street and rode south until they reached number 502, the old Murray mansion. They stood out front and stared up at the pointy roof peaks, the crumbling roof tiles, the broken and missing window shutters, and the peeling gray paint.

Jen shivered. Maybe this wasn't such a good idea after all.

Zeke took a deep breath. "Let's go," he said, sounding a lot braver than he felt.

They left their bikes on the pavement and passed through the creaking front gate. As soon as they walked onto the property, the sun went behind a cloud and everything became even gloomier. The front stairs groaned as they walked up them to the sagging front porch. A broken porch swing swayed in the breeze, one side of it still bolted to the ceiling of the porch.

"Think this is safe?" Zeke asked.

"No," Jen admitted. "But we have to find Lady before it's too late."

The front door was missing, so it was easy to enter the house. The high ceilings and dusty, dark drapes over the windows made Jen feel like she was entering a cave. It took a moment for their eyes to adjust.

Above them something creaked.

Zeke's heart slammed against his ribs. "What was that?" he hissed.

They heard another creak, followed by a loud thump.

Wide-eyed, Jen turned to Zeke. "It's either Lady or a ghost," she said with a gulp.

# 11

# Haunted?

The twins cocked their heads, straining to hear.

"We have to go look," Jen whispered after a few seconds of absolute silence. She headed for the wide staircase that led up into the darkness of the second floor. They climbed slowly, watching and listening the whole way. On the second floor landing, they stopped and listened.

Zeke heard a shuffling sound down the hall to the left. He pointed. Jen nodded, and they headed in that direction. What if they came face-to-face with a hungry tiger? She gritted her teeth and kept moving. Now she could hear the noise again. It was getting louder.

Suddenly, Jen stepped on a loose floorboard. It screeched like a frightened cat, sending chills from Jen's toes to the top of her head.

"Nice going," Zeke whispered.

The shuffling sound stopped. Then they heard the sound of running feet. Jen and Zeke rushed down the hall. It zigzagged, then led to a second set of stairs heading down. Before they started down the stairs, they heard a bang below them.

Jen ran to one of the tall, dusty windows and peered out into the backyard. She gasped. "It's Mrs. Watson!"

The twins watched as their science teacher ran across the yard and scrambled through a gap in the back fence. Mrs. Watson took one last frightened look back at the mansion before disappearing from view.

"I wonder what she was doing here?" Jen said.

"She's been snooping around a lot," Zeke said. "She must be up to something."

They searched the rest of the house, but they didn't find Lady, or any ghosts, much to their relief.

Outside, it took a few minutes for their eyes to get used to the bright sunlight. When they could see again, they rode up and down every street, keeping their eyes open for any likely hiding place for Lady.

Jen gave a sigh of disgust as they reached Main Street. "Maybe we're completely wrong about what's going on. Maybe Lady really did escape on her own and the truck is for transporting goats or something."

Zeke gave his sister a look. "Are you kidding?

We've pieced the clues together perfectly so far. Everything makes sense."

They passed the Mystic Café on their left. Then they rode by the self-serve laundry and the Smith Sisters' Salon. Just after they crossed Front Street, Zeke whistled with appreciation. Mr. Richards's awesome roadster was parked in front of Perfect Pets. It gleamed in the bright sunlight. He had to stop and admire it close up.

"That is so great," Zeke said with longing.

"Yeah, and you only need, like, a million dollars to get your own," Jen said dryly. She looked around. "I wonder where he is?" Then she spotted him in Perfect Pets. "Let's see what he's buying."

They leaned their bikes against the wall, and stepped inside the store. Several people were in the store looking at the Persian kittens. One boy was begging his father for a pug. Mr. Richards stood near the counter with a large, bright blue-and-yellow bird on his arm.

"Nice parrot," Zeke said, walking up to him.

Mr. Richards turned and smiled at the twins. "It's a macaw. I've never seen one with such a beautiful blend of colors and such bright eyes."

As though the bird knew they were talking about him, he bobbed his head and squawked loudly.

Jen laughed. "He sure is a noisy guy."

"Oh, that's nothing," Mr. Richards said. "When you get thirty birds together in one aviary, now *that's* noisy!"

"Thirty of these guys?" Zeke asked.

Mr. Richards nodded. "I can't seem to stop buying them. My menagerie just keeps growing." He paid for the bird, then asked the twins if they needed a ride back to the B&B.

Zeke groaned. "I can't, I have my bike here."

"Maybe some other time, then. See you later," Mr. Richards said.

Jen and Zeke followed him out of the store and watched him pack the birdcage onto the passenger seat and zoom off.

Jen sighed. "We may as well head home, too. We haven't found out anything more and we're running out of time."

"We need to make suspect sheets," Zeke said. "It's the only way to sort everything and *everyone* out."

Back at the B&B, the twins settled themselves in Zeke's room. Jen grabbed a couple of pens and several sheets of paper and started writing.

# Suspect Sheet

**Name:** PIERRE THE MAGNIFICENT

**Motive:** TRYING TO MAKE HIS SHOW BIGGER AND BETTER; INSURANCE MONEY?

**Clues:** Why would he want to steal the star of the show? Is it worth it?

WAS HE THE ONE TALKING TO THE TRUCK DRIVER?

THE TIGER WAS PROBABLY INSURED. MAYBE PIERRE WOULD RATHER HAVE THE INSURANCE MONEY TO UPGRADE THE SHOW?

What did he mean by telling Terra he was counting on her and why did that make her upset? Counting on her to steal the tiger?

Was the tiger stolen while he was distracting everyone with his ruined trailer? Is he working with someone?

# Suspect Sheet

**Name:** *Mrs. Watson*

**Motive:** *Hates to see the tiger in captivity*

**Clues:** *Admitted she's against animals in captivity and says she'd do ANYTHING to let the tiger go free.*

WHY WAS SHE SNEAKING AROUND THE SHOW AND NEAR THE TIGER CAGE? TO LET THE TIGER OUT?

WHAT WAS SHE DOING AT THE MURRAY MANSION?

# Suspect Sheet

**Name:** Terra the Tiger Trainer

**Motive:** Working with Pierre?

**Clues:** What was she talking to Pierre about after the trapeze accident? What did she mean by "You can trust me?" Trust her to steal the tiger? And what money was she talking about?

SHE WAS A CRYING WRECK AFTER TIGER DISAPPEARED—WAS SHE FAKING IT TO THROW OFF SUSPICION?

Was her key to Lady's cage really stolen or was she just trying to make it look like someone else could have done it?

# Suspect Sheet

**Name:** Mr. Richards

**Motive:** He collects exotic birds, could he collect other exotic animals, too?

**Clues:** WHY IS HE LURKING AROUND THE CIRCUS? WHAT CONNECTION DOES HE HAVE?

He admits he loves cats. Could he want a tiger? But he was on the phone all morning when the tiger was stolen.

Who is he talking to on the phone all the time?

HE TRAVELS ALL AROUND THE WORLD AND HAS BEEN TO SIBERIA. THE MISSING TIGER IS A SIBERIAN TIGER. ANY CONNECTION?

# Suspect Sheet

**Name:** ZAMBINI THE GREAT

**Motive:** MAD AT PIERRE FOR REPLACING THE GREAT ZAMBINI ACT WITH A TIGER?

**Clues:** Who cut their trapeze rope?

WHERE WAS MR. ZAMBINI WHEN HE WAS SUPPOSED TO BE IN HIS TRAILER RESTING?

Did he really hurt his leg, or was he faking it so he wouldn't have to perform? But why?

When the twins finished, they shuffled through the sheets again and again, but nothing seemed to sort itself out.

"Have we missed something?" Jen wondered out loud.

Zeke checked the clock on his desk. "I don't know, but we're running out of time!"

# Note to Reader

Have you figured out who stole Lady? Is it the same person who is causing all the accidents at the circus?

If you review this case carefully, you'll discover important clues that Jen and Zeke have missed along the way.

Take your time. Carefully review your suspect sheets. When you think you have a solution, read the last chapter to find out if Jen and Zeke can put all the pieces together to solve *The Mystery of the Missing Tiger*.

Good luck!

# Solution

## Another Mystery Solved!

"It's five o'clock!" Zeke said. "The truck will be ready at five-thirty."

"Think!" Jen commanded.

"I *am* thinking," Zeke protested. He looked over the suspect sheets again. Something was niggling at the back of his mind. Something they hadn't written down on the suspect sheets. . . . Mr. Richards's ring!

"What?" Jen asked, sensing her brother's growing excitement.

"The Pyramid Group owns the truck, right?"

Jen nodded.

"Well, Mr. Richards wears a diamond pinky ring in the shape of a pyramid!"

Jen frowned. "That's not exactly solid evidence."

"Think about how he travels all over the world. He loves animals, right? He *collects* them."

Slowly, Jen nodded. "And he loved Slinky, even though she was leaving cat hairs all over his expensive clothes. And he sure is rich enough to buy a Siberian tiger."

"Exactly," Zeke agreed. "Tigers are so rare that if he couldn't find someone to sell him one, he'd have to steal it!"

Suddenly, Jen frowned. "But he couldn't have stolen Lady. He was on the phone all Friday morning, remember?"

For a moment, Zeke paused. Then he snapped his fingers. "He must have someone on the inside working for him. One of the clowns must be his partner. Which one? Who needs the money?"

Jen closed her eyes and thought about the clown clues. Which clown? Mitchell had said he didn't think any of the clowns would do it. And the shoes with the blue paint on them belonged to . . . no one.

"It's not a clown," Jen said finally.

"But what about the clown footprint?"

"It was an old costume. And remember how hard it was to recognize Mitchell without his makeup on? I only recognized him by the way he moved his arms around when he talked. Someone was wearing the clown suit as a disguise."

Something flashed in Zeke's head. "I saw a

clown," he said slowly, "on the morning Lady was stolen. I thought it was weird that he was in his costume already since none of the others were. He walked with a limp."

"*What* did you say?" Jen demanded.

"I saw a clown—"

"Did you say he limped?"

"Uh, yeah."

"Who is the only performer in the circus with a limp?"

Then it dawned on Zeke. "Mr. Zambini!"

Nervously he checked the clock again—5:07.

Jen also looked at the clock, then she jumped up and headed for the door.

"Where are you going?" Zeke called.

She motioned for him to follow her. As they raced down the stairs, she hurriedly told Zeke her plan between breaths. "The truck. We have to sneak into the back. It'll go pick up Lady. We'll find Lady. It's the only way—we'll get to her—before they get her out of town."

Zeke grabbed Jen's arm and hauled her to a stop. "Are you nuts?" he demanded.

"Do you have a better idea?" Jen asked, moving on again.

Zeke fumed. No, he didn't have a better idea, but

he didn't exactly want to be eaten by a tiger, either. On the spur of the moment, he stopped at the beehive-shaped kitchen phone.

"What are you doing?" Jen asked. "We don't have time for phone calls."

Zeke motioned for his sister to hang on for one second as he dialed Tommy's number. Busy. He tried again. Still busy. He tried Stacey's number and she picked up on the second ring.

Tripping over his words, Zeke tried to explain what was going on. "You need to find Pierre and call the police. Then get them to follow the truck that's at Tommy's uncle's garage. The one with the black triangle on the side. Tell Pierre it will lead everyone to the missing tiger!"

Stacey started to ask questions, but Zeke knew she could talk forever if he let her. "Just get going," he interrupted. "It could be a matter of life or death." *Ours*, he thought as he slammed the phone down and dashed after Jen.

With her wavy brown hair flying out behind her, Jen zoomed down the hill and headed for the garage, pedaling like crazy. They hoped the truck wouldn't have been picked up already.

As they rounded the corner, Jen sighed with relief. The truck was still there! The twins ditched their bikes and ran toward the truck, hunching down in hopes that no one would notice them. Zeke couldn't breathe until they had managed to lift the back door a crack and slip into the dark truck. When they slid the door back down, they were left in complete blackness.

Zeke breathed with relief.

"I hope the driver won't check back here before he takes off," Jen said, positioning herself against the wall so she wouldn't roll around when the truck started moving.

Zeke groaned. "Great. I never thought of that. And what are we going to do when they open the door to let Lady in? They're not going to be too thrilled to see us here."

"Don't worry. Stacey will call the police."

At that moment, the truck rumbled to life. Jen braced herself as the driver backed up and took a left out of the driveway. She tried to imagine where they were heading, but after several rights and lefts, she got lost.

Suddenly, the truck lurched to the right and Jen hit her head against the side as they bumped over a rough road before coming to a jerky stop. The motor cut off.

Jen froze. All of a sudden this did not seem like a great plan. She heard voices outside. Someone grabbed the handle of the back door and lifted. With a loud rattle, it flew up. Jen and Zeke stared right into the eyes of Mr. Richards and Mr. Zambini.

Zeke looked beyond the two angry men, but no police were in sight. They were doomed!

Jen recognized where they were right away. *Of course!* she thought. *The old, abandoned ballfield.* A dreadful thought was sinking in. What if the police hadn't followed the truck? Would anyone think to look for them here?

"What are you two doing in there?" Mr. Richards demanded.

"I—we—" Zeke began.

"We know everything," Jen blurted out, raising her voice to compete with the crashing waves nearby. "And you're not going to get away with it."

A slow smile spread across Mr. Richards's face. He smoothed one hand over his oiled hair. "Of course I am. I always do. How do you think I have collected so many exotic creatures for my menagerie?"

Mr. Zambini stood nervously at his side.

Then Mr. Richards's smile turned nasty. "Go get Lady," he ordered.

Mr. Zambini blanched. "What about the kids?"

"Exactly," Mr. Richards said. "We'll find out if Lady has any wild instincts left in her."

Jen gasped.

"You're going to be in big trouble for this," Zeke said boldly.

Jen looked at her twin in amazement. He sounded so sure of himself. Then the faint sound that Zeke had obviously already heard reached her ears. Sirens!

Very soon, Mr. Richards and Mr. Zambini also heard the sirens, but it was too late for them to escape. Two police cars zoomed down the dirt road and slammed to a stop, surrounding them. Right behind them a circus van kicked up dust as it stopped and Pierre, Stacey, Mrs. Watson, and Terra jumped out. The police immediately put handcuffs on Mr. Richards, Mr. Zambini, and the truck driver.

"You have a lot of explaining to do," one of the police officers growled.

"We can explain most of it," Jen offered. She told everyone how they had figured out all the clues and discovered who was behind Lady's cat-nabbing. She looked around. "But we didn't figure out that this old abandoned sports field would be such a great hiding place. It makes sense. No one comes here now that there's a brand-new field, so no one would see Lady, and the Atlantic covers up most sounds."

Zeke turned to Terra, who now had possession of Lady's leash. The immense tiger lay down patiently at her feet. "We thought you might be guilty," he admitted.

Terra's green eyes opened wide. "Me? Why?"

"We heard you arguing with Pierre, promising him money."

Terra smiled. "I was promising to make him money with Lady." She bent down and scratched the tiger's ears. "We make quite a team."

"The circus wasn't doing well," Pierre said. "I needed a new act to revive ticket sales. I was nervous that Terra's act wouldn't do it," he said sheepishly. "I'm afraid I was rather on edge and not very kind."

Jen faced Mr. Zambini. "You were the one who stole Terra's keys for the cage, right?"

Mr. Zambini nodded, not lifting his face to look at anyone.

"You were that jealous of the new act that you wanted to get rid of it?" Zeke asked.

"No, no," Mr. Zambini protested in his slight accent. "I needed the money for my son. He is in medical school and the cost is very high. He wanted to be a veterinarian. It was his dream and I wished it to come true. But I couldn't afford it. When someone told me Mr. Richards would pay one hundred thousand dollars for the tiger, I made my plans."

"You cut your own rope," Jen guessed out loud.

"And caused all the little problems like missing clown costumes and painting Pierre's trailer blue."

"Yes," Mr. Zambini admitted. "I thought if there were many things going wrong, and one of them happened to me, no one could suspect me. They would just think someone was trying to ruin the circus."

Jen and Zeke glanced at each other. "It worked," Jen admitted. "It wasn't until Zeke remembered seeing a clown who walked with a limp that we figured out it was you."

Zeke turned to Mr. Richards. "And we thought you were a banker."

"Why a banker?" Mr. Richards asked.

"We heard you talking about bucks," Jen said. "You said the more bucks the better."

Mr. Richards frowned. "I was talking about male rabbits."

Jen shook her head. "Rabbits?"

"A buck is a male rabbit. My supplier found several bucks with extremely unusual markings. I wanted them for my collection."

"What do you do with all your animals anyway?" Stacey asked. Jen noticed that her best friend had her pen and pad of paper out.

Mr. Richards shrugged. "Not much. I just collect them."

"Like a zoo?" Stacey persisted.

"A *private* zoo," Mr. Richards said. "I don't like anyone else looking at my animals."

"I think we've heard enough," the police officer said. He pulled on Mr. Richards's arm. "You three are under arrest. You're coming with us."

After they left, Jen looked at her science teacher. "What are you doing here?"

Mrs. Watson looked embarrassed. "I was at the circus to see if Lady had been found when the call came. I just jumped in the van before anyone could say anything, and here I am. I had to be sure Lady was safe."

"But why were you at the old Murray mansion?" Zeke asked. "We saw you there."

"That was you?" Mrs. Watson exclaimed. She laughed. "You scared the daylights out of me. Like you, I was searching for the tiger. I was afraid she was being abused."

Terra clucked her tongue. "I've examined Lady, and she's in perfect health. The robbers didn't hurt her, thank goodness."

Lady rubbed her massive head against Terra's legs. "Yes, I missed you too," Terra said with a laugh.

Mrs. Watson sighed. "It seems that Lady really likes you."

"Of course," Terra said. "I raised her from a cub,

saving her from terrible people who were trying to illegally raise white tigers for their pelts."

"How horrible," Mrs. Watson said. "I guess she really is better off with you. I'm sorry I made such a fuss."

Terra waved away her apology. "I understand. And believe me, I treat Lady like a *queen*."

Stacey moved closer to the tiger trainer. "Can you tell me where you were born?"

Terra looked confused. "What does that have to do with anything?"

"It's background for the article I'm writing," Stacey explained, holding her pen poised above the paper.

"Always looking for a front page story," Jen said with a chuckle.

"Let's go to the circus," Zeke said. "With everything going on, we haven't had a chance to really enjoy it."

"We can look for Tommy," Jen said.

Stacey grinned. "Not that we'll have to look very hard."

"He'll be at the food stand," Jen and Zeke chimed in together. Then they burst out laughing.

# About the Author

Laura E. Williams has written more than twenty-five books for children, her most recent being the books in the Mystic Lighthouse Mysteries series, *ABC Kids*, and *The Executioner's Daughter*. In her spare time she works on the rubber art stamp company that she started in her garage.

Ms. Williams loves lighthouses. Someday she hopes to visit a lighthouse bed-and-breakfast just like the one in Mystic, Maine.

Mystic Lighthouse

# Suspect Sheet

**Name:**

**Motive:**

**Clues:**

# UNDERCOVER GIRL

## #1... secrets

by Christine Harris

To Marci, an expert on spies

Thanks to Mount Barker, Mount Barker South, Littlehampton, and Meadows elementary schools for their enthusiastic help in the research, and to Dyan Blacklock for a great idea.



ISBN 0-439-76125-5

 Published by Scholastic Inc., 557 Broadway, New York, NY 10012, by arrangement with Omnibus Books, an imprint of Scholastic Australia.



12 11 10 9 8 7 6 5 4 3 2 1 5 6 7 8 9/0

Printed in the U.S.A. 40

First American edition, September 2005

# 1.

A knot twisted in Jesse's stomach. Her target hadn't spotted her so far, but that could change in a second. He knew she was close. He knew she was watching him.

Without turning her head, she swiveled her eyes to the left. Passersby would simply see a girl window-shopping in the mall. Jesse checked her watch. She had to tag him in the next ten minutes.

"Got a dollar, miss?" A gruff voice rumbled into her ear. She looked up. A man with ratty dreadlocks and frayed fingerless gloves held out his hand. The flesh around his eyes was red-rimmed and crinkled. His eyeballs seemed too small for their sockets.

"Pick on someone your own size," she said and shot him a look that made him back away. She mustn't lose her target now. It was too important. If she got this right, she'd have more freedom. If not, it was back to "the fishbowl."

Again, she inspected the shifting crowd of shoppers. Yes, there he was: black pants, gray open-necked shirt, cropped hair gelled to stand up like a miniature yellow lawn. He stopped, fingered an apple from a fruit stand, then carefully scanned the people near him.

Then he was on the move again, sauntering as though he had all the time in the world. But he didn't. Jesse smiled. He had only . . . oh . . . about eight minutes left.

Jesse loosened her hair-tie and fanned the long, blond hair over her shoulders. She slipped off her jacket, reversed it, and put it back on. If he was looking for a glimpse of red, he would be wrong. The lining of her jacket was green. *Change something about your appearance, even if it's a little thing,* she'd learned at training.

Casually, as though she were daydreaming,

she strolled along the edge of the mall, beside the store windows. She closed the gap between her and the man. Her fingers curled around the can in her pocket, ready to aim.

He quickened his pace and turned right into a parking garage.

Jesse went left, into a shoe store opposite the parking garage. She turned her back and slipped on her sunglasses. The mirrored side strips allowed her to see clearly behind her.

"How may I help you?"

Jesse flicked a glance at the sales assistant, who had tight lips and thick makeup.

"What do you get if you cross a dinosaur with a pig?" asked Jesse, as she watched her target pay for his parking ticket across the mall.

"Excuse me?"

"Jurassic pork."

The assistant snorted. "Are you trying to be smart?"

*I am smart,* thought Jesse, but she didn't say it. The sales assistant would not understand.

Across the mall, the man pressed one of

the buttons outside the elevator. He checked all around him. Jesse pursed her lips. *Bet he thinks he's safe. Think again, Lawnhead.*

He stepped inside the elevator and the doors closed.

"*Yoo-hoo.* Earth to space cadet." The sales assistant waved a hand in front of Jesse's face.

Jesse didn't answer. She ripped off the glasses and jammed them back into her pocket. Then she ran across the mall, the soles of her sneakers slapping against the pavement.

The numbers lit up above the elevator — one, two, then it stopped at three. Jesse opened the door to the stairs and took them two at a time. She began to puff, and her chest hurt. By the second flight of stairs, her legs were screaming at her to stop. *Floor two . . . three.* This was it.

She edged open the door, just a crack. It made only the slightest of sounds as the latch clicked back. *There he is, digging in his pocket for keys.* Two minutes to go, maybe three.

After a couple of deep breaths, she dropped to the ground, squeezed around the partly open door and let it close quietly. Crablike, she scuttled across the oil-stained floor and around cars. She pressed her body flat, peering underneath the car beside her. Two legs, covered by black pants, stood on the other side. His shoes were scuffed at the front.

On a lower level, car tires squealed as someone gunned the engine.

Suddenly the elevator pinged. Jesse heard the doors open, then voices. The man's feet spun around so he could face the elevator. She knew, without looking, that his hand would be inside his jacket pocket. His heart, like hers, would be pounding and he would be ready to lunge.

Children's voices, high and irritated, echoed off the walls.

A deeper, older voice snapped back, "Be quiet or I'll take the toys back."

The man's feet did not move. He stood rock-still, ready for anything. Was he wondering if this woman with the arguing children was his hunter?

Jesse grabbed the can from her pocket. *Now! Get him while he's distracted.* She leaped to her feet. Instinctively, he half-turned. But he was too slow. Jesse squeezed the nozzle and blasted the man in the face. A similar can dropped from his fingers onto the cement with a *clack,* then rolled away. The man crumpled, unconscious. His head met the concrete with a thud.

# 2.

Three levels belowground, in a gray hallway, Jesse stood still while a light beam scanned her retinas. The square panel beneath her feet monitored her heart rate and weight.

"Jesse Sharpe, you are cleared for entry," came an electronic voice from a hidden speaker.

Behind her, two bulky guards, muscled arms folded, stood on each side of the underground hallway. The doors slid open silently. She stepped from the hall into the Director's waiting room.

His office manager, Prov, sat behind her broad, oak desk. She wore a yellow, fluffy sweater. Her black hair was teased high and her brown eyes were rimmed by eyeliner. Red stick-on nails made her fingers look extra long. Jesse didn't know how she could type with those nails.

A warm smile lit up Prov's face. "Jesse!"

Jesse smiled back. She couldn't help it. Prov's smile was like a fire on a cold day.

Prov beckoned Jesse to her desk and whispered, "I have something for you."

Within a few seconds, a bite-sized candy bar was whisked from Prov's handbag to Jesse's hand, and into her mouth. The chocolate flavor burst on her tongue as she bit down. *Mmm.* She wasn't allowed junk food. "Healthy body, healthy mind," her carer, Mary Holt, always said. Well, Mary didn't know everything. This organization dealt in secrets. Chocolate was just another one. Prov glanced over her shoulder at the closed door. "I think Director Granger's in a good mood. As far as I can tell, anyway."

Prov said he refused to use the shortened version of her name. He insisted on calling her Providenza. It was Italian for *providence* — the protective care of God or nature. Her mother had almost lost Prov when she was pregnant, so the doctors packed her in ice for four months. The baby — Prov — was born with pneumonia. Yet she lived.

The new Director of C2 was hard to read. Jesse had only met him once, when he gave her the test assignment. There were whispers that he intended to make changes. Whether they would be good or bad, she didn't know.

Prov raised one eyebrow. "He's got someone in there with him."

Jesse wished this appointment was over. Then she would know what was going to happen. She had tagged the big, blond man within the time limit. That was good. But what if he had been seriously injured from the bump on his head? That would be bad. Jesse wiped her moist palms on her jeans.

She thought of Rohan, her C2 "brother." Where was he now? "He was sick," was all they told her. "He went to a place where doctors heal the mind." Rohan had not seemed sick to her. But he had asked a lot of questions. He'd dropped hints about hacking into C2's computers. Even at eleven, he knew more about computers than most people would learn in their entire lives. Then Rohan was gone.

"Jesse."

She jumped. *Granger!* She hadn't heard his office door open.

Behind his back, Prov gave Jesse the thumbs-up sign and mouthed the words, *Go girl.* But there was an extra worry line between her eyes.

Jesse stood and entered Granger's spacious office. Because it was underground, there were no windows, just framed maps on the walls.

A man stood in the center of the room. He was dressed in black pants and a gray shirt, and his blond hair stuck up like a newly mowed lawn. A feeling of dread spread through Jesse as she recognized him. He turned. A bruised lump stood out from his brow.

The door snapped shut behind her.

# 3.

Jesse stared at the man she had tagged in the parking garage.

His eyebrows rose. He looked from Jesse to the Director, and back again.

*He doesn't know who I am.* She had knocked him out with the spray before he had seen her. Besides, she looked a lot different now. Jesse sighed. She'd been holding her breath without realizing it.

"Take a seat, Jesse." Director Granger walked to his desk and sat behind it. "You too, Liam."

Jesse chose the seat closest to the door. She sneaked a look at the lump on Liam's forehead. *Ouch. That had to hurt.* He didn't have a face that would win prizes, anyway. Liam's nose was wide, unusually flat, and leaned to the left. His yellowish skin was pockmarked. The expression on his face would sour milk.

"Liam," said the Director. "Meet your hunter."

Liam turned toward the door, but it remained shut. Director Granger said nothing. Neither did Jesse. Every second seemed etched into the air. Then Liam's gaze settled on Jesse. A strange look entered his eyes. "No."

The Director nodded and pressed his long, white fingers together.

"I was tagged by a *kid*?"

Liam said *kid* as though it were a disease. Jesse felt less guilty about the lump on his head.

"I don't believe it." He turned in his chair for a better look at her.

"I was wearing a wig," said Jesse. Long blond hair and green contacts had changed her appearance. Now, she knew, Liam would see her light brown hair, cropped short, and brown eyes.

"Don't feel too bad, Liam," said the

Director. "Jesse is a prodigy, a genius. Like the famous William Sidis, she read encyclopedias at three years of age. She speaks five languages and learned to play the clarinet in one day. Her memory is remarkable. We put her with a surveillance expert for two hours and she followed you without detection."

Liam did not look impressed.

"Jesse is part of Operation IQ," added Director Granger.

She sat silently, but her mind was whirring. C2 was riddled with code names, not just Operation IQ. Everything had a hidden side. It was a world of shadows. Sometimes she found it hard to tell what was real.

Director Granger smoothed down his green silk tie with one hand. "If we can discover what makes child geniuses, we can encourage our own. If we learn what they're capable of . . . well, it's an important contribution to science."

*A contribution to science?* Jesse's mind erupted with questions that she dared not ask out loud. She felt like a starving person being fed grains of rice one at a time.

Liam fingered the lump on his head.

"I'm sorry you were hurt," she said. "I didn't mean . . ."

Director Granger cut across her apology. "You were following orders, Jesse. Tag and run."

"You should have told me you'd sent a kid." Liam sent her a withering stare. "I was looking for someone who didn't suck her thumb."

"I have never sucked my thumb," said Jesse in a calm voice that hid the churning of her stomach. "It ruins the arch of a person's upper teeth." She pointed to his untidy thatch of hair. "Is that a wig, too?"

The way his lips pressed into an angry line told her that it wasn't. That figured. If he had a choice of disguises, he wouldn't have picked that one.

"Liam, despite your hurt pride, Jesse did well today. In one hour she had you tagged and unconscious. Not bad for someone who, until now, has been nurtured, kept separate from the annoying trifles of life."

*Nurture?* In her mind, Jesse saw a dictionary definition of the word. It meant *fostering care.* Is that how the Director described years of questions and uncomfortable experiments in the laboratory?

She felt more like an animal in a zoo — stared at, prodded, examined, and spoken to without anyone really knowing the Jesse that was more than her quick mind. Once she had tried to run away, to escape into that noisy world outside, full of other children and toys and chocolate stores. But only once. What happened afterward gave her nightmares.

# 4.

Director Granger tapped his fingertips together. "No one sees children, Liam. They're often overlooked. That's what we need. Someone who is watching, listening, but doesn't stand out."

Jesse felt a prickling at the back of her neck. Did this mean she had passed the test, that he would give her more freedom?

"Liam. Meet your new partner."

"What?" Liam leaped to his feet. "You can't send me out with *her*!"

"Yes, I can. And I am. A situation has come up and Jesse is the perfect choice to help us." There was an expression in Granger's narrowed eyes that made her think of black, slimy mold. Despite his fancy suit and formal manners, he was dangerous.

Liam might have thought so, too, because he didn't argue further.

"Jesse, I am sending you out with Liam on a field assignment."

She exchanged looks with Liam. Neither of them smiled. He was grumpy and rude, but also her means of discovering the outside world for herself.

"But a warning for you, Jesse. Never let down your guard. Remain alert. Suspect everyone." Director Granger opened a drawer in his desk and pulled out a large photograph. He held it out to Jesse.

Her fingers trembled slightly as she took it. There she was, in the long blond wig, talking to a beggar with dreadlocks and fingerless gloves in the mall. She remembered his gruff voice. "Got a dollar, miss?"

"He's one of our field agents," said the Director. "You were tagged."

She had been so busy looking ahead that she had not checked behind.

Director Granger shook his head. "If that was a real situation, you'd be dead."

# 5.

Jesse opened the door to her room on the tenth floor of the C2 building.

Mary Holt, her carer, was bent forward, arms outstretched, searching under Jesse's mattress. At the sound of the door, Mary jumped and dropped the mattress back into place. Her cheeks flushed red. She opened her eyes wide as if to say, "You can trust me."

*Yeah, right,* thought Jesse, *and I'm a Martian.* "All you'll find under there are snotty tissues," said Jesse. She walked across to stand in front of the large windows.

"I was checking if your bed needed stripping."

"Sheets are usually on *top* of the mattress."

"I thought the mattress might be musty." As Mary recovered from her surprise, the red on her cheeks faded to pink. Jesse knew it was not the first time Mary had searched her room. Although she was not usually clumsy enough to get caught.

Sometimes it was only a small object out of place that revealed Mary's snooping. Jesse's excellent memory gave her an advantage. She knew exactly where she had left everything.

At least her computer was safe. She had set it up with fingerprint recognition and changed her four passwords every day. Even her screensaver had a password. If anyone but she broke through a gateway, the whole system would shut down and eat the files. She sometimes wondered if someone from C2 would confiscate her computer, but so far it hadn't happened.

Mary dusted her hands and pushed her frizzy hair back from her face. "Atlantic salmon for dinner tonight, and organically grown vegetables. Fish has omega-3. It's good brain food."

Jesse wished that one day Mary would offer a hamburger. But it would never happen.

"How do you know it's been to the Atlantic?" asked Jesse. She imagined a large fish with a sticker on its back — I'VE BEEN TO THE ATLANTIC.

"That's just the name of it." Mary looked at Jesse suspiciously. "Is that a joke?"

Jesse shrugged.

"I'd better get going. Busy. Busy." Mary moved toward the door like a cobra about to strike. She pushed her head forward with every step, as though she wanted her face to get somewhere before her feet. As usual, she left Jesse's door open. To her, privacy was only another word in the dictionary. Still, it didn't matter this afternoon. It was almost time for Jai to arrive.

Jesse adjusted her telescope and examined the passersby, ten floors below. She liked watching families: parents with baby carriages, children with pets.

She zoomed in on a mother and daughter. The girl was about Jesse's age. Mother and daughter were dressed alike, with T-shirts and faded blue jeans. Even their hair was cut in a similar way. The mother rested one hand gently on the girl's head. Jesse looked away. She could never be that girl.

Soon the lights would come on, Jesse's favorite time. Then she couldn't see the littered streets or grimy buildings. The city would sparkle.

*Tomorrow I'll be out there in the real world.* Excitement rushed through her. For a little while, she would be free from this room she called "the fishbowl." She sometimes thought of herself as a goldfish, trapped behind glass, staring out. But it was dangerous outside. Her partner, Liam, already disliked her and called her a "thumb sucker." What if this assignment went wrong and she didn't come back? Then a scarier thought hit her. What if it was a trap to get rid of her? Is that what happened to Rohan?

# 6.

*I won't think about it.* If Jesse was too scared, she couldn't think clearly. And like a tightrope walker with no safety net, she needed to concentrate to stay alive.

She looked up at the wall clock, with its counterclockwise numbers. A Christmas present from Prov. Jai would arrive precisely on time. She could set her clock by his routines. Her C2 "brothers" were opposites in that way. Rohan had little idea of time. Jai was obsessed with it.

As though her thought had conjured him up, Jai entered the room. They had shaved his head again. The regrowth looked like a brown stain. He lifted his violin to his left shoulder. Eyes closed, his small fingers delicately holding the bow, he began to play one of his own compositions.

Some people said he made the violin talk. Jesse disagreed. It was more than that. He made it *feel*. It laughed, cried, and teased. This piece made her think of water dancing down rocks and, finally, swelling into a deep pool. He finished on a long, soft note that drifted into silence.

Jai opened his eyes. His voice was soft and high-pitched. As always, he spoke in a formal way, no clipped sentences, no slang. "How would you improve this piece of music?"

"Stop playing it," said Jesse dryly.

"For a child prodigy, your jokes are quite bad."

"Mary doesn't think I tell any."

"Mary does not think," he said. "She only obeys."

"I can't be perfect at everything."

"Why not?" Jai tilted his head to one side.

"Then I'd be a pain and no one would like me."

"Who likes you now?"

"You do."

He smiled. Then, stepping carefully, he followed the massive blue footprints Jesse had cut out of cardboard and stuck to the carpet. They led across the room and around her circular wooden table. The last print was on a chair. As he did most nights, Jai climbed onto the chair, stood in the center of the last cardboard footstep, and took a bow.

Jesse closed her door.

Jai climbed down and carefully placed the violin and bow on the table. "Did you know that the mother of Janos Starker, the cellist, made tiny sandwiches and left them on his music stand so that he would not have to stop practicing to eat?"

"That's cute."

Jai took a small metal tube the size of a pen from his left pocket and scanned underneath the table and chairs.

"She also trained a parrot to say *Practice, Janos, practice.*"

"Not so cute."

Jai scanned the bookcases, four-poster bed, fridge, video player, and the large painting of an eagle soaring over a high mountain.

Jesse watched silently.

Then he checked the computer desk, the exercise bike, her clothes hanging from a metal rail, the orange sofa, and the massive bird kite pinned to the wall.

"There are no listening devices today." Every time Jai found one, he had an "accident" with it. It would fall under his foot or drop into the toilet bowl.

Jai returned the scanner to his pocket and patted it.

A small silence stretched into awkwardness.

Jesse struggled to think of what to say. Usually they had no problem talking to each other. However, so much had happened in the last couple of days, and she could not tell Jai any of it.

"Did you hear about the two cannibals who ate a clown?" she said. "One said to the other, 'Does this taste funny to you?'"

Jai aimed a penetrating stare at Jesse. "What are you hiding?"

# 7.

Jesse laughed too loudly. "What makes you think I'm hiding something?" How could she explain that she was going outside, while Jai remained here?

"I am a genius."

"So am I," she said.

"Yes, but you are not as clever as I."

Jesse did not argue. "I . . . I can't tell you." Earlier, Director Granger had fixed his iceberg eyes on her and demanded total secrecy. Besides, if this was a trap, information could put Jai in danger. Jesse had to keep him out of it.

The look in Jai's eyes reminded her of the

Labrador she had seen on one of her guarded "test runs" outside. It had been hit by a car and lay injured in the gutter. The dog's eyes had pleaded for help.

"Jai. You're the closest thing to family that I have. We're like brother and sister. I want to tell you, but . . . I *can't*. You might be in danger."

"Look where we live. I am always in danger."

Jesse nodded. "This could be worse."

"You are going outside."

She nodded. "But I'll be back." Even though the words came from her own mouth, she felt reassured when she heard them.

"It is now six-thirty P.M. by your foolish clock. We must begin our Yahtzee game." Jai tugged at his bangs. Any change in routine worried him, especially if he was upset.

Jesse opened a drawer in the video cabinet and took out a score pad, pen, and five green dice. Jai couldn't handle playing with dice of different colors. It didn't matter *which* color, but they all had to be the same.

They sat at the table.

Jai pressed his palms flat to the surface. "Why do you use a score pad? We will both remember the sequence of numbers."

"I don't want to argue with you about the scores. You like to win."

"As do you."

"I like to compete. Winning is extra. Your turn to start." Jesse pushed the dice across the table. "Have you beaten your computer at chess yet?"

"No. But I programmed it, so I still win." Jai rolled the dice three times. "Yahtzee."

Jesse wrote down his score, then took her turn.

Jai pursed his lips. "The statistical probability of your attaining a high straight at this point is poor."

"Sometimes you have to take a risk."

"Jesse." Jai cleared his throat. "Do not take too many risks . . . out there, will you?"

"I won't," she said.

But she didn't believe it. Nor did he.

# 8.

Goosebumps dotted Jesse's skin. Anything could happen today. She lengthened her steps. Keeping up with Liam was like chasing a tree blown along by a typhoon. He turned right, following the tunnel. Jesse stayed close behind him.

No one who worked for C2 left by the usual doors. They took tunnels to a secret garage. People who came and went through the front doors were real customers seeking insurance. They had no idea that Trust Insurance Company covered a more secret business.

Liam stopped suddenly and Jesse almost ran into the back of him. He ignored her. *Do*

*I care?* she thought, then decided she did. A few kind words would have helped a lot this morning. But she would never admit it.

He stopped at a set of elevator doors and placed his palm against the identification scanner. No one passed in or out without C2 authorization.

"What's that supposed to be?" Liam glanced sideways.

"A backpack. For school."

"Give it here."

Reluctantly she handed it over, then followed him into the elevator.

Liam dropped the backpack. Then he raised one foot and stomped on it, scraping his boot backward and forward.

Jesse gasped. "What are you doing?"

He flipped the backpack over with the toe of his boot and scraped the other side. "It's too clean and new-looking. You'll look like a loser. You're supposed to blend in." He inspected the scuff marks and nodded. "That's better. Now it looks like a normal kid's bag."

Smothering her disappointment, Jesse snatched her backpack. It looked as though a herd of wild animals had trampled over it.

She glared at Liam. Well, maybe not a herd. Just one.

He took a long look at her neat, brushed hair.

"Don't even think about it," she said. "I have a black belt in tae kwon do." He still had a bruise on his forehead from his fall in the parking garage. If he touched her hair, he'd have another one.

Liam's scowl lightened. Was he going to smile? That'd be a first. "So do I, as a matter of fact."

The elevator stopped and the doors opened. Liam held out one arm as he peered left and right. "Looks OK."

His car was parked close by. She had hoped for a red sports car with ejector seats and buttons that fired missiles. But Liam's car had spots of rust and a dented bumper.

She saw her reflection in the side mirror. Her school uniform of navy track pants and white T-shirt was comfortable, but boring.

Inside the car, she kicked paper and cardboard containers aside. Liam ate a lot of takeout.

*The car matches his hair.* Today he had

gone easy on the gel. His blond hair pointed wherever it liked. He wore jeans that were too short, leaving a gap above his socks, with a hint of hairy legs.

Jesse stretched the seat belt across her body and locked it.

Liam turned the ignition key.

Jesse sneaked a look at him. His lips were pressed together in a grim line. She wished he would say something. *Anything.* Her first assignment outside, and she was with a zombie. It walked, it moved its eyes, but it didn't speak.

She placed the scuffed backpack at her feet.

Back in the tunnel, Liam had said that the school kids might think she was a loser. Is that what *he* thought?

She took a deep breath. "You think I'm a freak, don't you?"

# 9.

"We're all freaks." Liam shrugged. "Otherwise, why would we work for an organization like C2?"

"I don't work for them," said Jesse. "They adopted me."

"What happened to your parents?"

"There was a car accident. My parents were killed but I survived. I was one year old."

"You don't have other relatives?"

Liam's voice had an edge of doubt, and it disturbed her. It was a question she had often wondered herself.

"I don't think so," said Jesse. "I don't know anything about my family."

"So, who is this William Sidis that Granger mentioned?"

She stared through the window as they drove out of the garage, not wanting to miss a thing. "William Sidis read books when he was two. At six, he spoke Hebrew, German, Greek, French, Russian, and English. He wrote four books between the ages of four and eight. And when he was eleven, he went to Harvard University."

"Kinda slow, was he?" Liam braked and put on the right blinker.

Jesse smelled exhaust fumes. The air conditioning in "the fishbowl" filtered out odors. This morning there were dozens of smells to identify: coffee, toast, stale chips, and a touch of something spicy. Liam's deodorant or aftershave, maybe.

"Humans can distinguish ten thousand different aromas," said Jesse.

Liam sniffed.

*OK,* thought Jesse, *so you can also use your nose to say, "Who cares?"* She was tempted to stir him even further by adding, "If your nose runs and your feet smell, then you're upside down," but she didn't think he'd find it funny.

"Do you understand what your job is?" asked Liam.

"Yes."

"You cover the school and I'll do the house. I've got a position as a groundskeeper. Make friends with the target. Get as close as you can."

Without taking his eyes from the road, he slipped his left hand into his pocket and took out a watch. "Here. Take this."

"I've got a watch," said Jesse. The one Liam offered was chunky, more like a man's watch.

He dropped it into her lap. "There's more to it than meets the eye. If you press the alarm-set button, it changes the face. You can use it to send me a message."

She swapped it for her own watch, slipping hers into an outside pocket of the backpack.

"Contact me if you need help. But make the messages short. If someone is looking for you, they can triangulate where you are by reading the signal. But you'll be OK if you're brief."

*Oh, great. Contact me if you're in trouble, but the enemy might find you if you do.*

"My contact number is already recorded there. It's easy to use. Especially for a megabrain like you. And be careful out there. Watch your back."

She had learned that from her encounter with the dreadlocked man in the mall.

"At this stage, we don't know how to tell the good guys from the bad. And even good guys can be as ruthless as the bad."

"Wouldn't being ruthless make you one of the bad guys?"

Liam's hands gripped the steering wheel tightly. His knuckles stood out. "Nothing is that simple, especially with this kind of work. We infiltrate. We seek information. We obey orders. Period. Do yourself a favor and don't try to figure it all out. Just do your part and forget the rest."

But what if those orders included something she didn't want to do, something that might hurt someone?

"Last year a friend of mine, interstate, worked with a kid from Operation IQ," added Liam. "This kid went nuts, turned into a wacko who stayed in his room, making models out of lollipop sticks. Don't go nuts on me, will you? You could get us both killed."

Jesse's heart pounded in her ears. She turned her face away from Liam, hiding her confusion. *A kid from Operation IQ? Interstate?* All this time she thought there were just the three of them: her, Jai, and Rohan. But there were others. What did this mean?

Her head spun. Terrorists worked in what they called "cells." Most of the cells or groups didn't know about the others. If someone from one cell was captured, he could not give information about the others. Is that how it was with Operation IQ? But why?

# 10.

Thirty faces stared at Jesse. She had never been with so many other kids. They all wore similar navy track pants and white T-shirts. It was like being in a room full of clones, except the faces were different. There were paintings of fish and a poster of an Egyptian pyramid tacked on the classroom walls. A musty odor hung in the air. A boy in the front row shifted his feet and the smell became stronger. Was it his sneakers?

"Class, we have a new person joining us today. Jesse Sharpe. Let's welcome her." The teacher, Mr. Rathbone, clapped his hands. Most kids joined him. A few looked bored. The boy with the smelly sneakers rolled his eyes.

Mentally, Jesse checked each face in the room against the class photo she had been shown at C2. Someone was missing.

"Excuse me, sir." The kid with smelly feet put up his hand. "There's something wrong with my finger."

"What, Hugh?" barked Mr. Rathbone.

"It keeps going up my nose!" The boy snorted loudly through both nostrils. He looked around to see how many of his classmates thought he was funny.

The teacher sent him a glare that would wither stone.

"Excuse our bad manners, Jesse." Mr. Rathbone smiled at her, revealing the unusually pale gums of dentures. He had a large head that bobbed up and down as he spoke. He was bald on top with the side hairs cut short. It looked as though a horseshoe was curled around his skull. "Tell us a little about yourself."

A crumpled ball of paper flew through the air and hit Hugh on the back of the head. He twisted around to see who had thrown it.

Jesse cleared her throat. "I live with

a carer. A nanny. Whatever you want to call her."

Several girls sat up straighter and looked at her more carefully.

"My parents are overseas. They work in a circus, looking after the elephants. Mom polishes their toenails, and Dad's a vet. He's especially interested in teeth. Elephants' teeth are as big as house bricks. If an elephant's teeth wear down too far, it can't eat and it dies."

Doubt sat like a FOR SALE sign on Mr. Rathbone's face.

A ripple of whispers circled the room.

The door opened suddenly. A girl bolted inside in a flurry of arms and legs. Strands of hair like tiny tentacles framed her face. "Sorry I'm late, Mr. Rathbone." She held up a small black case. "Flute lesson went overtime."

Long brown hair, blue eyes, a tiny scar above the right eyebrow, and a small mouth.

*Yes. This is Jasmine Carrillo, the girl in the photo. The one who's going to be kidnapped.*

# 11.

Beside the playing field, Jesse sat with her back against a wall. From there she could see most of the school grounds, yet no one could sneak up behind her. How long would it take Jasmine to find her?

Jesse took a bite of the fruitcake Mary had prepared for her snack. Even though Jesse chewed it well, it still felt like lumps sliding down her throat. It surely had organically grown whole-wheat flour, free-range eggs, and no sugar. Jesse wouldn't put it past Mary to slip in some bran.

The sunshine warmed Jesse's face. She watched the boys play football. They seemed to get more fun out of tugging each other's shirts and tackling each other to the ground than handling the ball.

To her right, a small figure broke away from a group and headed toward her. Every nerve was alert. She wanted to appear relaxed, but she needed to be ready for anything. Jesse didn't look up. She didn't want to seem too eager.

A shadow moved across Jesse's outstretched legs.

"Hi." Jasmine sat beside Jesse, a paperback book and a plump paper bag on her lap. "Is it true that your parents look after elephants?"

Jesse nodded.

"I *love* elephants." Jasmine's blue eyes sparkled.

"Really?" Jesse pretended surprise. She knew a lot of things about Jasmine. "Elephants have feet like Nike Airs, you know. They're kind of spongy. Their feet squash out when they step on the ground, then shrink when they lift them back up. That's why they don't get stuck in the mud."

"Cool." Jasmine opened the paper bag and took out a chocolate doughnut.

Jesse stared at it, saliva pooling on her tongue.

"Want some?" Jasmine broke the dough-nut and offered half to Jesse.

*I have to take it to be friendly. Liam would tell me to eat it, I know he would.* Jesse bit into the piece of doughnut with anticipation. It was even better than she had imagined.

"What have you got?" Jasmine pointed to the fruitcake.

"A brick."

Jasmine laughed. "Let me try it." She broke off a corner of fruitcake with two fingers. She chewed. And chewed. Then swallowed as if she hadn't chewed at all. "Definitely a brick."

The two girls exchanged grins.

*Get close to her,* Liam had said. *Become her best friend, her shadow.*

The football soared in their direction, then bounced off the wall. Jesse and Jasmine ducked. Two boys thundered after the ball. One of them was Hugh with the smelly sneakers.

"They did that on purpose," said Jasmine. "Because we were here."

"But they didn't even look at us."

Jasmine nodded. "That's how I know they did it on purpose." She wiped her sticky fingers on the paper bag.

Jesse blinked. *I've got a lot to learn about people. I know more about elephants. And there aren't going to be many of those around here.* Although she had noticed the principal was overweight and wore a gray suit.

"Have you seen a real elephant?" asked Jasmine.

Jesse considered making up another story but decided against it. "No, only photos. My parents think it's a better life for me here. They're always traveling to different places and they live in a trailer. I don't want to live in a trailer, anyway."

"Me, neither."

"I've seen lots of photos of elephants," added Jesse. "My parents sometimes e-mail them to me. I had one from them a week ago when they were in Bangkok. This elephant had a reflector light on its tail, like a car, and its head was inside a nightclub doorway. All you could see was this fat elephant butt sticking out of the door, swaying to the music." It was only half made up. She had seen the photo on the Internet. "How do you know if there's an elephant under your bed?" asked Jesse.

"I don't know."

"Your nose scrapes the ceiling."

Jasmine chuckled. "I have a book of elephant pictures, and an elephant quilt cover. And I have a collection of elephant statues. Some of them are really small, but I've got sixty-seven. I might stop when I get to a hundred. But maybe not. You should come over and see them sometime."

"Sure." Jesse tried to sound casual, but she *had* to visit Jasmine's house.

Jesse looked at the field, then the playground. There were just kids fighting, eating, and playing. And a couple of teachers trying to ignore them.

Jasmine scrunched up the paper bag tightly in her palm. Jesse turned at the sound.

Over Jasmine's shoulder, she saw a white van parked across the street. A man in overalls sat on a fold-up stool. His dark hair hung down under his broad-brimmed hat to touch his shoulders. A junction-box door was open and the wires were exposed. *Power or phone company?* Yet something about him was odd. What was it?

She focused carefully, paying special attention. The man didn't seem to be doing any work. He was staring right in their direction.

# 12.

Jasmine opened her book. "My oral report is due after recess. I haven't read it, so I'm just going to look at the last page of each chapter. That should tell me what happens. I *hope*."

A flash of light drew Jesse's attention back to the man in the overalls. The sun glinted off something small that he held up to his right eye. *That's a magnifier.*

If this man was in on the plan to kidnap Jasmine, would he take her from school? Wouldn't it be easier to catch her on her way home? Or couldn't they wait? Jesse felt frustrated. She didn't even know who "they" were. All Granger had told her was that they were enemies of Jasmine's father.

The man across the street turned slightly. His lips appeared to be moving.

Jesse unzipped her track pants pocket, took out a tissue, and pretended to blow her nose. Then she brushed an invisible hair back from her face. As she did so, she slipped a tiny listening device called a spy ear from her palm into her left ear and pressed it.

Instantly, the playground noises were exaggerated, deafening. She tapped the spy ear to turn it off. Her head still rang with the *boom, crash, squeal* of the school yard.

She had to get closer to the man, away from these other sounds. "I'll be back in a minute," she told Jasmine.

Jasmine nodded and kept turning the pages of her book. Jesse walked to the girls' bathroom, entered the stall nearest the road, and quickly locked the door. She lifted the plastic seat, then stood on the porcelain bowl. Her head was level with the frosted window. Someone had scribbled on the wall, *Eat prunes and get a run for your money.* She tapped the spy ear. *That's better.*

A male voice, faint but audible, came from across the street. "Yes, sir . . . both here.

I can see them from my position. . . . Excuse me? You'll have to speak up. I'm sure . . . one of them has gone to the bathroom . . . no problem."

Jesse was tempted to leap down and hide. It was as though he could see her perched there like a bird in a tree. *Don't panic. Even with the best magnifier, he can't see through brick walls.*

"Neither of them has left the school. They're being good little girls."

Jesse ground her teeth. The way he said "good little girls" sounded like an insult. She wanted to take that cute little phrase and wrap it around his head.

"No, sir . . . they have no idea."

*That's what you think.*

"She's sticking with the other girl so far. . . . If I see that, I'll let you know."

*See what?* Hearing one side of the conversation was worse than hearing none. *There's no way this jerk is getting his hands on Jasmine.*

"Yes, sir. I understand. Watch Sharpe."

Jesse gasped. *Sharpe* wasn't Jasmine's last name. It was hers.

# 13.

After school, Jesse watched as Jasmine squeezed through the school gate. Her overloaded backpack bounced off a post.

There was no sign of the long-haired man who knew her name, or his van. Who was he? Another C2 agent checking on her? Or had the people who threatened Jasmine discovered who had sent Jesse? But how could they have found out so quickly?

Jesse called out, "Hey, Jasmine!"

Jasmine turned.

"I think this might be yours." Jesse held out a calculator.

Jasmine flipped it over to check the

initials on the back — JC. "Thanks. I didn't realize I'd dropped it."

"That's OK." It had taken Jesse only a second to slip it from Jasmine's backpack when she wasn't looking.

"You going this way, too?"

Jesse nodded.

"Let's walk together."

"Great idea."

Jesse kept a sharp lookout for the man with long hair or anyone else who might seem suspicious. Why was Jasmine walking home alone if she was in danger? Hadn't Director Granger warned her family? They might not want to scare Jasmine, but wouldn't it be better to be scared than kidnapped? *Typical. Can anyone at C2 even walk in a straight line?*

A maroon car cruising too slowly caught Jesse's attention. The driver wore a hat and dark glasses. A man, judging by the broad shoulders. The license plate of his car was covered in mud, unreadable.

*It could just be someone looking for a parking spot or a house number.*

Just in case, Jesse swapped sides with Jasmine to walk nearest the curb. That way, someone in a car would have to get past her to grab Jasmine.

"I have to walk near the road or I feel all squashed," said Jesse. "Weird, isn't it?"

"Maybe. But I make all my shoes face the same way in my closet — so I can't talk about weird."

Hot pins and needles shot through Jesse when she heard the word *closet*. Closets were dark places where things were locked in, kept away from the light. Her bedroom had only a long rail from which to hang clothes. She would never, *ever* have a closet.

The driver of the maroon car accelerated and turned a corner. Jesse relaxed a little. He must have been looking for a particular street.

She followed Jasmine past busy stores and cafes. *So much noise.* Jesse couldn't hear anything like this from her room ten floors up. Car horns, the *va voom, va voom* of a CD player that was turned up too loud, a dog barking, and human voices that faded in and out as they passed other pedestrians. It was exciting and confusing. *What would Jai think about all these colors?* Most things in his room were either black or white.

"So what's the woman who looks after you like?" asked Jasmine.

"Think of the fruitcake."

"You said it was a brick."

"Yeah." Jesse smirked.

Jasmine smirked right back at her. "We're going to be best friends, I can tell."

A warm glow fired inside Jesse. No one had ever said that to her before. Not just a friend, but a *best* friend. All she had to do was keep Jasmine alive.

# 14.

Jesse caught a flash of maroon reflected in a department store window. The muddied car was back. Her instinct kicked into action. *I have to get Jasmine off this street — now.*

"How many seconds do you think it would take us to run from this end of the store through to the other?" Jesse grabbed Jasmine's arm.

"I don't know. . . ."

"Thirty?"

Jasmine bolted. As the double glass doors slid open, she disappeared inside the store. Jesse gasped, then chased after her. Jasmine had reacted faster than she'd expected.

Jesse's backpack thumped against her spine as she ran. Her feet made little sound on the carpet. Left and right, directly behind her new friend, Jesse darted around customers. Faces were a blur of raised eyebrows and O-shaped mouths. *Oops — a baby carriage.* Jesse leaped sideways, then continued toward the back doors.

Running gave her a sense of being free and wild. Her legs pumped like motor pistons. Her hair whipped her face.

Jasmine stopped abruptly. The automatic doors were too slow. She almost collided with the glass. Jesse ran into Jasmine's backpack. *Oofph.* They both squealed, then shot through the open doors like two bullets fired from a gun.

Outside, Jasmine bent double, gasping for air. "Forgot . . . to check . . . the time we . . ." She took a deep breath. "Started."

"Me, too."

Jasmine giggled.

"Which way is your place?" asked Jesse.

Jasmine pointed, without speaking.

After a quick check over her shoulder,

Jesse followed Jasmine down a narrow lane and out onto another street.

In the short wait for the pedestrian light to turn green, Jesse took a few deep breaths. Her legs stopped trembling.

They were halfway across the street when Jesse heard the roar of a motor, then the screech of tires. To her left, a maroon car shot straight toward them. The driver hunched down, both hands gripping the steering wheel.

"Look out!" she shouted at Jasmine.

Jasmine hesitated.

The maroon car closed in. In only a few seconds, it would smash into them.

Jesse dropped her bag, leaped forward, and shoved Jasmine in the back. Jasmine flew forward.

The momentum tumbled Jesse across the asphalt. Finally she stopped. She lay on her back, dizzy and disoriented. A deafening horn blared. Jesse opened her eyes to find the world was upside down. A huge, roaring monster approached. She blinked once before realizing what it was. A truck. She had rolled into its path.

# 15.

There was no time to get out of the way. Jesse pressed herself flat against the asphalt and covered her face with her hands. There was a mighty roar and a blast of hot air as the truck drove over her.

Fumes from hot oil and diesel fuel caught in her throat. She smothered a cough. Hard, gritty asphalt pressed against the back of her scalp.

As abruptly as it had approached, the truck passed. The air around her was fresh and open. Still she kept her hands glued to her face.

"Is she breathing . . . did you get a license plate number . . . stop the traffic . . . call an ambulance . . ." A babble of voices floated above her. Fingers gently grasped her wrists and moved her hands away from her face.

"Are you all right?" asked a kindly female voice.

*I can't see.* For a second, Jesse panicked, then she realized that her eyes were still closed. She blinked rapidly. The sky seemed too bright.

A woman with wide green eyes and vivid red lipstick knelt beside her. "I'm a doctor. Are you hurting anywhere?"

"I don't think so." Jesse felt numb all over.

The doctor gently felt Jesse's head, arms, and legs, then told her to take a few deep breaths. "No broken bones." The doctor held up a finger. "How many fingers do you see?"

"One."

"Now follow the movement." The doctor waved her hand from left to right. "Do you feel sick?"

In the background, drivers impatiently tooted car horns.

Jesse sat up. "No. I'm OK."

"Let's get you off the street." The doctor took hold of Jesse's right arm while a man in a striped suit took the left. Gently, they helped Jesse to her feet. "Move back, please."

Jesse looked around. "Where's Jasmine?"

No one answered. There was a ripple of movement, but none of the spectators retreated.

The doctor spoke again, this time more sharply, "Out of the way."

Jesse felt like a beetle mobbed by insane ants. She and her helpers shuffled toward the sidewalk. None of the faces peering at her were familiar.

A siren screamed louder and louder. An ambulance stopped.

Was Jasmine hurt? What if she'd hit her head or broken a bone? Jesse's heart pounded. Had the kidnappers staged the whole stunt, using the maroon car to separate them and snatch Jasmine?

Jesse screamed, *"Jasmine!"*

# 16.

*"Jesse!"*

Her knees wobbled at the sound of an answering cry.

Jasmine forced her way through the crowd.

A man and a woman in uniform, ambulance attendants, walked through the gap behind her. The woman carried a first-aid box.

Jasmine slipped past them, dumped two backpacks at Jesse's feet, and threw her arms around her in a fierce hug.

"You're all right!" said Jasmine.

"I would be if I could breathe."

Jasmine stepped back and grinned. Her palms were red where blood seeped through grazes.

The ambulance attendants took latex gloves from the first-aid box. Jesse winced. The slapping of gloves reminded her of the C2 laboratory. The male attendant put out one hand. "You young ladies had better come with us."

Warning bells rang in Jesse's mind. "No!"

The two attendants frowned.

Jesse was determined. Jasmine was not going anywhere with two strangers. That long-haired man had been watching them, talking about them on his phone, and he knew Jesse's name. The maroon car had followed them, then almost run them down. How could she trust these ambulance attendants? They, too, could be part of a trap.

"I don't want to go to a hospital," said Jasmine. "I've only grazed my hands."

"Good thinking," said Jesse. "They jab you with needles, feed you mush, and make you pee into cups."

Jasmine flinched. "I want to go home."

"We're fine. Look!" Jesse wriggled her arms and legs, flicking her head from left to right. *Ouch. Shouldn't have done that.*

A large man with a hairy chest peeking from a checked shirt stepped to the front. A frown brought his thick eyebrows dangerously close to his eyes. His hands were clenched. "I was driving that truck, missie. What did you think you were doing?"

*Does he think I rolled onto the road for fun?* She could think of better ways to have fun. Rolling under trucks wouldn't even be in the top fifty.

"You could have been killed!" he said.

*No kidding. Don't stand in a puddle — you'll get a brain wash.* She was trying to be patient. He'd had a fright, too. But being yelled at right after being driven over by a truck was too much.

The man in the striped suit said, "I saw it happen. A maroon car came out of nowhere and ran the red light. This girl . . ." He pointed to Jesse, "leaped out of the way, but rolled straight into the path of your truck. The car's brakes must have failed."

A second siren began to wail. *Police? Uh-oh.* Jesse wanted to avoid police officers. For starters, they would ask where she lived. And the questions would only get worse after that. Jesse could not give them answers.

With a grunt, the truck driver said, "Police will sort it out."

The female ambulance attendant stepped toward Jasmine. "Your hands need attention." She gestured toward the vehicle. "This way."

"We get sick in cars," said Jesse.

"Both of you?"

Jesse nodded. "We're really close."

The siren wailed louder.

Unnoticed, Jesse reached into her backpack and slipped a small object into her hand. She leaned forward and whispered into Jasmine's ear, "Please do as I ask. Shut your eyes."

Jasmine obeyed.

*She'd make a good spy. She runs fast and doesn't ask dumb questions.*

Jesse aimed the object at the faces around her. Gasps erupted. People flung their hands over their eyes and cried out, "I can't see . . . what happened . . . it's a comet . . ."

*Actually it's an illuminator.* It caused temporary flash blindness, like looking through dusty glass into bright sunlight.

The siren told Jesse that the police car was close. She grabbed Jasmine's arm, pulled her through the crowd and down a side alley. They turned left and right several times before Jesse felt safe.

"What happened back there?" asked Jasmine.

"Flashed a mirror," said Jesse. "They couldn't see for a minute."

She thought about what the man in the striped suit had said. He was wrong. The car driver had not braked. He had accelerated.

# 17.

"Oowww."

"Keep still, Jasmine."

Jesse watched as Eva, the Carrillos' housekeeper, washed gravel and blood from Jasmine's hands.

"You should have seen Jesse. She moved like a rocket. I'd be squashed on the road if it wasn't for her." Jasmine's voice was high-pitched and excited.

Eva raised an eyebrow at the word *squashed.*

Perched on the huge black spa bath, Jesse looked at her reflection in the mirrored wall. A graze showed on her forehead. Her white T-shirt was filthy. *No big surprise.* It had been stepped on, rolled on asphalt, and driven over. Her track pants had a hole over her right knee. She bent her right arm. It was tender. Bruises might show tomorrow. She put her special watch to her ear and shook it. No rattling. That was a good sign.

Gently, Eva taped a gauze bandage over each of Jasmine's palms. "There. All fixed. Now I'll make you two hot chocolate. And you'll both drink it."

Eva had an air of authority. She was tall and broadshouldered, and her legs were almost too long to be real. *If Eva were a dog,* Jesse decided, *she'd be a Great Dane.*

"Are there any chocolate-chip cookies?" asked Jasmine, a gleam in her eyes.

"Of course. Otherwise you'd gnaw the furniture." Eva winked at Jesse. Then she washed her hands and rinsed out the sink with fresh water. "Jasmine, I called your father. He should be home soon."

Jasmine screwed up her nose.

"I had to call him for something like this. You know that." Eva left the bathroom.

"Jesse, you're a hero," said Jasmine.

"No, I'm not." Jesse felt her face go hot. "A hero wears tights and has a big *S* on his chest. I'm not wearing tights for anyone."

"I can't believe you weren't squished by that truck." Jasmine shuddered.

"I'm thin. And I was in the middle of the lane." Jesse shook her head to clear the mental image of a giant black wheel making her even thinner. She looked around the room. "Is this really your own bathroom?"

It was huge, with mirrored walls, hanging potted plants, and a spa bath big enough to fit a whole basketball team.

"The rest of the house must be like a castle." Jesse was determined to see it all. She had a plan and she wasn't returning to C2 until she had completed it.

"My mom thinks she lost Dad in here for two days once. Couldn't find him. This house was Dad's idea. He has loads of money. He sends me to a public school because he doesn't want me to grow up soft."

Jesse didn't comment, but she thought plenty. *Is that a normal Dad thing to say or is Mr. Carrillo strange?*

"Come on. I'll show you around." Jasmine beckoned Jesse to follow her back into the bedroom. It was elephant heaven. Her quilt cover had gray elephants marching across a yellow background. Wooden shelves held row after row of elephant statues, and there was a giant poster of a mother and baby elephant. Jesse wished she could show Jasmine the special things in her own room, including the large blue footprints. But that was impossible.

"This is my family." Jasmine held up a photograph, careful to keep her bandaged palms away from the frame. "This is Dad." He had a square jaw, dark hair with gray flecks, and smallish eyes. His stomach bulged over his belt.

"This is Momll."

"Momll?"

Jasmine nodded. "When I was little and learning to talk, I'd hear Dad say, 'Mom'll do this' or 'Mom'll do that.' So I started calling her *Momll,* and it stuck."

Jasmine's mother had blond hair curled up on top of her head, a longish nose, and full lips. Her hands were folded gracefully on her lap. They looked as though they'd float into the air if Mrs. Carrillo didn't hold them down.

"Momll's in London for a few weeks. There's an Elvis display that she really wanted to see. You know what they've got in there? A vial of Elvis' sweat, a toenail, and a wart on a pink cushion."

"A *wart*?"

"She's a fan," Jasmine said, as if that explained everything.

That was a long way and a lot of money to see a wart from a fat man with greasy hair.

"Miss Jasmine." A male voice drifted down the hallway.

"Yes?" Jasmine went to the open doorway.

"I heard what happened. Are you all right?"

Jesse listened carefully. *Is that voice familiar?*

Jasmine held up both her hands, palms out, to show the gauze bandages. "I'm OK. Thanks to my friend Jesse."

A tall man with longish hair moved into the open doorway.

"Tom is head of security," said Jasmine. "He drinks lots of coffee and jangles keys."

The hairs on Jesse's arms stood at attention. She had seen Tom before. This morning he had sat beside a white van, spying on them.

# 18.

“This hallway is the same size as a soccer field,” said Jasmine.

“Do you ever play soccer in here?”

“No, but it feels cool saying that.” Jasmine lowered her voice to a whisper. “Dad has this alarm system with these light beams across the hallway. Once Eva forgot and went downstairs to get her glasses and set them all off. Dad got such a fright he ran into a wall and gave himself a bloody nose.”

Jesse filed the fact about the alarm system in her mind.

“This is the dining room.” Jasmine led her into another room on her right.

The walls were the color of an apricot. A

large framed mirror hung on one wall and a painting of red flowers in a field on another. Dark polished wood sideboards lined the walls, and there was a long table to match.

Running one hand along the shiny table, Jesse imagined the three Carrillos at one end, eating pasta. Or did they sit at opposite ends and shout? She touched the frame of the flower painting and quietly attached a metal listening device, the size of a lentil, to the back of it.

Jasmine spun around.

Jesse's heart thumped.

"Want to be fancy and have our hot chocolate in here?" asked Jasmine.

"Great."

"You wait here and I'll go tell Eva, OK?"

Jesse nodded. It was more than OK. It was great. She would have a few minutes alone.

She counted to twenty, then sneaked a look down the hallway. It was empty. Jesse crossed it and opened the opposite door. A sitting room, with a phone. *Excellent.* She pushed the door closed without actually clicking it shut. Then she picked up the phone and tried to unscrew the mouthpiece. It was tight. She took a deep breath and tried again. *Whoever put this together was on steroids.*

She stopped, listening for footsteps. None. Although with this thick carpet, they would be hard to detect. "Make sure you get at least one into a phone," Liam had said.

Hot prickles on her skin made Jesse feel uncomfortable and sweaty.

One more twist and the end of the mouthpiece gave way. She fitted in the bugging device and screwed the top back down.

Abruptly the door swung open.

With the phone still in her hand, Jesse froze.

A stout man stood in the doorway. Jesse recognized him from the family photo. It was Jasmine's father, with a look on his face that would shrivel plants. "What are you doing in here?"

# 19.

"I was calling . . . home to say I was all right." Jesse put down the phone.

"Dad!" A hand snaked around the door and grabbed his sleeve.

He looked over his shoulder. "Jasmine."

She squeezed past him into the room. "This speeding car almost hit us. Jesse pushed me out of the way and a *truck* drove right over her."

Mr. Carrillo focused on the graze on Jesse's forehead. His face hardened. Jesse guessed that he was angry at the careless driver. Except that the driver hadn't been careless. He had driven straight at them.

Who was he? C2 or an enemy of the Carrillo family?

"Are you both OK?"

Both girls talked over each other to reassure him.

Mr. Carrillo advanced toward Jesse. Not sure what he intended, she was ready to run. But he smiled and held out his right hand.

She shook it.

"Thank you for looking out for my daughter."

"*Yoo-hoo.* Where is everyone?" Eva's voice, along with the chink of mugs, drifted into the room from the hallway.

Jesse's spirits lifted at the thought of chocolate-chip cookies.

Back in the dining room, Mr. Carrillo sat and watched the two girls drink hot chocolate and devour cookies. He tried to make conversation. Jesse wished he wouldn't. He ran through a list of questions, ordinary for most people, but dangerous for her. *Where do you live? What do your parents do? How long have you known Jasmine? Where were you before this?*

Was he like this with all of Jasmine's friends?

Jesse sipped her chocolate. It was thick and sweet. "What is your job, Mr. Carrillo?"

"Trade." Absentmindedly, he rubbed at the back of his neck.

*When is an answer not an answer? When Mr. Carrillo speaks but doesn't tell me anything.* "What do you trade?"

"Goods."

She wanted to ask more, but it would seem too nosy.

"Jasmine. Question for the week," he said.

Laughing, she explained to Jesse. "Every week Dad gives me a question and I have to find the answer."

"Are the North Pole and the South Pole the same temperature?"

Automatically, Jesse shook her head.

"Jesse," he said. "You know the answer?"

"Elevation. One is higher than the other and . . ." Suddenly Jesse realized that Jasmine and her father were staring at her. She swallowed the rest of the answer. Most people wouldn't know facts like that. Jesse shrugged. "At my last school I had a project about it. That's all I remember."

Curiosity satisfied, Jasmine concentrated on her hot chocolate.

Mr. Carrillo stood up. "Well, now that I know you're all right, I'll head back to work."

Nodding, Jasmine bit into a cookie.

"And thank you, Jesse. I'm glad my daughter has such a good friend."

Jesse smiled. *What would he think if he knew who I really am?*

He walked toward the door, stopped beside a cupboard, and opened the top drawer. Unexpectedly, he spun around. "Catch!"

Jesse felt, rather than saw, a small blur shoot through the air toward her. Instinctively, she threw up one hand and batted the object back. *A tennis ball?* Mr. Carrillo tried to catch it in return, but he was too slow. The ball bounced off his forearm onto the floor, then rolled under the table.

"Good reflexes," he said.

"Dad!" Jasmine's aggrieved voice rang out.

Jesse stared at Mr. Carrillo's shirtsleeve. Blood seeped through the blue material. He covered the patch with one hand. "It's nothing. I cut myself at work. I should have put a bandage over it. The ball just hit the spot. My own fault." He glanced sideways as he spoke.

*Is he embarrassed?* thought Jesse.

"Dad's always goofing around. He thinks he's funny. You see why Momll wanted to get away and look at a wart?" Jasmine giggled. A second Carrillo who thought she was funny. But this time Jesse agreed.

Jesse sighed. Her first visit to Jasmine's house, and already she'd narrowly missed being caught planting a bug in the phone and made Mr. Carrillo's arm bleed. Although Mr. Carrillo didn't have to throw the ball that hard. It was a full-on pitch, aimed straight at her face. What if she'd missed?

# 20.

"You've got a mark on your head." Liam's hands, which held the steering wheel, were grubby, the nails stained brown around the edges.

"Got to expect that when you're run over by a truck." Jesse kicked aside a cardboard container and stretched out her feet. After today, Liam's clunky little car seemed familiar, safe.

"Nasty. How's the truck?"

Jesse glanced sideways, but Liam's face was impassive.

"What happened?" he asked.

As he drove back to C2, she told him.

"Did you get into the main rooms?" he asked.

"Yes. But I was almost caught by Mr. Carrillo while putting a bug in the phone."

"Almost is OK. Means he missed. You'll get better at it."

*Better?* Jesse hoped she'd never have to do that again. It still made her shiver to think of that moment.

"I saw you go into the house with the girl," said Liam.

"Her name's Jasmine."

Liam grunted.

"I didn't see *you,*" said Jesse.

"You weren't supposed to."

"That security man, Tom, who spied on us at school, knew my name. Is he from C2?"

"No. But part of his job is to keep an eye on the girl. . . ."

"Jasmine."

He braked to avoid a puppy with long ears, who scampered willy-nilly across the street. "Don't get personally involved. It'll only cause you heartache and you won't do your job properly. We complete our assignment. We go home. The next shift goes to work. Then we move on to the next job."

"Ever thought about changing jobs?"

"You don't leave C2."

*Want to bet?*

Liam turned the car right. Soon they would be at the C2 parking garage.

"But if this Tom was watching Jasmine, that means he knows about the kidnap threat," said Jesse. "I thought the family didn't know."

"Maybe he was watching her for other reasons."

*What reasons?* To Jesse, it seemed bizarre that a family would assign someone to watch their kid at school. *But what do I know about families?*

"So if Tom is just security . . ."

"Nobody is *just* anything. Not even us. The friendliest face can hide the most treacherous thoughts. Don't trust him."

"But you just said . . ."

"Don't trust *me*."

"I . . ."

"Don't trust yourself."

# 21.

"What did you think of Carrillo?" asked Liam.

Jesse shrugged. "He's a bit strange."

"How?"

Immediately, she thought of the tennis ball. "His jokes aren't funny."

"Most jokes aren't. People laugh because they want to please the person who told the joke."

"I think he could have a temper. He cares about Jasmine. He's intelligent."

The lights changed. Liam accelerated. "Carrillo has some shady business partners. I wonder if this kidnap threat has something to do with that. It's all so vague. I've learned that he's arranging a shipment this weekend.

I'd like to know what's in it. His background check shows no arrests. Just a few speeding tickets. He gained distinctions at college. Lived in Switzerland for several years. Has a beautiful wife, an adoring child, a mansion. It's all too perfect. Too clean. Most people's lives are a mess. Not his. What's been covered up?"

Jesse was confused. How could someone look suspicious because they *hadn't* done anything? "The kidnap threat might be about money."

"Possibly. But thugs don't usually ask for the ransom *before* they kidnap the victim."

"So we don't know who made the threat?"

Liam shook his head. "It was a tip-off. Granger wouldn't give away his source. Must be someone under deep cover. But if C2 is involved, then this Carrillo is important to them. He must be providing a service or product they don't want to lose."

"Or he knows something about them that's secret."

"In that case, he might just disappear."

A chill ran through Jesse as she thought of Rohan.

"The kidnap threat could be to manipulate him, to make him do something . . . or *not* do something. The child is his soft spot, perhaps — his weakness."

If so, Jesse could understand why. Jasmine was great. Even if there was no assignment, Jesse would like to be her friend. *Does that make Jasmine my weakness, too?*

# 22.

Jesse had her smile ready as the office waiting room door opened. In her mind, she had practiced this moment, but actually saying the words was harder. She had never asked Prov for anything really big. CDs and videos, sure. The ones Mary supplied were boring. But this was different.

Prov wore another short-sleeved mohair top. This time it was pink. *Does she have a rule — any color, but must have lots of fluff?*

"Here's my daily report for Director Granger." Jesse placed a large envelope on the desk. Inside were several sheets of paper and a computer disk.

Prov punched a list of numbers into the

small safe beside her desk and slipped it inside. "He's out. I'll give it to him when he returns. . . . What's that mark on your forehead?"

"Stupid door. I should have looked where I was going." Jesse wondered if other field agents blamed doors for their injuries. Maybe she should have come up with something more creative.

Prov gave her a penetrating look, but asked no more questions.

Jesse leaned forward and whispered. "Is this room bugged?" Her breath did not disturb Prov's hair one bit. Prov used so much hairspray, Jesse doubted a hurricane would ruffle it.

Prov whispered back, "I presume you don't mean cockroaches?"

Jesse cupped one hand to her ear to mime *listening*.

Prov shook her head, but kept her voice quiet. "Director Granger is strict about that. He's fanatical about security. At the end of every day we back up files, twice, and someone sweeps these rooms for listening devices. The walls and doors are especially thick and constructed of special materials, so longer-range devices won't penetrate."

"What if the person sweeping for bugs actually planted one?"

"I doubt it." Prov frowned. "No, I'm *sure* of it. It's always a different agent who does it. They'd all have to be in on it to keep a bug here." Sympathy softened her face. "What's wrong?"

"Who am I?" Jesse knelt beside her. "Mary won't tell me. I don't know who my parents were or how the car accident happened. Do I have other relatives? How did C2 find me? I was only one year old. How did they know I was a prodigy?"

Prov touched Jesse's hair with one hand. "I can't answer those questions. I don't know. When I came here, you'd already been here two years and that woman was looking after you."

To Prov, it was always "that woman" and not Mary.

Jesse peeked at the computer screen. "There must be records. The scientists, Roger and Michael, have done tests in the laboratory. They write things down. If I've been legally adopted, there'll be information about it."

Prov flushed as though someone had turned up the heating. "I can't access many of the files. If they're marked *Top Secret* or *Director's Eyes Only*, then I'm shut out."

Jesse had hacked into other computer systems outside C2. However, they were simple compared to this one. There were electronic safeguards that she couldn't break through.

"There must be other ways to get some information."

"Some of the older material is on paper, down in the basement. Not on computer." Prov chewed on her bottom lip. "I only have access to basic material."

"You have security clearance and you're the only one I trust," said Jesse. "What happens to the backup disks?"

"I shouldn't tell you this . . . but if I were you, I'd want to know about my family. And it's time someone looked after you better." Prov looked over at the closed door. "One set of disks is locked in a safe in the Director's office, and the others go to the archives. The archives have more security devices than his office. Sensitive files and disks have a tag attached, which gives out a radio signal. If one is removed, security would know in a second."

"Oh."

"You'd better go. Granger will be back any minute. But a good office manager might make another copy of special files, just for safekeeping. . . . I can't promise. . . . I'd have to be careful. So would you."

"I don't want you to lose your job."

Prov's pupils grew so big they became black holes. "Honey, it's not my job that I'm worried about."

# 23.

The hands on the counterclockwise clock showed Jai was late. Jesse spun on her chair to face the door. Was he sick?

*He has one more minute, then I'm going to find him.*

Just then, soft footsteps announced Jai's arrival. His shoulders were slumped and his arms dangled loosely at his sides as though he didn't know what to do with them.

"Where's your violin?" asked Jesse.

"Michael took it away. He wants to see how it will affect me to be without my music."

Not well, judging by the dark shadows under Jai's eyes.

It still surprised Jesse that freaky men

in white coats, who spent their lives doing experiments on children and inventing bizarre weapons, would have ordinary names like Michael or Roger.

"They didn't hurt you, did they?" Jesse locked the door.

He shook his head.

"Why don't you sit down? We can talk tonight. No games."

He didn't argue, just flopped onto the orange sofa, ignoring the giant blue footprints.

"I can play my clarinet for you if you like." Jesse had only learned it so that the scientists could gauge her aptitude for music. She proved she could play. Now she didn't need to do it.

"I am not that distressed," he said with a slight smile.

Jesse understood completely.

"I was in the laboratory all day."

"Want a drink?" Jesse opened the small fridge in the corner of her room and took out a jug of fresh orange juice and two glasses. She took one glass across to Jai and kept the other for herself.

He drained the juice in the same time that Jesse had taken two sips.

"Do you have anything to eat?" His eyes showed that his stomach was more demanding than his polite voice.

Jesse pulled out a couple of apples, an orange, a boiled egg, and a slice of pizza with red dots. "Mary's into lentils this week." Jesse dropped the slice into the trash can.

Jai crunched the apple like a piranha attacking a carcass. The color returned to his cheeks, although the smudges beneath his eyes stayed.

"What happened to your head?" *Crunch,* another lump of apple disappeared into Jai's mouth.

"Um . . ."

*Munch.* He shook his head. "Forget that I asked."

*Fair enough.* She couldn't tell him the truth, anyway.

"You have a question to ask me?"

She started with surprise. "How do you know?"

*Crunch.* "It is in your eyes even if it is not

yet on your lips. Your movements are faster than usual. You are slightly agitated." He put a finger to his lips and raised his eyebrows.

"I've already scanned for bugs. The room is clean."

"What is your question?"

"Has anyone told you about where you come from? Which country? Who your parents were, anything like that?"

"No. Jesse, we have had this conversation before."

"I know. But I want to be sure. Why haven't they told us anything?"

"They may think it would unsettle us. Perhaps we are more docile if we know nothing."

"Don't you think it's strange?" she asked.

"This place is all I have ever known. Sometimes it is hard to know if things are strange or perfectly normal."

"The man I'm working with told me there are more child prodigies in C2. In other branches."

Jai blinked several times. "Who are they? How many are there?"

"I don't know. He only told me about one boy. Interstate. But the way he said it . . . I think there are even more."

"Did you ask him about it?"

"I couldn't," said Jesse. "I don't think he likes me. And he hates questions. Even if I asked him, he'd probably just lie."

"He might have been lying when he told you there were more of us."

"I don't think so. And if I ask too many questions, they'll know I'm interested. They might bury the truth even deeper. We'd never find out anything."

Jai nodded. "Agreed."

"How can we all be orphans? And I want to show you something." She sat on her computer chair, gave her fingerprints, then her four passwords, and logged on to the Internet. "I entered the words *missing children* into a search engine."

Jai ditched his apple core into the trash. It looked like a tiny animal spine without flesh.

"This is about Operation Babylift. In nineteen seventy-five, after the war, nearly three thousand orphans were taken from orphanages and child-care centers in Vietnam.

Some of those children had parents. They were stolen. There was a big court case about it," she explained.

"We are too young to be connected to that. And you are obviously not Vietnamese."

"No." Jesse turned her head to look at him. "But you could be. Jai, if one government ordered their agents to do that, why not others? And if they've stolen children once, they might do it again. It wouldn't have to be in Vietnam. There's always a war somewhere. Kids go missing."

He stared at the computer screen.

Jesse thought of C2's laboratory. "This says they used these kids for experiments."

"You cannot believe everything you read on the Internet," he said, yet there was curiosity in his tone.

"Jai, what if we're not really orphans, but were stolen from our families?"

# 24.

Jesse's stomach rumbled as she peered through Liam's car window at a hamburger joint. Today, she hadn't fallen under a truck, balanced on a toilet seat to eavesdrop, or injured her only friend's father. *I might be getting the hang of this spy stuff.* Part of her felt she shouldn't be going back to C2 yet. Not enough had happened. Yet spending another day with Jasmine had been a treat.

"What do you think of school?" Liam asked.

"Boring."

"Ha. This was only your second day. You should try a second year or a second decade. I was always in trouble in school. Had a learning disability. The dopey kid who didn't know what was going on. So I acted out to hide it."

*Did he have smelly sneakers like Hugh? Bet he did.* "You're not dopey now."

"No."

"You're cranky, though."

"Yeah. But only when I'm on assignment with an agent who sucks her thumb."

They both faced the front of the car, satisfied with the score — one hit each.

As they neared C2, Jesse felt herself tense, as though invisible ropes tightened around her chest.

Liam drove down to the level below the basement and stopped. He scooped up paper from the floor of his car and began shoving it into a cardboard container.

Jesse grabbed her bag, got out, and leaned against the car. Liam had enough paper in there to make a whole tree. Suddenly she became aware of something out of place. Without moving her body, she scanned the parking garage. What was it?

Liam was still in the car, head down, rummaging in trash. If she called out to him, it would attract attention. Better to keep still and listen. *There. It's scraping. Faint, but definite.* Jesse deliberately yawned. "Rats, my shoelace is undone again." Casually, she placed her bag on the hood of the car and knelt down. Fiddling with her laces, she looked left and right beneath the cars. *No feet showing.* She checked left a second time. Damp footprints led from a puddle to a parked car, then stopped. Yet no driver was visible.

*Here we go again.* Jesse wondered if every field assignment included crawling around in parking garages. She hoped not. Hands on the concrete, she scuttled wide around the suspicious area. Warily, she raised her head, gasped, then ducked down again.

A man crouched in the open doorway of a green car, knees bent, his feet still on the car floor. He balanced himself with his left hand. *That's why I didn't see his feet.* In his right hand he held a gun. It was aimed directly at Liam. In a moment the man would wonder why it took Jesse so long to retie her shoelace and become suspicious. She had to act now.

Still hunkered down, she slipped around

another car and came up behind the man. Hard and swift, she punched him exactly three inches below his right shoulder.

"What . . ." The gun fell onto the concrete.

Before he could respond, Jesse karate chopped him on the side of his neck. He crumpled backward in an untidy heap, still with a surprised expression on his face.

# 25.

Liam bent over the unconscious man's body. "What did you do?"

"I applied pressure to his brachial plexus tie-in, then chopped the brachial plexus origin," said Jesse.

"You did *what*?" He scratched his head.

"I paralyzed his arm so he'd drop the gun, then applied a karate chop to the base of his neck. An artery and several nerves run through that area. If you hit it, you disrupt the blood flow and the person falls unconscious."

"Thanks for the lesson, Master Karate Girl. I thought you did tae kwon do."

"I have a black belt in that. I've dabbled in karate. I didn't find it as interesting."

Liam picked up the man's gun, checked it, then slid it back into the man's pocket.

"You're giving him back his gun!"

"That's right."

"But he was going to shoot you."

"Jesse, meet Hans Faulkner. He's an agent with C2. You've just knocked out one of our own men."

Jesse gasped. "What'll we do?"

"Get out of here before he wakes up."

"But we can't just leave him here. He might be hurt."

Liam rolled his eyes, then knelt beside Agent Faulkner. He pressed two fingers gently under his jaw. "Strong pulse. He's fine." Liam stood and began to walk away. "Come on."

Reluctantly, Jesse followed.

"You're a funny one," he said. "You don't think twice about knocking people out, then you go weak at the knees in case they're hurt."

"Why was he trying to shoot you?"

Back at the car Liam grabbed Jesse's bag and thrust it into her arms. "Here, partner. Carry your own gear. This isn't a charity. Hans wasn't going to shoot. Sneaky bugger. I didn't know he was back. Caught me by surprise. We have this challenge between us, to catch the other unawares. Keeps us on our toes."

"I thought I was putting my life in danger to save you and it was only a game?" She glared at him. "I could have died from fright."

"I owe you one."

Jesse stared at Liam's neck and imagined the exact spot she would like to chop.

# 26.

Jesse stomped along the hallway toward her room.

"Jesse!"

She looked up to see Prov. Had she found something in the files? Jesse's eyes flicked toward the security cameras fixed to the ceilings. They would be following everything that happened out here. But Prov knew that.

She held something in her hands. "Honey, I made you this no-bake cheesecake."

Now that she was close, Jesse could smell the strong sweetness of Prov's perfume. A speck of eyeliner sat like a freckle on her eyelid. A pulse beat rapidly in her neck.

*She's nervous.*

Prov leaned forward to plant a peck on Jesse's cheek and whispered, "There's a special ingredient."

Jesse wondered if she had red lipstick on her cheek now, but she didn't mind. She took the cheesecake and sniffed it. "Thank you. It smells wonderful. Just like lemons."

"Hold it right there," came a tight voice from behind.

Prov and Jesse spun around.

Mary Holt stood like a soldier guarding a treasure. "What is that?"

"A cheesecake." Jesse held it closer to her body.

"Give it to me." Mary held out both hands. "You are not permitted such appallingly unhealthy food. Healthy body, healthy mind."

She'd said that so often, in the same singsong tone, that Jesse wondered if her voice was actually a recording. If the food police were after new recruits, Mary should be number one on their list.

"It's not for me personally, Mary." Jesse used her sweetest voice. "It's for . . . well, I can't say where I'm going each day. But I need this for tomorrow."

A frown wrinkled Mary's brow. "Why would you need a cake for a field assignment?"

"Top secret. Prov doesn't know what I want it for, either. . . ."

"No, I know nothing." Prov's voice was too loud and shrill.

Mary pouted. "I don't believe that a cheesecake could be top secret."

*Why not? Everything else is around here.*

"I wouldn't, either, if I were you," said Jesse.

Prov gasped.

"Sounds silly. But it's true. Why don't you check with Director Granger, if you're worried?"

If Mary called her bluff and went to Granger, she was sunk. Jesse watched the expressions on Mary's face change as she imagined herself confronting the Director of C2 to ask if Jesse could take a cheesecake on her secret assignment. She also saw the moment Mary decided to stop arguing.

"Why didn't you ask me? I'm your carer."

"I know you prefer healthy food. I thought you might feel bad making something like this."

Mary's face settled into its normal discontented lines. "Yes, well. I do my duty. But you . . . Provincial, or whatever your real name is . . . you're not supposed to be on this level. Off you go." She made shooing noises as though she were rounding up chickens.

Prov didn't argue. She patted Jesse on the back and retreated.

*Slow down, Prov,* Jesse told her silently. *You look like you're running away.*

Mary sniffed. "I hope you will be responsible and not nibble any of that. It will rot your teeth. And too much sugar gives you a false energy high, then you crash and feel more tired."

"Yes, Mary."

"You'd better put it in the fridge right away." She looked at her watch. "You're late. They want you in the laboratory."

Jesse felt a sick taste at the back of her throat.

# 27.

"Ten more, Jesse. You can do it."

Puffing, her arms beginning to wobble, Jesse tried another push-up. "Thirty-one, thirty-two . . ." She was sick of seeing carpet pile under her nose.

Michael stood beside her with a clipboard, watching. Sometimes Jesse felt like doing something totally outrageous, just to see his reaction.

"Thirty-nine, forty." She flopped on the carpet, sweat running down her temples. That was it. She'd been exercising for an hour. At least this session hadn't included anything weird or too uncomfortable. Her regular exercise routine was bearable.

Michael scribbled on his clipboard.

*You'd think he'd be more into computers than clipboards.*

"Wrist."

Jesse held out her wrist. Michael felt for her pulse, checking it against his watch. Then he wrote on the clipboard again. "You know what's next."

Grudgingly, Jesse scrambled to her feet. "Do I have to?"

He nodded.

"But I hate needles."

"A vitamin B12 supplement is good for you."

"Someone who has a perfectly balanced diet, as I do, does not need vitamin supplements."

He rubbed a small spot on her arm with disinfectant on gauze, then inserted the needle.

*Ouch,* thought Jesse, but she refused to flinch.

"We've missed you, Jesse."

*Yeah, right.*

Two good things came from her field

assignment. Making a friend and being away from C2.

Someone appeared in the gymnasium doorway.

Jesse turned.

"Good afternoon," said Director Granger. "Glad to see you're keeping fit."

*As if I had a choice.*

"Michael. Would you leave us for a few minutes?"

Michael retreated to the back room and closed the door.

*If only it were that easy for me. Michael, would you go away? Great. Michael, stick that needle in your own arm. Excellent. Michael, a hundred push-ups, now. Michael, lock yourself in that tub of water with no light or sound and see how long before you crack. Fantastic.*

The Director slipped his hands into his pockets. "Liam tells me you have asked permission to stay at the target's house tomorrow night."

Jesse felt hope sink like a heavy weight at the coldness in his voice. "Yes, I can be closer to her there, watch what goes on at the house."

Jesse wiped sweat from her brow with her right forearm. She wanted to stay at Jasmine's so much it hurt. But if Director Granger knew that, he might say no.

He pursed his lips.

*If the answer's no, then just tell me.*

"It's a good opportunity to observe the household at close range," he said. "And Liam says you can be trusted."

"He *did*?" Maybe this is what he meant in the parking garage by "I owe you one."

Granger raised one eyebrow. "You sound surprised."

"I thought he didn't like me."

"He doesn't have to. He just has to do his job. That's all. Every action has consequences. Liam would not enjoy the consequences of failure. Neither would you."

# 28.

The door was locked, the room was free from listening devices, and there was half an hour till lights-out. Jesse slid her fingers under the cheesecake, hoping she was right about Prov's "special ingredient."

The crumbed base was rough on her fingers. *Nothing hidden there.* She looked at the soft, yellow mixture in the middle. It was going to make a big mess, but there was no other way. *One . . . two . . . three.* She plunged her hand into the middle, not sure whether to say "yuck" because it was gooey or "yum" because it was probably delicious.

No wonder Prov worked in the office and not on field assignments. There must be better ways to hide something than in the middle of a cake. But then, how many people would think of searching a cheesecake for secret material?

*Ah, there it is.* Jesse pulled out a computer disk protected by a plastic bag. She placed it carefully on a tissue beside her computer. The disk itself was perfectly clean.

She looked at the ruined cheesecake with regret. If Mary saw it like this, she might guess the truth. Reluctantly, Jesse picked up the plate, held it at shoulder height and turned it upside down. It splattered onto the floor, splashing onto Jesse's trousers.

"Oops. Sorry, Mary. I had an accident," she said under her breath, then licked her fingers. Yes, that was a definite *yum*.

She washed her hands at double speed, eager to get to her computer.

It was only seconds before the machine was fired up and ready to go, but it seemed longer. With trembling fingers, Jesse inserted the disk. Her hand hovered over the mouse. What if she discovered something she would rather not know?

# 29.

The file began with facts about Jesse's weight and height at different ages. And a series of photographs. She didn't have a camera, had no photos of her own. Michael and Roger had conducted hundreds of tests and refused to tell her the results or why they did them. So when they took the annual photographs she never asked to see them.

Looking at this toddler, then the bigger child, was like staring at a stranger. *Is that really me?* Through different hairstyles and facial expressions one thing remained the same — a determined glint in the eyes.

If only there was a photo of the three of them, Rohan, Jai, and herself, together.

She checked the time. *Twenty minutes till lights- out. Better hurry up. I can look at these again later.*

A quick scroll down brought her to Personality Profile at Four Years of Age.

Jesse Sharpe has an extraordinary memory.

She is a natural mimic.

The child shows signs of stubbornness, a trait that could lead her either to become a determined, hardworking adult or to develop an inability to compromise.

She interacts well with the other children and acts protectively toward them.

She seems distrustful of adults. She may be a cautious adult, or she may become cynical.

Her language skills are outstanding.
She reads a wide range of books and has mastered Spanish, English, and French.
She shows an advanced interest in mathematics and physics.
This child does not like to be given orders. She responds better to suggestions.
Currently, there is no sign of mental instability.
We feel that Jesse Sharpe has proved a good candidate for Operation IQ.
However, she will need discipline and close supervision to ensure that her individuality does not affect her usefulness.

Recommended to continue with the

program.

Jesse sat back in her chair. *Recommended to continue with the program.* What if their conclusion had been different? What would have happened to her?

And why would they look for signs of "mental instability"? Were they expecting some?

She clicked on a scanned newspaper article. The headline read, "Child Found in Car with Dead Parents." A man and woman had been driving in their car. Another vehicle, speeding, had not given way and rammed into this couple's car. The car rolled and the couple were killed. A baby girl was found alive, but unconscious, strapped into a car seat.

Jesse felt the strength drain out of her. Her legs were heavy and useless. It must be true. She really *was* an orphan. Until now, her parents had been shadows. If she turned, they weren't there, had *never* been there. But now she had a sense that they had been real people. Sadness swept through her. She felt as though she had glimpsed them, for a brief second, then they vanished again.

There was no copy of adoption papers.

Near the bottom of the file it read, FURTHER INFORMATION CLASSIFIED TOP SECRET. RESTRICTED ACCESS. OPERATION IQ.

Jesse tapped the screen. *That's where the real information is kept and I can't touch it. Not yet.*

Then she read CROSS-REFERENCE OPERATION IQ and it listed four different states. Were all the C2 child prodigies orphans? That was impossible. Maybe their parents had volunteered them for the project. But why?

But Jesse, Rohan, and Jai had been told that they were orphans and had no one to look after them. C2 had stepped in to save them — so they said.

Jesse took out the disk and prepared to hide it in her secret place. She wouldn't tell anyone where it was. Not even Jai. If anyone found the disk, Prov would be in danger. And no matter how much Jesse wanted to find out about her past, she couldn't let that happen.

The information on the disk was a beginning. There was a lot more. Jesse resolved to find out everything. Not today. Not tomorrow. But she *would* find out.

# 30.

Jesse tugged the blanket up to her chin. She wasn't cold, just relished being wrapped in a soft blanket. Jesse was still shocked that Director Granger had given permission for her to stay overnight at Jasmine's house. *But here I am.*

It was Jasmine's turn to ask two questions. "Favorite color?"

"Yellow."

"Favorite food?"

"Um . . . hamburger." *Because I've never tasted one,* Jesse added silently.

Jasmine laughed. "Your turn."

Jesse stretched, touching the end of the trundle bed with her toes. "Best TV show?"

"Documentaries on elephants."

"Scariest person you've ever met?" Jesse wondered if Jasmine's answer would give her a clue about who was threatening her.

"Me. Because I have to take myself everywhere I go. So if I don't like myself, I'm stuck with me."

*Cool answer, but no help as a clue.*

In the pale glow from the night-light, Jesse saw Jasmine turn over. "I'm glad you came to our school."

"So am I," said Jesse. "Do you get scared in this big house at night?"

"No. Security patrols outside. And inside, there's the alarm system upstairs and downstairs. When Dad's out, like tonight, Eva or Momll are usually home. Besides, who'd want to break in here?"

*Good question.* Jesse felt comforted that her own security patrol of one — Liam — was also outside.

Jasmine's voice softened, became fuzzy. "I'm nearly asleep."

"Me, too. Good night." Jesse waited till Jasmine snuffled in a way that suggested she was truly asleep.

Adrenaline kicked in, making Jesse's heart race. Carefully, she eased back the blanket and stood up.

Jasmine didn't move.

First Jesse slipped on her jeans, then a pair of goggles, then a pair of latex gloves. Her stomach turned at the feel of the gloves, but she didn't want her fingerprints to show up in the wrong places. She hoisted her shoulder bag, then crept to the door and peeked out. Through the goggles, she saw beams of infrared light criss-crossing the hallway. If she touched any of them, an alarm would sound.

The first beam was about a yard above the floor. Jesse flattened herself on the carpet and wriggled like a worm. The carpet smelled dusty, but she didn't dare lift her head. Clutching her shoulder bag firmly to her side, she stepped over the second beam. Gradually she worked her way safely along the hallway.

She listened for sounds. Nothing. She turned the handle of Mr. Carrillo's office. Locked, as she'd suspected. She took a thin metal tool from her shoulder bag, hoping the door itself wasn't alarmed. How would she explain standing in the hall, wearing this wild gear and fiddling with the lock?

Quietly, she pushed the tool into the lock, easing it left, then right. Sensing the moment it clicked, rather than hearing it, she turned the door handle a second time. This time it swung open. Jesse sighed with relief. No alarm.

Stepping inside, she closed the door gently behind her. She took off the goggles, placed them in the shoulder bag, and took out a small flashlight. *Ah, there's the computer, in the corner near the window.*

Once the screen lit up, she didn't need the flashlight and switched it off.

*OK, what would Mr. Carrillo's password be?* People usually chose predictable, easily remembered passwords, their birth dates or names of family members. What about his wife's name, *Julianna*? Incorrect password. His daughter, *Jasmine*? Incorrect password. Jesse swung on the chair. *Ah, I know.* She typed in *Moml1.* The computer whirred. She was in. Only one password.

That was slack, and dangerous. People could break in.

She went straight for his e-mails. Mr. Carrillo had deleted his messages. *So he thinks.* Silently, Jesse thanked Rohan for all the computer tricks he had shown her. She used to tease him by saying he had an electronic mouse instead of a pacifier when he was a baby.

As always, the thought of Rohan made her sad. She shook her head. *I must concentrate.*

Nothing on computers was truly deleted. It was electronically chopped up and scattered. She searched among the debris on the hard drive. The scraps she found were mostly boring — business-meeting arrangements, a birthday greeting, chatty nonsense. Then she found a large part of a message to his wife. There was no word about Jasmine's tangle with the maroon car. It did say Jasmine had a new friend, so it must have been sent recently. Maybe he didn't want to worry his wife while she was away.

*What's this?* She found part of a sent

message that made her eyes grow wide. *This must be a mistake.* She reread the message, twice. It wasn't all retrievable, but it was enough to make her sweat. She couldn't think of another way to interpret the information. Mr. Carrillo had arranged to have his own daughter kidnapped.

# 31.

*Is Mr. Carrillo crazy?*

If he didn't like his daughter or wanted her out of the way, why didn't he send her overseas with her mother or put her in a boarding school? He didn't have to kidnap her. Unless he wanted her hidden from someone else who threatened her. They couldn't take her if she had already disappeared. *This is so weird and so complicated.*

*Just a minute.* Jesse's brain spun like a satellite out of control. *C2 is smart enough to have bugs planted inside the house and agents watching the Carrillos. Liam says they're using scanners to eavesdrop on his mobile phone conversations. How could they overlook e-mails?*

Suddenly suspicious, she checked further for hidden software designed to pick up e-mails. Mr. Carrillo might not think to look for something like that.

*There it is. C2 must know about that e-mail. Why haven't they taken Carrillo away? And if they think he's going to fake a kidnapping, to remove Jasmine from the real danger, why haven't they told me?*

Until she knew what was going on, she had to get Jasmine out of here. But where could they go? If C2 was involved, Jesse couldn't take her there. *One step at a time. When we're away from here, we'll figure out what to do.*

*What do I say to Jasmine? "Excuse me, but we have to run away, right now, because your father plans to kidnap you."* Jesse could hardly believe it herself, but somehow, she had to convince Jasmine.

Shaking slightly, she closed down the computer and refitted the goggles. She opened the door and looked out. Every nerve in her body jumped to attention. No beams of infrared light crisscrossed the long hallway. The alarm was off. Had Carrillo's security team discovered her presence in the office? Or did this mean something worse?

She ripped off the goggles and gloves, stuffed them into the bag, and shot down the hallway. One hand on the door frame, Jesse swung into Jasmine's room.

A soft glow from the night-light showed crumpled blankets and a pillow half-hanging off the mattress. Jasmine's bed was empty.

The door swung open and caught her on the arm. She staggered sideways. Rough, heavy material was thrown over her head. Strong arms wrapped around her tightly. Jesse struggled. The material pressed against her face, making it hard to breathe. Her knees buckled.

# 32.

Jesse felt consciousness return slowly. She opened her eyes but her vision was still cloudy. A few blinks and a deep breath later, the room cleared. She lay on her side on a couch, her wrists and ankles tied together. Wide tape covered her mouth.

*I'm still alive. That's a good sign, isn't it? But wait till they find out they've kidnapped the wrong girl. They'll be furious. Or did they take me because I blundered in before they could escape? In that case, they have Jasmine captive, too.* Jesse's stomach turned. *Please be all right, Jasmine.*

Answers to those questions would have to

wait. Her priority was to get out. She lifted her head. The room was neat, clean, and had no windows. There was a sink, the couch on which she lay, a rickety cupboard against one wall, and not much else. The concrete floor was swept clean.

Jesse tugged at the bindings on her hands. There was some slack there. Whoever had tied her up had left a short strand of tape between her wrists. She could move a little and it didn't interfere with her circulation. A kind captor — or one who hadn't had much practice? Still, the ties wouldn't break. Fiercely, she tried to snap the duct tape by forcing her wrists apart, until they began to ache with the effort and the tape ripped at the tiny hairs on her arms.

Maybe it would be easier to nibble through the mouth tape first. She rested a moment, then tried to open her lips. Little by little, she pinched the tape between her front teeth. It was tough stuff. She felt like a giant rabbit gnawing at bark.

A key turned in the lock. Someone was coming in. She closed her eyes, forcing herself to relax, as though she were still unconscious. *Breathe slowly. Don't let your eyelids flicker.*

The door opened with a squeak. Footsteps approached. Jesse longed to peek, but she didn't dare. A second set of feet, probably belonging to a heavier person, stepped inside the room and stopped. Cool fingers felt under her neck for a pulse, then pressed gently against her forehead.

"Pulse is fine, no temperature. Her color's good. She should come round any time." The voice was female and Jesse recognized it. *Eva, the Carrillos' housekeeper.*

"Lucky for you," added Eva. "Did you have to be so rough? You could have suffocated her."

"What was I supposed to do — let her kick her way free and run straight to C2?" said an unfamiliar male voice.

*C2? They know where I'm from.*

Eva spoke again. "I'll check her again in half an hour. By then she'll need the bathroom and something to eat. The procedure will have to wait till tomorrow."

*What procedure?* Jesse felt sick.

The two sets of footsteps retreated, and the door was locked again.

Jesse opened her eyes. A terrifying thought ripped through her mind. The target hadn't been Jasmine Carrillo — it was Jesse Sharpe.

# 33.

She had half an hour to figure out a plan. First she had to break free of this tape. She couldn't open her mouth wide. *There must be another way.* Her hands were useless at her back. *If I can get them to the front, it'll be much better.*

Squeezing her knees up into her chest, she rolled herself into a tight ball. Then she forced her hands down, trying to ease them around her body. Her arms screamed at her to stop, to release the pressure. *You can't dislocate a joint doing this, can you?*

*Come on, you can do it. One more try.* She let out her breath and curled up a fraction tighter. *If only my arms were longer.* Suddenly, they slipped around her body.

Jesse grabbed the wide tape over her mouth and ripped it away. *Oooww!* Her eyes watered. The pain was excruciating. *Jesse, don't ever try waxing, even if you're as hairy as a goat.*

Open, shut, open, shut — she exercised her stiff jaw. Now her teeth were free to work properly. Like a ravenous animal, she tore at the tape binding her wrists together. It gave way. She used her fingers to tear the tape from the opposite wrist. It was only a few seconds till her ankles were also free. The tape stuck to her fingers. *That might be useful later.* She rolled the strips into sticky balls and put them in her jeans pocket.

Jesse stood and shook her arms and legs. They tingled a little but worked just fine. *So far, so good. Now, how do I get out of here?* A careful check of each wall showed no windows, chutes, or trapdoors. Her shoulder bag was not here. Any gadgets that might help her had gone along with it. Despite tae kwon do and karate, Jesse knew she couldn't fight her way out of here alone. She wasn't strong enough. *But I have a good brain, better than most. I can use that.*

She looked at her special wristwatch. The face was broken and it rattled. *Useless.*

One hand on her chin, she considered her small prison. Why were there no windows? Was this a storage room? There wasn't much in here if it was. Then she remembered Director Granger's office. That, too, had no windows. Why? It was underground. A flash of inspiration swept through her. If she was belowground, there was only one direction to escape. Up.

# 34.

With her feet balanced on the arm of the couch, Jesse stretched above her head to reach the ventilation-shaft cover. Using the metal clip from her hair, she loosened the two screws that held the cover in place. She held the first screw between her lips while she undid the second. *Faster. There can't be much time left before they check on me.*

Firmly, she tucked the cover into the waist of her jeans, placed both hands on each side of the duct opening, and hauled herself upward. For the first time, she was glad she worked out in the C2 gymnasium.

The shaft was a long silver tube that snaked up into the distance. She couldn't redo the screws from inside. But if the cover was back in place it would take her captors a few minutes longer to work out where she had gone. It might make the difference between escape and capture. She extracted the tape from her pocket and stuck several strips to the sides of the ventilation cover. *It'll have to do.*

Jesse felt a sickness deep in her stomach. She loathed enclosed spaces. But if she sat here, frozen with fear, that would be the end of her.

The shaft swung as she moved. Bracing her body by using her feet, back, and hands, she edged upward. *Just as well this shaft tilts sideways and up, rather than straight up. Otherwise, my arms would drop off.*

Soon the shaft leveled out more. Slowly, wriggling on her stomach like an earthworm, she advanced. She wasn't sure where this would take her, but it was her only option. *If this building is out in the country, I'll be totally lost.*

Then she heard the sound of voices — muffled, male, and nearby.

*It's OK, just another vent. I'd better be*

*careful or they'll hear me crawling past.* She peered down to the room below.

There was another face she knew. Mr. Carrillo sat on a stool.

Jesse had a clear view of the top of his head. *He's going bald. Good. He deserves it.*

A man in a white coat bent over Carrillo's extended arm. "What happened, Al?"

"Hit by a tennis ball. It didn't bother me then. But it's still bleeding."

The man in the coat lifted a flap of skin on Carrillo's arm and prodded with some kind of instrument.

*Gross. What is he doing?*

"It's red. Don't want it to become infected. I'll give you something for it. But the connection to the mainframe is still working."

*Mainframe? That's a computer connection in his arm. He's into cybernetics.* She had read about people who had terminals inserted surgically in their bodies. They could open doors, read e-mails, and know what others connected were feeling.

"How's the neck?" The man lifted Mr. Carrillo's hair and inspected the back of his neck.

"Working fine."

"Good. And the girl?"

*Does he mean me?*

"Eva says she's OK. But the procedure is best done tomorrow. Let her rest."

Carrillo rubbed his hands together. "Do you understand what this means? A cybernetically enhanced genius. A marriage of genes and technology. She could be of tremendous use to us here at Cybervision."

*No way. I'm not having bits of machinery stuck into my flesh. Gross.*

"And C2?"

*Good question. And how did he know I was a genius? It's top secret.*

Carrillo puffed his lips in a gesture of contempt. "They don't suspect me. Why should they? I'm their best deep-cover agent. I'm just the best for two different sides." He chuckled. "C2 is falling behind the times. Cybernetics is the way of the future, and those who realize that will be the leaders of a new society. The implant gives me eyes in the space station, ears in the most secret submarine. It gives me an endless supply of information. Once I learn how to control the implant properly, I can manipulate machinery and information with just my mind. Think about the possibilities."

The man in the white coat nodded as though he had heard all of this before, and agreed.

"It's all worked out rather well. Who else would they send to guard a child? Another child, of course. It was the perfect lure to get the kid outside of the building."

"And Jasmine?"

*Yes, what about her?* It hurt to think Jasmine might have been pretending to like her, to get close, then betray her. A twinge of guilt stung Jesse. That was similar to what she had tried to do. Except her intention had been to save Jasmine, not to hurt her.

"She knows nothing. She should be at the airport, on her way to London."

Relief surged through Jesse.

The door below burst open. Hair disheveled, face tight with tension, Eva shouted, "The girl's disappeared!"

# 35.

Jesse flinched. She'd heard enough. It was urgent to get out. She wriggled past the vent and farther into the shaft. It wouldn't take them long to figure out where she was. But she still had a head start.

She passed two more vents over empty rooms, then stopped when she reached the third. A man lay on the floor. It was Tom, the head of Carrillo security. By the angle of his neck and the stillness of his body, she could tell he was dead.

*These people don't mess around.* Jesse's heart thumped. She edged along the shaft as fast as she could. Dust danced in the silver shaft, making her nose itch. *If I sneeze over a vent, I'll give myself away.* She pinched the end of her nose and waited for the urge to pass.

She was in big trouble, and not just because she was trapped in a ventilation shaft with maniacs below. Even if she escaped, it would not be over. Those Cybervision people would still know who she was and would try again to catch her. Either to turn her into a partial machine or to silence her.

Seconds later, she crawled over a vent that opened into a room that housed a bank of computers. *This is the mainframe, the brain.* A wild thought flashed through her mind.

The screws for the vent cover were on the outside. *I can kick it open. But when it falls, they'll hear it.* Jesse considered her options for a few seconds, then slid the belt from her jeans and fastened one end around the cover grating. Three hard kicks released the cover. It dangled harmlessly, and silently, from her belt.

Jesse dropped, catlike, to her feet and

placed the cover on a chair. She made sure both doors were dead bolted and dragged a table in front of each. *That should give me a few minutes.* Shouting and running feet told her that was about all she had left.

# 36.

Jesse sat at the computer terminal with a rising sense of panic. Nothing she tried had worked.

A knock sounded at the door. "Who's in there? Let me in."

It was Eva.

*No way, not even if you huff and puff.*

Jesse rested her head in her hands. What else could she try? She sighed and looked again at the screen. There was only one option left. The cyber implant specifications were on the screen in front of her. They were definitely all connected to this one big computer system. Like drones. Their strength was also their weakness.

Did Carrillo tell them what to do via the computer links? Could he force them, brainwash them? She didn't know. But certainly, they were all aware of each other, like ants before rain. Communicating without sound. Any other time, she would have been fascinated. Right now, she was desperate to stop them.

"The door's locked from the inside, Al," came Eva's voice. "Could she be in there, do you think?"

There was a loud bang as though something heavy was being aimed at the door.

"Blow it up if you have to," came Carrillo's voice.

*What happened to Mr. Smiling Dad?*

He bellowed again, "She must be using the ventilation shaft. Someone get up there. Now! And have security at exit points."

Again, Jesse hoped Jasmine was not a cyber girl.

Her fingers flew over the keyboard. *What do computer nerds always worry about? Viruses. If this mainframe got sick, everything and anyone joined to it would become infected. The connection should be broken.*

Grateful for her photographic memory, Jesse typed in one last command, then hesitated. But she had no choice. She hit ENTER. The light in the ceiling flashed and zigzags shot across the screen, followed by an electrical hiss.

Someone outside the room gave a short scream, then there was silence. A single cursor flashed off and on against the blank computer screen. *That's it. Scrambled, like a carton of eggs.* Jesse hoped the power surge had blown all the circuits, including those embedded in human flesh.

Jesse dragged a chair under the hole in the ceiling and climbed back up into the ventilation shaft. Again, her skin crawled at the idea of being so closed in. She swallowed her fear and forced herself to go on.

She checked in the next room, where the pounding had originated. Below her, Eva and Mr. Carrillo wandered in little circles as if they didn't know what they were doing. Their faces were blank, like windup toys.

There was no time to feel sorry for them. Jesse was still in danger. Some of these people might not have implants. As fast as she dared, she headed onward again and came to a dead end. Well, almost a dead end. The shaft went upward at a sharp angle.

Jesse wanted to cry from frustration. Her lips felt twice their normal size and still stung from the sticky tape, her wrists were red and raw, and she was tired.

Then she thought about Jai. What would happen to him if she didn't return? He was smart but he wasn't strong emotionally. He needed her. And what about Rohan? Who would search for him if she couldn't? No, she had to get out.

Teeth gritted with determination, Jesse began her ascent. Using her feet to lever her body upward and her back to steady and balance herself against the opposite wall, she inched upward. Her breath came in tired puffs. Her legs trembled. The silver shaft trembled along with them. Its movement made her queasy.

*Ah.* She slipped. The sweat on her hands made it difficult to brace herself.

She had no notion of time, just pushed upward, bracing herself for rest every so often. *This isn't as bad as some of the laboratory experiments at C2, and I survived them.*

Suddenly, shockingly, the ventilation shaft evened out again. Jesse slumped, breathing deeply, relieved to have the pressure gone from her legs. *They'll ache tomorrow. If there is a tomorrow.*

When she caught her breath, she edged forward to another vent and looked down. The room below her was familiar. Jesse stifled a giggle, worried she wouldn't be able to stop.

# 37.

"Hello!" Liam stood in the doorway to Jesse's room at C2, a paper bag in his hand. The door was open, ready for Jai's visit.

"Come in," said Jesse.

Liam followed the blue footprints around to a chair at the table and sat. As usual, his blond hair stuck out crazily.

He looked at Jesse's face intently. "How are you?"

"All right."

"I brought you a hamburger." He placed the bag on the table. "Don't tell that Mary woman. She'll have me executed."

Her mouth watered instantly. "Thanks."

"What you did back at the Carrillo

house . . . it was gutsy. Of course, I could have done better." He raised one eyebrow. "But you did all right for a thumb sucker."

Jesse tucked her knees up on the chair and wrapped her arms around them. "I got a shock when I looked down and saw I was still in the Carrillos' house, over the dining room. I had to stop myself from laughing. I think if I'd started, I would never have stopped."

"Nervous reaction."

"I think I hate the color apricot now."

"Yeah. Too fruity," said Liam. "I'm not fond of anything that's good for me."

"Thanks for . . . rescuing me."

"I didn't. You rescued yourself. All I had to do was drive you back here while the team swept in to remove a few security guards." Liam shrugged. "The zombies were no trouble."

"How are they . . . the Cybervision people?"

"Alive and physically well. But no memories. You blew their fuses. Clever. I guess there are advantages to working with a midget genius."

"I'm not a midget," she said. "I'm average height for my age."

"Do you have to argue with everything?"

"Pretty much."

"Director Granger is . . ." Liam's lips formed an impolite word, then he changed it midsentence. "He didn't suspect Carrillo was a double agent. Me? I didn't know he was even supposed to be one of ours. Under deep cover, only Granger and a couple of others knew. If they'd told us, it might have been different. But they can't work that way. Honesty is too hard an idea for them to grasp."

Jesse nodded.

"I've been given a new assignment," he said.

*So that's why he's here, to say good-bye. Another person leaving my life.*

"I've been asked to pick a partner. . . . What are you doing next week?"

"Me?"

He looked around the room. "I don't see anyone else in here, unless they're invisible."

"I suppose it's OK." Actually it was perfect. She could get away from here for a few days. The more successful she was in her assignments, the more the Director would trust her. She could search for Rohan and a way to freedom. Maybe even find out about their real families. It would take time, but she would do it.

"I was also hoping you would karate Hans again for me. He's got an attitude."

"You mean he beats you."

"Something like that." Liam drew an envelope from his jacket pocket. "You've got mail."

"Me?"

"That your favorite word today?"

"But I don't know anyone."

"A letter was sent from London to the school you attended. The sender's initials are J.C."

*Jasmine Carrillo.*

"Prov kind of forgot to pass it on to Granger. I read it. Sorry, but I had to make sure it was OK. You know, no letter bomb or poisoned glue. If you're smart, you won't answer. It's too dangerous to form attachments from assignments. And although she seems innocent herself, she was involved with some nasty people. Be happy she remembers you and move on."

He was right, of course. Jesse stared at the envelope. *My first letter.* She took it, but didn't open it. Later, when she was alone, she'd read it.

"Tell me about our next assignment."

Hello

i've sneaked out from C2 for a little while and my friend, Christine Harris, has now set up an e-mail address for me:

jesse@christineharris.com

Any secret communications should be safe. i hope lots of readers will write to me after they read my books.

– jesse Sharpe,

child prodigy and hamburger lover